TRICKERY

JAYMIN EVE
JANE WASHINGTON

Copyright 2017 © Jane Washington and Jaymin Eve.
All rights reserved.
The authors have provided this book for your personal use only. It may not be re-sold or made publicly available in any way. **Copyright infringement is against the law.** Thank you for respecting the hard work of these authors.

Washington, Jane
Eve, Jaymin
Trickery

www.janewashington.com
www.jaymineve.com

Edited by David Thomas
www.josephinebanksofficial.com/editing

ISBN: 978-1544094014

For Jane: thanks for nothing, asshole.
Also for Jaymin: go home, you're drunk.

GLOSSARY

click – **minute**
rotation – **hour**
sun-cycle – **day**
moon-cycle – **month**
life-cycle – **year**
minateur – **soldier**
bullsen – **beast**
sleeper – **spider**
furline – **caterpillar**
sol – **dominant race**
dweller – **serving race**
minatsol – **world of the dwellers and sols**
topia – **world of the gods**
luciu – **floating city of the gods**
soldel – **first city of the sols**
dvadel – **second city of the sols**
tridel – **third city of the gods**

ONE

Some things in life were a given. It was a given that the sols were the bridge between the dwellers and the gods. It was a given that some of them would *become* gods, after they died—while the rest of us would only become ash. It was a given that they would always be more important, and that the dwellers would remain their slaves until there were no dwellers left, and the sols had taken over everything.

It was also a given that I'd never be picked to go to Blesswood Academy, because I never got picked for anything. I was still going to go to the selection ceremony, though. To support Emmy. *She* would get picked. She was smart like that, and lucky like that, and people loved the hell out of her. They didn't love the hell out of me; they ran the hell away from me. It wasn't like I was a bad person or anything, I just ... had a lot of accidents. I didn't mean accidents like I ate glue and then peed myself on a regular basis. I just tripped more than usual, and accidently set things on fire more than what would be considered 'normal'. I got kicked out of the village school only one moon-cycle before graduation for accidently making one of the teachers bald. *How do you accidently make someone bald?* That's a good question. All you really need is a bucket of warm tar to accidently toss onto the back of their head. *How do you get a bucket of warm tar?* You don't go looking for it or anything—or at least I didn't. It was just sitting on the road outside the school and I thought I should carry it inside to ask what it was.

None of us had any experience with tar. All of our roads were dirt, but the leader of our village was always trying to make us famous, and he had all these random engineering books to give him ideas. Books that he probably stole from somewhere. As if the gods gave a shit about whether our roads were gravel or dirt. We had no sols in our village, and we were so far out from the centre ring—the centre of our society. So the gods wouldn't even notice if we painted our roads purple and started walking around naked.

Anyway, back to the tar.

Apparently, when your hair gets covered in tar, the only way to get rid of it is to shave your entire head, and that's how I made my teacher bald. The whole 'making a teacher bald' incident was pretty much the reason that nobody was expecting me to go to the selection ceremony. I was the embarrassment of the village, the *village fool*, the cursed child that they all secretly wanted to be rid of. But they could all suck-it-the-hell-up, because Emmy was my best friend, and I needed to be there when they announced that she would be chosen. Mostly, I just wanted to see Casey's face when she *wasn't* chosen, but that wasn't even halfway as noble a motivation as cheering on Emmy.

Casey might still be chosen—each of the outlying villages were allowed to send two of their best dwellers to Blesswood, where they would serve the smartest, bravest, and most powerful sols in the world. Blesswood was Minatsol's most holy city, housing the only academy dedicated to the gods. The gods even came down to Blesswood once a moon-cycle to survey the sols—to watch them fight it out in the arena, or outsmart each other in strategy games. Not every sol would get chosen to join the gods, but those that did were always chosen from Blesswood.

None of us dwellers really understood how the process worked, but it wasn't our business to understand. The majority of us would never step foot inside of Blesswood. Instead, we would remain in our outlying villages, studying to become teachers, or working in our family trades to keep ourselves afloat. But two insanely talented dwellers would always be chosen to lead a different life. To *be* different. To enter the world of the sols. Emmy was definitely one of those dwellers; there was no doubt in my mind about it. She was beautiful, intelligent, steadfast, and brave. She once re-built the woodsmith's shop overnight, all on her own. There wasn't a thing in the world that she couldn't do.

Well ... except for becoming a sol, or a god.

That was pretty much impossible.

"Willa!" The girl in question had just skidded into the house, her eyes widening at the sight of me, a shriek in the form of my name leaving her mouth.

"It's nothing," I managed, jumping away from her before she could grab me.

"You're bleeding, idiot!"

"Since when does bleeding make a person an idiot? We all do it. It's totally natural."

She rolled her pretty brown eyes, making another grab for me. I huffed, giving up my hand. I wasn't actually bleeding, but the burn on my hand was all red and angry, so it had probably appeared that I was bleeding, at first. She dropped my hand and spun to the stove, tossing a pot of water over the licking flames that I had lit beneath the cooking cupboard. As steam filled the room, she started rummaging around in the drawers of my mother's tiny kitchen. The first three drawers that she opened contained small medical packs made of cloth, but they had all been depleted.

"Over there." I decided to help her out, jerking my head in the direction of the bed in the corner of the room.

It was the only proper bed in our cottage—my mother had bought it when Emmy's parents had died, saying that she could live with us and that the two of us could share it, while she slept on the mattress on the floor. It didn't take her long to kick both of us to the floor instead, to the thin stretch of foam that had always been my bed in the past. Emmy found the fourth medical pack tucked beneath the bed, and brought it over to me, making quick work of bandaging my hand.

"I told you not to use the stove anymore," she chastised, a frown furrowing between her brows. "That's why I cook enough to last for the week, if you keep it properly."

"I wasn't cooking, I swear. I would never. Not even if you forced me."

"Why was the stove hot?"

"There was something inside it. I thought if I made it hot, it would crawl out."

"With the door shut?"

"Whoops."

She laughed, finishing up with my hand and spinning to face the stove. It was made of stone, a long and bulky structure reminiscent of a fireplace, with an area to light a fire below a stone cupboard with a cast-iron door, which filtered into a chimney. She wrapped her hand in a cloth and popped open the door. That was what I had done wrong—not wrapping my hand before trying to touch the hot metal.

Emmy winced, and then closed the door again. "Guess we're having rat for dinner."

I inspected my hand, totally impressed with her bandaging skills. "Can't I keep you here, Emmy? You're so handy. What am I going to do without you?"

"I might not get picked," she reminded me, her voice soft.

She was afraid. I didn't know why. Maybe she was afraid of leaving me alone, or maybe she was afraid that she *would* get picked. Blesswood was a whole other world to us outlying dwellers—a world that we had barely any knowledge of, and absolutely no experience in. A form stumbled in through the doorway, and we both turned to watch my mother slump down onto the twin bed with an incoherent mumble.

"Mum," I groused, walking over to the bed and shaking her leg. "The selection ceremony is this sun-cycle, remember?"

"Just leave her." Emmy grabbed my hand, pulling me away. "We're going to be late."

I was pissed. I didn't want my mum to stand Emmy up on her big day, but she'd obviously been at Cyan's tavern all night. *Again*. I tried not to think about it in certain terms—they were *her* life choices after all—but I was pretty sure that she was having sex with travellers passing through the tavern to earn enough tokens to keep us all alive.

Okay, those were pretty certain terms.

That would have been bad enough, but I was also pretty sure that she was drinking away most of the tokens that she earned. She wasn't a very responsible mother. She barely seemed to notice that we were around. Emmy kept her fed, and I sometimes pulled her shoes off when she stumbled into the house with the dawn. That was the extent of our relationship now. Maybe it would have been different, if Emmy hadn't come to live with us. Maybe I would have needed her more, and that would have forced her to act like a mother.

Emmy started to drag me out of the house, but we both stopped on our way to the door, looking down at the broken timepiece on the floor. Each of the village households were permitted a single timepiece to share, and I must have accidentally dropped ours after I had burned my hand. The glass cover was shattered, and the two pointers were struggling to move. The longer, thinner pointer, which moved slowly around the timepiece to measure *clicks* in time, was just twitching back and forth over the same number. The shorter, thicker pointer, which would rotate to the next number after sixty clicks—indicating a *rotation* in time—had broken off completely.

"Don't worry about it," Emmy said. "We can deal with it later."

She finally succeeded in dragging me out of the house, and we took off down the road, our backpacks thumping against us with each step. Hers was probably full of books and practical things. Mine had practical things in it, too. But things that would only have been practical for me, specifically. Among those things were a fire blanket, a pocketknife, a general-poisons antidote that I'd basically traded my soul for at a travelling circus. And by my *soul*, I mean every token that I had ever saved up.

Tokens were the currency of our people, and I'd managed to save up a total of three. Well ... two and a half. Not sure where the other half of the last one was. It kind of looked like someone had taken a bite out of it, but that was both impossible and unhygienic. The tokens were made of bronze metal, and they were always pretty filthy. So, I had traded my precious two and a half tokens for what was most likely a scam-potion. I was almost positive that it wouldn't work, but I'd never come across anything like it before, so it was far too easy for them to convince me that it was the rarest of potions, and worth much more than I was paying for it. I also had another medical kit in my backpack, and a banana. Just in case I got hungry.

"Maybe they'll choose you to go with me," Emmy joked, peeking at me sideways.

"*Pfft*," I huffed, a little out of breath, because she was so much faster than me. "They wouldn't even let me graduate."

"They did, though."

"Yeah but only because I broke into the records office and made myself a star pupil."

"I still can't believe you did that." She chuckled.

"You graduated above everyone else. Almost above me, even, and they couldn't do anything about it."

"Nope." I let my lips smack together in satisfaction as I said the word. "Those documents are official. Binding."

"They just didn't want to admit to Leader Graham that you managed to break into their records office and tamper with everything. He would have fired all of them."

"Okay yeah, that's probably a more likely explanation."

We reached the school—which was a collection of stone houses, connected by dirt pathways—and wove through the people toward the back field, where everyone was gathering. There was a stage set up, and Leader Graham himself was standing there, a bunch of papers in his hands. I snorted, pointing at him, and Emmy glanced in the direction that I indicated, a smile breaking out across her face. Leader Graham was always trying to look important. He had easily ten pages of notes in front of him, but he only needed to learn two names. He had a whole team of village advisers behind him, but he would only *announce* two names.

"Good evening, dwellers," he began, just as we took seats toward the back, peering around the heads in front of us to try and get a better glimpse of him. "As you all know, we've reached the end of another life-cycle, and will be sending off two of our best to attend to the sols of Blesswood." He paused, allowing the front row of dwellers to jump out of their seats, cheering excitedly. I recognised most of them as our classmates.

"Emmy." I poked her. "I think we're supposed to be sitting up the front."

She nudged me back and I slid out of the seat, creeping up the middle aisle with her right behind me as Leader Graham started talking again.

"As you all know, Blesswood was the original birthplace of the first sol family, many hundreds of thousands of life-cycles ago. The original family did not work to strengthen themselves for the gods, so they were not chosen to ascend to Topia to be with the gods. The sols of this age know better, and throughout Minatsol, they are even now gathering the best amongst their own people to send to Blesswood, to train for that very purpose. To impress the gods. Just as we are striving to serve the sols, the sols are striving to serve the gods. And we must always keep in mind that some of those sols *may* be chosen to join the gods, which means that our chosen dwellers will be attending to not only the most respected sols of our world, but also the future *gods* of our world. There is no more noble profession for a dweller in all of Minatsol."

"Except maybe just staying put and probably accidently burning the village down," I muttered to

Emmy over my shoulder. "I think my future profession is super noble."

She snickered, but hit my shoulder kind of hard, which wasn't surprising. She didn't like it when I said stuff like that. The boy whose chair I was currently crouched next to shot me a glare, and I shut up, turning my attention back to Leader Graham.

"So," he shook out his top sheet of paper, clearing his throat, "without further ado, the selected dwellers both graduated with perfect marks in all classes, and are even siblings of the same household. May they bring honour to their family, and to this village. Emmanuelle and Willa Knight ... please come up to the stage."

I froze, the breath rushing out of my chest in a groan.

Shit.

Shit!

I didn't think they would use those records to decide on who to send to Blesswood.

"Willa?" Emmy muttered from behind me, her voice a squeak. "You altered my forms too?"

"Just your last name." I was on autopilot, my mind spinning too fast for logical thought. "You're my sister. You needed my last name."

"Oh, Willa ... what have you done?"

I didn't get a chance to answer, because she was standing, grabbing my arm and pulling me up with her. I tried to crouch down again, but she wouldn't let me and *holy gods*, she was strong. She dragged me all the way up to the stage and planted me directly beside Leader Graham, who shook my hand, and then her hand, before presenting us to the village people. They weren't even clapping. They were sitting there, mouths hanging open, while metaphorical crickets chirped in the background.

Leader Graham frowned, having no idea what was going on, because he really didn't get involved with the people he was supposed to be leading, unless it was to force us to do something he wanted. Or on the rare occasion that the Minateurs—the governing body of the sols—inspected our village.

He grabbed my shoulders and forced me forward a step. "Would you like to say something?" he asked me, in a way that didn't really make it a question. "Thank your teachers, maybe?"

"Thanks, er, teachers," I managed, my voice strangled.

His frown deepened, and he turned to Emmy, who stepped up beside me, clearing her throat confidently.

"We will not let this village down," she promised, her strong voice carrying over everyone's shock, and stirring them back into motion. "We will work harder than any other chosen dwellers, and we will return to this village with the blessings of the gods. That is a promise."

It was such a short speech, but Emmy had been the one to deliver it, so it was enough to force a few cheers from the people. The rest were all still staring at me. Leader Graham seemed to give up on us, pointing to the side of the stage to dismiss us while he rambled on for a little bit longer about a few of the most legendary sols to ever ascend to Topia.

Emmy was laughing by the time the people cleared out. I mean *really* laughing. She was sitting on the stage, her knees brought up to cradle her face as she hung her head and veritably *lost it*. When she looked up, there were tears streaming down her face.

"I can't believe our luck," she told me. "I just can't believe it. This was something I didn't even dare to dream about. We're going to Blesswood, Willa. *Both of us*. Together!" She started laughing again, and I started worrying about her sanity.

"Are you okay?" I asked, kneeling beside her, my hand on her back.

Immediately, she started sobbing. *What the hell*?

"I've been losing it inside my head," she admitted between hiccupping sobs. "Ever since you got kicked out of school. You were so smart, you could have made it, but then ... then it all came crashing down. I thought ... I thought I'd have to say no, if I got chosen."

I felt my own tears welling, then. I had to bite them back as I cuddled her into my arms. I stroked her silvery hair, muttering things that weren't really things, like *you're fine, we're fine, it'll be fine*. What I really wanted to say was that I was probably going to die. Literally. I was the *least* appropriate person to throw into a school of elite sols. If I pissed one of them off enough, they would send me to one of the temples to be sacrificed to the gods. No joke. I was probably going to die.

"We're fine," I repeated. "This is going to be amazing. A whole new life. Just you wait, Emmy."

Within one sun-cycle, Emmy and I were standing on the edge of our village, single bag in hand, preparing for our big moment. Preparing to walk from the only home we'd ever known. I was leaving behind a mother who probably wasn't even aware that I'd been chosen; she'd barely been present or conscious since our selection. I wasn't sure she understood what had happened. Maybe she didn't even know that Emmy and I were leaving. That we would never return. Blesswood dwellers didn't come back to the outlying villages, despite what Emmy had promised—nope, they were destined for bigger and better things. Like being hogtied and sacrificed to the Gods for accidently tripping and punching the sacred balls of one of the sacred sols. Don't think it couldn't happen, because I was up to five cases this life-cycle alone. *Torture.* That was what my future had in store for me. I was going to be tortured.

The previous afternoon, after the ceremony, I had told Emmy that I couldn't wait. That it was going to be fantastic. The best ever. Sign me up for two lifetimes, and then for an encore. But when the sky grew dark and there was nobody around to see my false enthusiasm, the terrors grew particularly dark and vivid. Each nightmarish scene depicted one of the millions of ways that I might inflict disaster onto the sols. Onto Blesswood.

I tried to tell myself that it would be fine. That the academy had been coasting along with a perfect reputation for too long anyway, and that a little tarnish would do it some good. Spice things up. As long as they didn't use my blood to try and buff the stain ...

Crowds swelled around us as we waited by the oldest piere tree for our transport cart to arrive. This huge, gnarled, ancient thing represented the most northern point of our village, where the two dirt roads intersected. One leading to Blesswood in the north, and the other leading to the last vestiges of civilisation in Minatsol. Beyond that ... nobody really knew. Not a single person had ever travelled any further south than the last village and actually *returned*; and none of us were any wiser as to what lay in that most mysterious part of Minatsol. More death, I was sure. Or maybe it was paradise, and that was why nobody ever came back. The thing was ... that was a pretty big gamble: *death or paradise?* Only two villages lay further from Blesswood than ours, and both struggled to grow from the land. Water was scarce, but their leaders had expressed on more than one occasion how grateful they were not to have me, so that was something.

Minatsol was set out in a ring-like pattern. The very centre was Blesswood. It was there that the most fertile of life was. Each circle that extended out grew worse and worse. We were in the seventh ring, and there were nine in total, that we knew of. Beyond that was the south road, and the gamble of death or paradise.

Glancing up, I let the sway of red and green-tinged leaves soothe me. We were in the middle of the hot season, but despite a scarcity of water, this old tree continued to provide shade and shelter. As the folk stories told it, this tree was from the time *before*. No one liked to talk much of the time before. I'm not sure any of the stories really truly *remembered* the true beauty of our world. Apparently, all of Minatsol—not just Blesswood—had once resembled Topia; which was said to be the most beautiful of all worlds. Not that any of us knew about the other worlds. We just assumed that they were out there. Somewhere. Like Topia.

"You ready for this, Will?" Emmy gripped her bag loosely, her other hand wound tightly through mine.

"How long do you think it'll take mum to realise we're gone?" I continued to scan the crowd. It was common for the village as a whole to send the Blesswood recruits off, but there was no sign of my dirty-blond, tired-faced, red-eyed matron.

Emmy's silver hair slid across her cheek as the slightest of breezes lifted the strands. She looked extra pretty, having taken time and care with her appearance. I had worn my good shirt, and it was even mostly clean, except for a little sooty patch on the back from where I had accidentally sat in the fireplace.

"Probably around the time she realises that her medical kits are full, and that my dinners have run out," Emmy replied.

Yeah, my mother used those medical kits almost as much as I did, because believe it or not, there *was* another person out there capable of causing as much chaos as I did. She wasn't born that way, though—not like me. She got there with the help of alcohol and low morals.

Noises swelled in the crowds, and I could see the transport cart slowly moving toward us. Yellow, ochre-coloured dirt kicked up beneath the four spoked wheels. It was believed that within the sacred walls of Blesswood, they had transport systems able to move without the help of bullsen—the huge, black, pointy-headed beasts that now pulled the approaching cart. It wasn't called *Blesswood* for no reason, you see. The gods gifted them with magic and technology of the calibre that dwellers could only dream of. That must have been where the book on tar had come from: from a place where the reality was far beyond even our brightest sun-cycles.

Emmy started dragging me to the now-waiting transport, her grip on my hand tight with nervous energy. People reached out and touched us as we left. Dwellers were superstitious by nature and believed that these were the actions which would garner favour with the gods. This was why we served the sols the way we did—I mean, other than the fact that the sols would probably burn our villages to the ground if we didn't. We wanted the gods to reward us, to see our use, to recognise our people. So when any of the dwellers were chosen to serve the sols, the others always made a show of their support. They hoped that *eventually* the dwellers would find themselves recognised as more than just the bottom rung of sentient life in our world.

I had never reached out to touch any of the previous dwellers, because I assumed differently. I was the bottom feeder of the bottom feeders, and if my eighteen life-cycles had taught me anything, it was that nothing ever changed. Dwellers would always be worthless to the world, and I would always be worthless to the worthless.

As if I'd summoned the accident by thought alone, my feet tangled in a rough section of brush by the side of the dirt road, and before Emmy could right my balance—no doubt the reason she'd chosen to utilise her crazy, muscle-man strength and manhandle me in the first place—the bag shot from my hand and hit the side of the cart. A cart which bore the very regal crest of Blesswood; the mark of the creator, the original God. His mark was a staff, with a spear-head made of silver. Always silver, because silver was the colour of the Creator. I'd heard, once, that all the gods were defined by certain colours, but the only part of that particular lesson that had actually stuck with me had been the fact that Death's colour was black. It just seemed so ... predictable. *Where's the creativity, gods?* I didn't see why Death couldn't have pink. Or purple. What if he liked sparkles?

I was distracted from my thoughts as my bag dropped heavily into the dirt beside the cart, billowing up a plume of dust. An actual gasp was let out en-mass as the shock of what I'd just done wore off. *Come on, people.* They couldn't be surprised, right? Did they think that by just being chosen, I'd suddenly emulate the grace of a sol? Well, that would have been nice, but I was a pragmatic sort of dweller. The clumsy curse was going nowhere, although I did take a moment to be grateful that I'd neither killed anyone, nor disabled the vehicle in a way that would render it completely useless.

"Willa," Emmy hissed. "What the hell is in your bag?"

I took a closer look at the crest. There was now a dent in it, right in the centre. Knocking the pin-straight staff a little off-kilter. *Whoops.* Striding a few feet forward, dragging Emmy with me, I snatched my bag up again.

"I think it was the saucepan," I whispered.

"Why is there a saucepan in your bag?" she asked, glaring at the bag in question.

"Won't we need it to cook with?"

She slapped a hand over her mouth, but it was too late. I'd caught the start of her laugh. I brandished my bag at her, fully prepared to whack her with it—and the gathered people gasped, *again*.

Emmy only shook her head at me.

"How many strikes do you get before they bleed you?" I was half joking as we were forced to turn to the gathered villagers and wave.

She blinked a few times, her mouth opening and closing, before she was finally able to say, "It's your own fault, Will. What did I tell you about walking?"

"That I should leave it to the experts," I mumbled, trying to sound chastised.

The stark white of her skin was a little too pronounced, and I knew she feared for me, even though she was teasing me in the same way that she always had. I wasn't the only one who had been kept up last night by visions of the many ways in which I would almost definitely be tortured. Dwellers might live simple, menial, task-driven lives—but it was reasonably safe in the villages. My curse was barely tolerated here, but there was nothing that could be done to actually get rid of me. Most dwellers figured that one sun-cycle soon, I would simply take care of the problem myself, by tripping into one of the spiked pits that bordered the village to protect us from wild animals, or accidentally stumbling into untamed bullsen territory. *Pfft.* Been there, done that, wasn't even *that* close to dying.

"Come on." Emmy dragged me the last few feet.

My bag was now being stored in the back by the

guide ... though not before he searched it suspiciously. He didn't even open Emmy's. *Hardly surprising.* One look at Emmy and it was pretty clear that the most illegal thing she would be capable of smuggling into Blesswood would be a pair of underpants with an accidental rip in them. Not even a deliberate rip—an *accidental* one.

The guide was probably employed by the Blesswood academy. He would take us across the seven rings, a journey which would take many sun-cycles, and then he would deliver me to my doom. I examined the cart, worried that it wouldn't be sturdy enough to withstand my bad luck. It was one with a covered, round-top cargo hold. It would be there that we would sleep when night fell. Two bullsen were secured with a multitude of belts, which had been woven from the strongest of vines. Vines which I knew only grew in the two rings out from Blesswood. Not much else was able to contain the huge black beasts. I paused to admire them for a moment—because they could do no harm to me all trussed up in leather harnesses. They were relatively hairless, or at least they had really short, shiny coats. Their eyes were usually full of darkness, but I had heard you could occasionally make out the faintest ring of colour around the iris. I never had, but that was because I refused to get that close. They had four sets of legs, with knobby knees and hooved feet, and while they looked somewhat gangly, they were impressively strong and fast.

They were also wild and dangerous, but most people chose to ignore that fact by pretending that they had successfully 'domesticated' them.

"Greetings, dwellers." The guide was younger than I'd expected, probably around thirty life-cycles old, with a full head of orange hair, a spattering of birth spots across his nose, and light blue eyes. "My name is Jerath. I will be escorting you safely to Blesswood, where you will begin your blessed service to the sols."

A cheer went up from my village. It wasn't the first one.

"Crying would be much more appropriate," I side-whispered to Emmy. "They could at least *fake* sadness until we left."

With a shake of her head, she nudged me forward and both of us climbed up onto the back bench seat. The guide had the front, and he would use the belts to control the cart. From this high vantage, I could see the crowds and the edges of our village. The spot near the water well where I'd hidden during the most punishing sun-cycles of the heat season, so that the droplets of cool water would splash me as people pulled from the well. The stone buildings where I'd spent my formative life-cycles learning, and the healer's hut, where I'd sent at least five of the teachers who had laboured over my formative learning. The tar incident had been the final straw, but there had been so many straws before that. Probably too many straws.

Teacher Garat had actually been more patient than most.

The bullsen twitched as more noise erupted from the drunken crowd. They had to be drunk. There was literally no other excuse for grown-ass dwellers to act so freaking happy about us leaving. *None.* They had definitely moved past their shock over me having been chosen, and were now taking it as a gift from the gods.

The bastards.

Jerath was now speaking with Leader Graham; I saw the exchange of goods, and probably tokens. Villages earned tokens for their hard work, something like one million tokens got you the grand prize of more dwellers to do more work. Hardly worth the effort, if you asked me, but tokens were life around here. I was pretty sure that our leader slept in a bed of the round, shiny discs.

Jerath climbed back onto the cart, signalling the fact that it was now time to go. Leader Graham stepped to our side. "The seventh ring wishes you a long life of servitude. You have been blessed. You must now do everything in your power to bring pride to your people. Anything you do reflects on us; your village is rewarded for your hard work".

Right. Give me a moment to wipe my tears.

Emmy gave him a genial nod. "We will make our village proud. You can expect many tokens for our service."

So many. Except for all those subtracted away when

I accidentally glued one sacred sol's head to another sacred sol's backside.

Jerath lifted the belts, and with one last wave, we were moving. I sent a single glance back, silently bidding farewell to my mother. She was a bit of a drunk floozy, but she had always been in my life. I had very few things which were mine—she'd been one of those things. Emmy squeezed my hand, and it was enough for me to turn in my seat and face toward the new future.

Everything was about to change now. Whether it was for better or worse, no one but the gods knew.

TWO

In the first four sun-cycles of the journey, we'd suffered two cracked cart wheels, an escaped bullsen, and three wild animal attacks. Considering my propensity for disaster, I was considering it a roaring success. We were now in the third ring and it was the first time I could see the difference in the land. The sixth, fifth, and fourth rings had been much like ours: with yellow dirt roads, hard, unforgiving land, stone buildings, and bullsen pens. Sure, their villages might have had a few more trees, extra water wells and maybe even a pond which could be used for bathing ... but for the most part, it was familiar.

The third ring, however, was when the world started to change.

The roads were paved; the houses had proper glass windows set into decorative, mason-worked sills; and the people barely even blinked at the passing transport cart, even though it had the symbol of the Creator on it. It was something they apparently saw often.

"This is Tridel," Emmy whispered to me—even though nobody could hear us over the noisy turning of the wheels against the paved road. "The first sol city. Or the last, actually, depending on which way you're coming from. The next is Dvadel, Soldel, and then we'll be in Blesswood."

I didn't bother to ask how she knew that. She knew everything, because she clearly stole all the good genes from the rest of us pathetic villagers. I sat up higher in my seat, peering at the faces that were so completely oblivious to us. The sols didn't look any different to us dwellers, not really. I was staring at a group of them now, as they gathered around a shop-front, waiting in line for something with hempen sacks of produce loaded up into their arms.

"They don't look *that* sacred," I muttered to Emmy.

She followed the direction of my gaze, and then snorted on a laugh. "Those are dwellers, Will. The sols keep slaves even in Tridel."

I flushed, a tiny bit embarrassed, and turned the other way, staring out along the other side of the cart. There was a couple walking along the side of the road, close enough for me to examine. The woman was a few inches shorter than the man, her arm hooked through his. Either there were subtle differences in how sols appeared compared to dwellers, or else they were just a particularly attractive couple. Whatever the reason, the sun was shining right on them, highlighting them like a flattering spotlight. I felt my mouth dropping open, just a little bit. Her hair was *shiny*, her eyes were *shiny*, his teeth were *shiny,* their clothes were *shiny.* Maybe it was just the light, but it put me into a bit of a trance anyway.

"*Shiny*," I drooled, causing Emmy to laugh again.

The man must have heard Emmy, because he glanced our way, his smile growing for a moment, as he nodded in greeting. He knew where we were going. It was pretty obvious. We were *dwellers*, sitting in a cart bearing the Creator's insignia. We were going to Blesswood, to serve the future gods.

"He smiled at me," I tried to tell Emmy, speaking out of the side of my mouth, trying not to make it look like I was talking about him.

"I know, dummy," she replied blandly.

The cart veered a little then, probably dodging a crack in the pavers, and the wheel hit a puddle, spraying dirty street water all over the shiny couple.

"Whoops." I jerked back in my seat, fixing my eyes firmly in front of me, as though I had somehow done it deliberately.

The man wasn't smiling anymore—he was now loudly cursing poor Jerath, who either couldn't hear, or didn't care. I suspected that Jerath was another dweller, albeit one important enough to serve the sols of Blesswood. Did that give him a certain amount of status? And was the status high enough that he could accidently spray some sols with street water? *Apparently.*

Things were looking up.

"Remember what I told you, Will?" Emmy was watching me. I could feel the weight of her stare.

I had no damn idea what she was talking about, but she already knew that. I was supposed to say 'what?' and *cue preventative lecture about safety in Blesswood.*

"Don't sleep with a knife in the bed for safety?" I asked instead, a smirk lifting my mouth.

She narrowed her eyes on me, trying to convey that it was serious time. "Not that."

"Don't make out with Teacher Hardy's son? He probably has a disease because he's always itching his crotch?"

"Not th—"

"Don't leave the curtains open while I'm dancing naked? Don't eat *everything* that's put in front of me—especially if *I* was the one who put it in front of me? Don't—"

"Will—"

"Don't sew *all* the holes shut while I'm mending shirts, because then where do the arms go?"

"*Will—*"

"Don't drink pond water; don't believe everything I read; don't say no to everything; don't say yes to everything; don't—"

"Don't talk over me while I'm trying to lecture you!"

My smirk melted into laughter, seeing how red her face had turned, and I settled back into my seat, wiggling around a little bit to get comfortable.

"Okay, fine," I eventually said. "Bring it on. Lay it on me. Lecture away. I'm ready. I'm waiting. Let's do this."

She was getting frustrated. The smoke coming out of her ears was almost visible—but to be honest, I was trying to put off the serious-talk. I had been since we left the village. Emmy had been preparing for the possibility of eventually ending up in Blesswood, but I hadn't been. I didn't know anything, and I was terrified of what she was going to tell me.

"Are you done?" she finally asked, arching a single, silver eyebrow.

"No, wait ..." I reached into my pack, pulling out one of the honey sandwiches that she had packed to last the journey. "Okay, go," I allowed, freeing the bread from its canvas wrapping and stuffing as much into my mouth as possible.

Maybe I was being immature, but it would be easier to turn this into a one-way lecture.

Emmy didn't mind. She launched straight into it. "You have no idea what's going to happen when you get there, Will, but the rest of us do. They spent a lot of time going over this in the last moon-cycle at school, because two of us were going to get picked. It's important that we're prepared."

"Oghay," I managed around a mouthful of bread.

"Our sun-cycles will be split between the

classrooms and the dormitories—we'll be given a timetable just like all the sols, but we don't get to actually *attend* classes with them. We'll be attending *to* the classes. Each classroom is assigned five dwellers to be at the disposal of the sols and the professors. When academy classes are over, we'll each have an assigned dormitory room, and it'll be our job to service the room and the sols assigned to the room. I don't know when we're going to have time to eat ... they never explained that."

"What about sleep?" I quipped, swallowing what was in my mouth. "Will we have time for that? Or the other essentials, like breathing?"

"Bathing?"

"No. *Breathing*."

"You can multitask, can't you?"

I *huffed*, stuffing the rest of my sandwich into my mouth. "Hard-ass," I muttered, almost unintelligibly.

"What was that?" she asked, snatching the rest of the sandwiches out of my lap.

"Love you," I amended quickly, causing her to laugh.

Emmy held off on lecturing me any further, even when we passed through Dvadel and into Soldel, which was the first ring after Blesswood. This city was different to the other sol settlements. It was actually stepping up into a gradual incline, with several lower tiers of what seemed to be general housing, below several higher tiers of ... *what the hell was that?* It looked like they had taken a bunch of stone houses and stacked them on top of each other. There were buildings like this scattered all around, towering into the sky. How could they do that? How did it stay up so high in the air? Emmy noticed my slack jaw, wide eyes, and metaphorically drooling chin, and quickly leaned over to follow my line of sight.

"*Wow!*" Her voice got all breathy. "I've wanted to see skyreachers my entire life. Did you know that hundreds of sols can live in one building? It's ingenious."

All I heard was '*did you know that hundreds of sols can all die in one go?*' Ingenious clearly equalled insane in Emmy-talk. No way would I ever step foot into something like that. Temptation for my clumsy curse was exactly what that was.

"If sols are so blessed—you know, with all the shininess, and the gifts, and the chance to kiss-ass the gods of Topia—then why do they live all stacked up on top of each other like the Minateurs are waiting to sort them out properly later?"

It didn't make sense to me. I dreamed of living in my own home, surrounded by all my stuff. I'd have medical kits in the exact spot I last left them. You know, the little things. Emmy had her sol-worshipping eyes on, the deep brown colour as rich as the soil beneath the roots of the trees that we passed. She clearly loved the skyreachers.

"They're supposed to be so fancy, Will. Like *fancy*

fancy. Only the wealthiest of the sols are able to afford a skyreacher home. Can you imagine? Being so much closer to the gods?"

"Do we know that the gods live in the sky, though? I never really believed Teacher Hardy's theory. He ate sardines for lunch. It's never good to trust a person who eats sardines."

Emmy shrugged. "Maybe they don't, but I doubt they live in the ground, and whenever anyone talks about the gods coming to Blesswood every moon-cycle, they say that the gods are coming *down*."

"Okay, but back to the skyreachers just real quick. How do they even pee? I mean a hole in the floor is going to be a real problem for the sols below."

Even Jerath chuckled at that one, and he'd been a tough crowd so far. "They have indoor piping and proper bathrooms," he informed us, a broad grin strong across his fair cheeks. "They can even bathe inside, and the pipes make sure no one gets a pee shower."

Inside. *Inside?* Where did the water come from? Where did it go? Would my mind explode from all of the questions currently fighting for dominance? The higher we climbed, the more of the towering buildings surrounded us. Speckled intermittently between them were these huge, gated stone buildings. I had no idea why they needed gates. Sols were probably so badass they kept wild bullsen around their dwellings. Just for kicks.

It seemed that Soldel was coming to its peak; from our current vantage point we could see right out to the second ring, Dvadel. At the junction of this peak was another massive building, and it alone was almost the size of our entire village back home. It wasn't a dark grey stone like most of the other structures, but instead, something white and pretty with sparkling stones embedded *into* the walls. That was the leader of the buildings, the one which was all 'look at me, look at me,' making every other building in Soldel feel like crap about itself.

"Let me guess, that's Soldel's academy?" I pointed toward the show-pony.

Emmy shook her head. "Nope. Good guess, but that's the Minateurs' council chambers and training facility. They recruit sols during their graduation life-cycle at the academies. After that, it's another four life-cycles of training, and then they either become council members dealing with the disputes of the gods and the nine rings, or else they go into patrols. The patrols walk the streets, respond to distress calls, and keep the peace. It's a very honourable life-path and only the best of the best get to be a Minateur."

"Quick question." I leaned forward, trying to stretch out the ache in my back. It was taking forever to get to Blesswood. "How did we become friends? I've spent my life cycles trying not to become the great disaster of this era, and you've spent yours overachieving and learning way too much about the nine rings. They never specifically taught us this in school, so explain how you know everything?"

For most dwellers, there was absolutely no point learning about the inner workings of any rings except the one you lived in. There was no time off to travel; we weren't even allowed to travel without a tonne of tokens, thirty-five permits, special permission, and a sacrifice to the gods, or some crap. We weren't sols. We had no rights, and therefore, no need to learn anything more than the basics.

The basics being how to stay the hell out of the way of the sols, unless we were called upon for service.

"The information is there if you want it," Emmy told me. "I've been preparing for Blesswood my entire life. Did you know Teacher Howard was a former Blesswood recruit?"

Teacher Howard? Oh, right, he'd stopped by for one cold season in our sixth school cycle. We'd had a lot of teachers actually, when I thought about it.

"Six stitches and a mild concussion?" I double-checked that I was thinking of the right dweller.

Emmy was trying not to roll her eyes, which was fair considering I'd just summarised an incident that could have occurred with one of at least three other teachers.

I continued. "He loved yellow pants, wore the same socks over and over—despite the fact we could smell his feet even out in the snow—told crazy stories, learned the hard way to never take a weaving class with me. Or at least learned the hard way to never hand me cutters and belts at the same time?"

Still no eye roll. She was practising super-dweller patience.

"Yes, Will, that's him. He did something to annoy an important sol in Blesswood and as a punishment, he was directed to teach throughout the nine rings. A position of honour, but one which took him far from the blessed capital that he had been working his whole life to get to. He took a liking to me, said I reminded him of his sister, who now serves one of the most gifted of the sol families. He taught me so much. It's because of him that I worked so hard, studied, and made it my goal to be recruited."

"And somehow your clumsy-ass best friend got herself invited along on the journey. Very little work and at least one almost-world-ending-disaster per sun-cycle her only claim to fame."

"I don't think deliberately altering your records is a *somehow* thing, Will." Even as she said it, she was hugging me, hard. "At eight life-cycles I didn't love you like I do now." Her voice was muffled against my shirt. "Nope, at eight I was determined to go no matter what. Then you happened, and I knew that one sun-cycle I would have to leave you. It broke my heart. Every morning when I woke up, I questioned whether it was worth it. I would start off wanting to turn it down, and then I wouldn't be sure. No matter my doubts, I never stopped trying my hardest to be chosen. It was like I had to prove I could be the best, and then if I turned it down I'd know it was my choice." She pulled back to face me. "You getting chosen with me was the best thing that could ever have happened. For once your clumsy curse was a true gift."

A *gift*.

Those weren't words which had been used to describe my curse before. Nobody would have dared, even to make me feel better. Only sols had *gifts*, and my curse was enough of a slap-in-the-face-of-the-people as it was.

"Did you ever consider turning it down, Will?" The question from Emmy was a little hesitant, like she had been thinking about it but was afraid to ask. "I mean ... I know things have happened so fast, but ... *did* you consider turning it down?"

I hadn't. Not even once, actually. Which was odd because I was pretty certain I would die there. Although, the certainty of death was something I lived with every day, so it was understandable that it didn't have me in a panic. Well, not *that* much of a panic.

"Never even crossed my mind," I finally said to her. "This was meant to be, our friendship and journey was fated by the gods." I blew her a kiss, and when she was distracted by my sappy face, I reached out and snatched up the container of purple gaja berries she'd picked in the fourth ring. There were only half a dozen left, and she was being so stingy with her sharing.

She glared as I popped the first tart bite of goodness into my mouth. Berries didn't grow in the seventh ring, but we occasionally got some in trade. Emmy leaned across, but before things escalated into a girl-fight, the cart slowed, and our attentions were diverted to a huge fence across our current path, just to the side of the Minateurs' building. Standing spread out across the front of the tall barrier were six sols. I was assuming they were sols because they had the same dazzling thing going on, not to mention that one appeared to be holding a naked flame in his palm, and as far as I could tell, he wasn't in excruciating, screaming pain as his hand burnt down to a stub. Dwellers were great at lots of things: toiling from sunup to sundown; turning three figs into a pie for the entire village; and even dancing around a fire after copious amounts of liquor. But one thing we could *not* do was control the elements. Gifts of the sols. Lucky bastards.

Jerath pulled the bullsen to a complete halt and got off the cart. He crossed to the closest sol, a female who stood a foot taller than me, had better hair than me, and was altogether much more beautiful and intimidating than me. Not that I was comparing. Words were exchanged—words we couldn't hear—and then Jerath handed over some papers.

"Why are these sols eyeballing us?" I asked Emmy, trying not to move my mouth too much.

"Standard security checks before entering

Blesswood." She spoke normally, so my stealthy whispers were clearly not required.

They spent a few clicks examining our cart, checking the back sleeping area, and zapping me with sparks of energy which seemed to emit from their bodies as they crossed close by. Eventually, we were cleared to enter, and I found myself sneakily popping gaja berries in one by one as the gates opened. I had to do something to stem the rising tide of nerves which were threatening to erupt from me. Emmy had given up trying to get her snacks back, instead placing a hand on my knee to stop me bouncing it right out of the cart.

The gates took at least eighty-five life-cycles to open. By the time they did, I was over the nerves. Dragging things out helped no one. *Bad power play, sols, bad power play.*

The bullsen seemed hesitant to cross the final threshold of Soldel into Blesswood. Jerath had to be extra convincing, his belts flying through the air as he encouraged them along. The sols continued to watch us as we wheeled past. None of them smiled, or said anything, but I could feel their judgement.

You shouldn't be here.

You don't belong here.

You're not one of us.

The gate closed behind us. And suddenly ... the nerves were back. I twisted my hands in my lap as I tried to take in everything on this side of the barrier.

We were still at the very top of the hill we'd climbed and now it seemed it was time to start descending. To the right of our path was a long waterfall, which trickled down into the valley we were heading for. Yes, you heard that right—*water* just *trickling* out in the open for all to see. And everything was green. The land was covered in a vibrant green carpet of grass, which was almost too bright to stare at directly. The cart picked up speed and with a rapid warning from Jerath, Emmy and I had to hold on tight to the rails besides us.

After a brief dip, the land levelled out, and despite my need to appear unfazed, there might have been loud gasp slippage. Either that, or the air was thin here and I was having to work harder to breathe.

I knew Blesswood was the very centre of the nine rings and that there were multiple villages in each ring. Those were the things I knew. What I hadn't known was that Blesswood was pretty much an island. *An island?* The very concept was like a myth wrapped in a fable shot through with some sparkling magic. Ever since the great rivers and lakes had dried up—since the outer rings of Minatsol had turned into the land of dust and despair—we had no true islands. But Blesswood was doing its very best to come close.

"We'll need to cross on the barges now," Jerath said, halting his cart next to a bunch of other carts.

There were other carts! I'd been so caught up in the visage of the centre ring—a mass of land which went further than the eye could see and which seemed to be surrounded by a body of water that was connected to a series of waterfalls, like the one we had passed moments before—that I'd failed to notice the other carts, just like ours, all lined up in rows beside us. It looked as though all the recruits from the nine rings were converging there. They were all waiting for this barge thing to take us across the water.

"What's a barge?" I asked Emmy.

We were both off now, trying to balance on our half-dead legs. We were being punished for too many sun-cycles of too little use.

"I have no idea," she answered, as Jerath handed us both our bags. Emmy frowned down at mine, and I knew she was still trying to figure out how I got the pans and rock salt in there, plus enough changes of clothing for a week. If she was so worried about it, she should have packed for me. It was her own fault.

Wait a moment ... "You have no idea what a barge is?" I asked, astounded. "You know everything. I don't even bother trying to learn stuff myself, I just ask you and you give me the answer."

"Yeah, that's probably going to have to change," she advised, a laugh riding her words. "But I've never read about barges, and nobody has ever mentioned them to me."

"Wow. Guess you're not all that smart after all. Guess you're kinda silly. You feel silly right now, don't you? You feel a little embarrassed, because you don't know what a barge is?"

"No." She smirked, grabbing my arm and pulling me after Jerath.

She'd gotten into the habit of dragging me everywhere since they announced our names at the selection ceremony. She probably thought that I'd have a panic attack, steal a bullsen, and high-tail it as far away from Blesswood as possible at any moment. The thought hadn't even crossed my mind. But I didn't tell her that. It was too funny to watch her watching me out of the corner of her eye all the time.

We reached the first group of dwellers, all stuck together in groups of two. I wasn't sure how many dweller settlements there actually were in Minatsol—Emmy had told me once, but I'd forgotten. Either way, the number of dwellers gathered to the edge of the platform rising over the water hinted at a substantial dweller population. We all turned as one unit at the sound carrying over the water—like a horn, but long and drawn-out. There was a massive, floating platform coming toward us. Moving *over* the water.

"*Agh!*" I jumped back, grabbing Emmy's arm. "*What the hell is that?*"

"The barge," Jerath answered for her, folding his arms and grinning at the *thing* as it approached us.

Many of the dwellers closest to it jumped back, scattering away from the edge. Someone pushed me, another landed an elbow in my gut. Everyone was now scrambling back, trying to get away from the barge. Jerath was striding forward, so Emmy grabbed my arm and started dragging me again. I could make out people on the barge, now. Two of them were manoeuvring something down, snapping it against the edge of solid ground, forming a bridge over the water, leading from us to them.

"Come on," Jerath encouraged, moving toward the bridge. I could see many other dweller-guides doing the same thing, encouraging the rest of the gathered dwellers to cross onto the floating platform.

As soon as I stepped onto it, I let out a pitiful squeak. I could feel the water moving beneath, rocking me gently back and forth. It was terrifying ... until I noticed Emmy laughing, and then I quickly convinced myself that it wasn't scary at all, because I didn't want to look like a wimp. We moved to the side, allowing the wimpy dwellers to push us closer and closer to the water in their bid to all stand in the centre of the barge. I sat down on the edge, Emmy beside me, Jerath standing behind us. Our bags were piled together with a bunch of other bags, and I kept an eye on them because I was not losing those pots. I didn't care what Emmy said, they were important. Between watching my stuff, I studied the barge and everything else to do with this water marvel. The platform was too thick for our feet to touch the water, but I could feel the spray. It was cool and sharp, all at once.

We watched as the island drew near: displaying a patchwork array of water-front houses; along with giant, colourful stone buildings; and imposing skyreachers. A very strange kind of building sat in the centre of it all, making it the centre of the world itself. It was raised up, on a hill, with a giant stone wall creeping all around the valleys of the small mountain beneath, gradually enclosing the very tip, where the strange building sat.

"What's that?" I asked, pointing. I wasn't asking Emmy or Jerath in particular, just whoever answered me first.

"Blesswood Academy." Emmy was the one to answer, her eyes bright, her cheeks flushed. "It's exactly how they described it."

"The academy grounds contain more than just the academy itself," Jerath added, watching the peak with us. "The Temple of the Creator is inside those walls, and the Sacred Sand arena."

We stood as the barge slowed, I grabbed my bag before anyone else could think of touching it. The large water vessel eventually came to a standstill, and we moved with the rest of the dwellers hurrying to get their feet on solid ground again. They herded us toward a path carved into the side of the small mountain, and we climbed right to another set of gates. Two more sols stood guard, just as they had at the entrance to Blesswood. I looked up to the top of the wall and caught another sol face, briefly appearing over the edge.

"This everyone?" one of the guards grunted at Jerath.

We had managed to draw to the front of the long procession during our walk up, but it wasn't because we were particularly braver or stronger or faster than the other dwellers. It was because *Emmy* was particularly braver, stronger, and faster than the other dwellers, and she had been dragging me again. She was standing there now, not a single wrinkle in her expression as she brushed her hair over her shoulder and stood straight for the inspection of the guard. I was wheezing, my hands on my knees. The guard also inspected me, a small, sardonic smile on his face, before running his eyes down to the end of our procession.

"Go on in," he announced, jerking his head to the side and moving out of the way.

This was it. I was stepping into what would be Emmy's home for the rest of her life, and what would be my home for probably about half a sun-cycle. Maybe even an entire sun-cycle. All I needed to do was stay away from fire, tar, sharp things, pointy things, serrated things, hot things, breathing things, living things, and sacred things.

I paused, my feet stalling, my eyes flying wide. We had stepped into a courtyard with multihued stones underfoot and a giant, ancient piere tree standing in the middle, breaking up the cobblestones with thick, papery-white, gnarled roots. It figured that it was twice the size of the ancient piere tree back home, and that there were several more that I could see, spread around the winding cobbled pathways leading between academy buildings. It wasn't the tree that had surprised me, though. It was the guy *tied* to the tree, and the guy standing before him, holding up a crossbow. He was blindfolded, and the guy tied to the tree was laughing. They were clearly sols, because they were bigger than normal dweller men. Bigger, even, than what I would have expected of a sol. The one tied to the tree looked just a little older than me, his bright eyes sparkling with laughter. I wanted to draw closer, to see the colour of his eyes, or to confirm that his hair actually was the stunning meld of golden-black that it appeared to be from this distance. He glanced over as the dwellers behind us also came to a stop, and he started to laugh even harder.

"Turn!" he shouted.

The guy with the crossbow raised his arm, aiming the bolt directly at the other's chest, before slowly turning.

Turning ... to face *us*.

Jerath made a groaning sound, but nobody did anything to stop the crazy sol. He had the same golden tarnish to his hair as the one tied to the tree, though it was more golden-red, and his skin was a shade more tanned. He was also built like he tore up trees from the ground for a fun hobby. The blindfold over his eyes seemed to mask his face more than just his eyes, but I could still make out the infinitesimal smirk twisting his lips.

"Stop!" the one tied to the tree shouted.

The crossbow—and the guy holding it—paused. The bolt quivered ... and everyone turned to stare at me, because it was now pointed directly at me.

"Don't mind them," Jerath consoled, taking a step back.

"Are you seriously saying that while you move *away* from me?" I hissed out quietly.

"Those are the Abcurse brothers—or two of them anyway. Coen has a gift for Pain, and Siret has a gift for Trickery."

"The one that has a gift for pain ... is he the one holding the crossbow by any chance?"

"Yeah ..."

"Really?" I groaned, even though my heart was kicking up a riot inside my chest and my eyes were fixed to the annoyingly still crossbow bolt. "I didn't even last one *step* into Blesswood."

As the words left my mouth, Emmy kicked out a leg, knocking me into the ground. I felt the air brush past my face, something tugging against my hair, and then I heard the telling *thunk* of a crossbow bolt embedding itself into the wooden gate behind us. A gate that had obviously been nudged shut at some point, to protect the dwellers congregating around the entrance. I stared at the bolt, my mouth dropping open, my brain short-circuiting, and then I looked back to Coen, who had ripped the blindfold off and strolled forward a few steps. He had bright green eyes, smoking to a dark colour around the edges of the pupils, and I now noticed that the colour of his hair actually bled a deep, burnt red, with only a few golden strands. He glanced down at me on the ground, *frowned*, and then wandered away, resting his crossbow over his shoulder.

Siret, who had been left at the tree, struggled out of his ropes, jumping over the base of the tree and sauntering over to us.

"Dear little dirt-dwellers!" he sang, raising his arms and grinning as the gate creaked open again. "Welcome to Blesswood, and to the beginning of the rest of your lives! Try not to get in the way when my brother decides he's bored."

"Or when *you* decide you're bored," Jerath muttered beneath his breath.

Siret walked the rest of the way over, holding his hand out to me. I didn't want to take it. I really didn't. Emmy cleared her throat, though, her eyes full of panic, and I quickly grabbed his hand. He hauled me to my feet with far more ease than was really necessary to display to everyone, and I accidently stomped on his foot. He didn't seem to notice. He brushed off my shoulders as I tried not to get distracted by the green-gold tint of his eyes. They were lighter than his brother's, but just as stunning. *Did all sols have such stunning eyes?*

He almost had you killed! Right. His eyes sucked. He had *sucky* eyes, and so did his brother.

"See you round, Rocks," he said, sweeping his gaze over me before turning and jogging down the path his brother had taken.

"Rocks?" I managed, as the guides started ushering the other dwellers inside again.

Everyone was trying pretty hard to pretend that nothing had happened, but I could see the nervous expressions on their faces, and the sympathetic looks they shot my way. They were wasting their energy. Shit like this happened to me all the time. Maybe not on a *sacred sol of Blesswood almost murdering me for no reason whatsoever* scale, but close.

Emmy was chuckling beneath her breath, which meant that she had worked out my nickname.

"What?" I nudged her.

"You dropped like a bag of rocks."

"It wasn't *that* funny." I scowled.

THREE

It was a sombre, sweaty crowd that made its way the last few yards into the inner domain of Blesswood. Our first introduction to the gifted sols had been enough for all of us to realise that shit had just gotten real. *Really* real. Being a dweller in the village might be a lowly, unfortunate life, but we were all pretty equal there. Here, we would know every single sun-cycle that we were the dirt beneath the blessed feet of the blessed sols.

Dirt-dweller.

Punching a sol in the nose was probably frowned upon in Blesswood. I reminded myself to check the rule book on that one later, right after I learned how to punch. I should probably just stick with tripping and kneeing them in the groin, since it was one of my specialties. Maybe I could throw some tar on them. I was pretty sure that Siret and Coen wouldn't be so confident if they had to shave off all their pretty hair.

"Follow me," Jerath demanded, his voice loud enough to be heard over our panicked and rapid heartbeats. "There's no time to settle in, you'll find your bunk, dump your bags, and then get your assigned dorms, classes, and other duties. These were all decided long before you reached Blesswood, by the dweller-relations committee, so don't bother arguing, you won't get reassigned unless a *sol* requests it. No special circumstances."

Well *great*. What were the odds I pulled washroom duties for the rest of my life? Maybe being sacrificed to the gods wasn't the worst thing that could happen here. I focused on sucking up as much of the surrounding beauty as I could, before I was stuck cleaning urine-pots and bowing down to sols. The main room of this particular building was huge, with a dome-shaped ceiling. There were these scattered panes of glass, which allowed trickles of sunlight to wash down the marbled white walls and pillars. There didn't seem to be much in the actual room, furniture-wise. It appeared to be a central point, leading to a bunch of other buildings.

Jerath, who had somehow slipped into *leader* mode —and was definitely letting the power go straight to his head—was waving everyone forward. "Hurry up, there's no time for your slow, village backwardness right now."

We were roughly ushered through a small, dark archway, which somehow ended up in the corner of the beautiful building, and then down some dark, wooden stairs. I could see the staircase also went up, but apparently, they wanted us as far from the gods as possible.

Jerath's voice drifted back through the narrow stairs. "This is the dwellers' stairway. You'll use these back stairs to move around Blesswood as much as possible. The sols like their privacy; they want things done right, but without having to see or smell you."

I decided that *chatty leader-Jerath* was my least favourite of all the Jeraths—he was so much more fun when he was silent and spraying sols with street water.

It was dark and kind of damp in this section. I preferred wide-open spaces, and less elbows in my ribs. Also, the sweaty nerves thing was really starting to become an olfactory problem. The sols should probably cross off the *not smell us* thing. That just wasn't going to work. Finally, after climbing down four million and fifty stairs, we reached the dwellers' section. There was no natural light in this part; we were clearly far, far underground.

"Did anyone tell them about things collapsing on me?" I whispered to Emmy. "Someone should have warned them."

She shook her head, before her hand snaked around to cover my mouth. "We're one floor down, Will, you're going to be fine."

One! Was she insane? Those stairs had been never-ending!

"Female dorms are to the left, males to the right." Jerath was actually waving his hands now. Whatever chill he'd been channelling on the way here was long gone. "I'll be waiting for you back in the main foyer. You have until the bells ring for next class." He was gone then, back up the never-ending stairs.

Emmy was in the mood to get shit *done*. She had her arm around my entire middle this time, and was barrelling through all the poor dwellers who thought they were getting first pick of beds. From what I saw in our dash through, it looked like the dwellers' underground bunker was a small, dull room. Rocks under our feet, and above our heads. Real homey feel to it, what with all the dust and the lack of natural light.

"Are all the dwellers here?" I asked, trying not to breathe in the second-hand air. There was nothing fresh down there, that was for sure.

"Nope, this is just for the newbies. Although there are always a lot of newbies. Sols aren't very gentle with their play things."

Emmy hadn't answered that time. Someone else knew things too, which lowered my need to ever learn. I was good with that. I swivelled to see a petite girl with a huge mane of bushy, dirty-blonde curls. She was doing well to keep pace with my manic best friend. Her huge, azure eyes gave her face a cute-but-slightly-weird look. She seemed friendly enough though.

"So where do the dwellers who last longer than a life-cycle go?" I asked.

Emmy had told me on the way over that we would be considered 'recruits' for the first life-cycle, and that after that, we would become 'resident' dwellers. *Creepy*, I thought. *Hi! I'm just the resident dweller. I'll be waiting down here in the dungeon if you feel like some tea.* Anyway, using that information, it made sense that we'd be stuck down here for that long.

"Another building," the girl answered. "To the east of the academy estate. I heard that it's also underground, but slightly nicer. My cousin was here for many life-cycles; she now serves in Soldel."

We were in the female wing now, and it was about the same level of awesome as the previous room, just add in twenty or so small boxes masquerading as bedrooms. Emmy was dragging me toward the boxed room closest to the door, when I dug my feet in and pointed toward the name tags on the small edges above the doorway. It said *Janelle Brown and Samsa Neel*.

"Think we have to find our names," I said tentatively. I recognised her mood, so I was treading lightly.

She actually growled then, like a weird forest-cat growl. "We need to be near the entrance so that we don't miss any calls."

Right. That was my first thought also.

With a huff, I was dragged along each of the cordoned-off rooms, until finally Emmanuelle Knight came into sight. There was only one name above her door, which was odd. It looked like the two chosen from each of the villages were rooming together. Except for those who had a male and a female.

With a shrug, I followed her in, glad to see that there were two beds in the tiny box. "Guess they forgot about me. It happens." This was the start; I could feel it. The start of Willa Knight ceasing to exist at all.

A metallic tinkling sound broke the silence around us. It was a dull noise, like it came from far away. Back up the million-or-so stairs, I was sure.

Emmy's face went deathly white. She shot-putted her bag across the room, and I watched as it slammed against the wall before falling to the tiny bed on the left side.

"Was that really necess—"

She cut me off. "The bells. It's the goddamn freaking bells."

"I hate this place," I groaned, as she pulled her leg out and used her foot to nudge me toward the door. "Seriously, Emmy, did you just kick me?"

"Why aren't you moving? Why is your stupid bag filled with stupid pots still in your stupid hands?"

I lunged at her, tickling her in all the places where she was most vulnerable. Which was every place with exposed skin. She was the most sensitive person I knew when it came to tickling.

"You need to chill the hell out!" I demanded, while she snorted and fought off my hands, trying to stay mad. "I swear to the gods you look like you're forty life-cycles old right now!"

Footsteps sounded outside our little box, and I knew that Emmy or Jerath would actually kill me if we were late to our first assignment, so I straightened my clothes, dropped my stupid bag on the other bed, and followed my best friend from the room. I remained quiet and demure, not voicing my many opinions on what a shit-hole it was that they had shoved us into. I thought this was supposed to be an honour? I'd have preferred to stay in the village, if anyone wanted to know my opinion on it all. I hadn't stayed because I wouldn't leave my sister, but it was still my preference.

I'd give Emmy something: the trip up the stairs did seem a lot shorter than going down. We emerged from our rat-hole-in-the-wall and since I expected to see Jerath standing there, hands on hips, I was astonished enough to trip and knock down fifteen or so dwellers, because there were three sols waiting for us.

The dwellers who tumbled with me jumped quickly to their feet, all of them looking around, trying to figure out who had knocked them down. I was doing it too, looking around with a confused expression on my face ... because survival was kind of important. The three sols stepped forward, moving just a little closer to us, and I found myself caring less about my tripping and more about how shiny these people were.

There were two men and a lady. The female was in the centre, dressed in shimmering white, her dress floor-length, demonstrating how slim and tall she was. Her hair was bound in golden curls, her eyes a dark, stormy grey—scary and exotic, all at once. I couldn't look away.

"Welcome dwellers," she announced coolly. "I am Elowin, the Head of the Dweller-relations committee here at Blesswood. You are honoured to be here this sun-cycle, to serve the sols and the gods."

We are honour... was this speech for real?

"We only allow the best dwellers in all of Minatsol to attend our sols in Blesswood. Dwellers who have demonstrated their intelligence, skill, grace, and discretion. You speak to no one of what goes on inside these walls. You are not to be seen or heard. You do your job right and you will be rewarded. After you spend seven life-cycles here, you will be offered a position with a family of worth in Soldel, Dvadel, or Tridel. This is your future; don't mess it up."

The men were clearly her pretty arm candy. The one on the right, a brunette with longer hair that he had tied at his nape, started handing out sheets of parchment to us. We all knew how to read; it was one of the few things the villages made sure every child could do. Read and write the common language. Each ring had its own dialect, but everyone spoke the common language. The language of the gods.

It was a timetable, schedule, and assigned job list. I

ran my eyes over the list, noticing that Emmy had library and kitchen duties, as well as classrooms 325, 2010, and Study Hall 8. She also got the female dorms 10-15. I searched for my name next, hoping that I would at least be close to her. They were going to have us working for the entire sun-cycle, every single sun-cycle, and I was already fearing that I would never see her again.

Finally, I found it, way past all the girls' names. *Will Knight.* Oh crap, made sense for my curse to screw me like this. I was assigned to arena and training duties, classrooms 346 and 2213, Study Hall 8, and *male* dorms 1-5.

"I guess that explains the name on the bedroom then," Emmy said, her face drawn as she clenched her fists tight around the paper. "They think you're a boy."

"But—"

Emmy *shooshed* me. "Just take it, Willa, they said you can't ask for any changes. This is all preordained by the gods."

I snorted, unable to keep my voice down. "Actually this is preordained by our idiot village leader who was probably too drunk to notice he filled my name in wrong."

"It's no big deal." Emmy was lying through her teeth now, trying not to cause a scene as Elowin split us up into two groups to tour the grounds, sending the boys off with one of her henchmen, and the rest of us off with the second. "Just borrow some clothes from one of the male dwellers—maybe a hat, too? They probably won't even mention the fact that you look like a girl because that's super rude."

"Rude like ... I don't know ... *shooting a crossbow through my chest?*"

"It didn't go through your chest."

"I think it snagged a few hairs. From my head, I mean, not my chest ..." I trailed off, because one of the girls hurrying along with us was giving me a strange look. I blinked, momentarily stumbling over my own feet as something else occurred to me. "Dammit. *Boobs*, Emmy. I can't pretend to be a guy. What about my boobs? Or is it rude to mention that a guy has boobs, clear as the sun, standing right there—"

"Will!" Emmy was catching my arm every few steps now, because I couldn't seem to keep my footing with all the excitement. And by excitement, I definitely meant terror. "Can you stop talking about boobs, please? We're getting weird looks."

"Oh yeah," I drawled, "change the subject. Real smooth, Emmy, real smooth."

She rumbled with that chilling, forest-cat growl again, making me shut up. Okay, so maybe she was right. *I* couldn't change the dorm assignment, but maybe the sols would request a change themselves, after discovering that I was a girl?

"And this is the dining hall," Henchman Number Two announced to the group, pushing two heavy doors apart to give us a glimpse into a massive hall with floor-to-ceiling windows and heavy, velvet curtains. There were bronze chandeliers hanging from the ceiling, with so many candles stuck into their brackets that I was sure they had to be a hazard of some kind. Most likely the fire kind. Dozens and dozens of circular wooden tables were spaced apart around the room, with a long bar of empty aluminium dishes stretching along one wall, a kitchen area barely visible behind it.

"The final prep-kitchen is on this level, allowing the sols to request certain dishes outside of the set menu each mealtime, but most of the work is done below, in the basement kitchens. No recruits are allowed in the basement-kitchen. Resident dwellers only."

He backed away from the doors, letting them fall shut, and then proceeded to drag our group from one end of the academy grounds to the other. We also toured the female dormitories and the bathing chambers attached to the ends of each dormitory corridor. I could only pray to the gods that the male dormitories were set up in a similar way, but that was kind of futile ... because the gods had allowed me to get assigned to the male dorm in the first place.

Correction: they didn't really *allow* it, so much as they just never paid any damn attention to me in the first place.

I mean, I got it, I did. I wasn't that important. I was just a little dirt-dweller with a little *Danger!* sign hovering over my head. Why *would* the gods bother to watch over me, unless it was for entertainment?

Oh my gods ...

"Emmy!" I bounced up from her bed—the one we had collapsed against as Henchman Number Two allowed us a short break after the touring. "Do you think they do it deliberately?"

"Who?" She blinked, her head snapping up, her eyes flying open. She had fallen asleep, apparently. She jumped up with me, finding her feet, her eyes darting about wildly. "What? Who?"

"The gods!"

"The gods *what*?"

"Do you think they do this crap to me deliberately? All the accidents?"

Emmy groaned, her posture deflating as she sank back onto the bed, her hand wiping down her face. "Dammit, Will ... of course they don't do it deliberately. Why the hell would they do that?"

"Well they're supposed to love the sols fighting against each other; that's why they come down to the arena every moon-cycle to watch them battle, right? So ... what if they're making my life hell just to laugh about it?"

She sighed again, but this time it was a pity sigh. She grabbed my hands, pulling me down onto the bed beside her. "Will ... just stop thinking about it, okay? It is what it is. We can't change it, so we need to live with it. I know this whole ..." she shook her hand around, indicating the stone walls surrounding us, "*situation* has shaken you up a bit, but the gods definitely aren't making you *clumsy* just to amuse themselves. If they really wanted that kind of entertainment, they'd be doing it to the sols. We're just dwellers. It'd be like poking ants just to see them scatter. It's really not that entertaining. Certainly not for eighteen life-cycles on end."

I opened my mouth to answer—probably to say that she could call herself an ant, if she really wanted to, but I was totally an eagle, or basically anything cooler than an ant—but I wasn't afforded the chance, because the bells were ringing again.

"Free time is up," Emmy unnecessarily announced.

Henchman Number Two had told us that we would be expected to attend the dining hall for the Commencement Celebration that night, in the presence of every sol at the academy. Apparently, they had a feast at the beginning of every academy life-cycle, and the new dweller recruits were one of the main attractions. Emmy was staring into the tiny, oval reflection glass stuck to the wall between the two single beds, fussing with her hair. She would have changed, too, if she hadn't already been wearing her best clothes. I waited until she was done before moving over to the reflection glass myself and peering at the image of my own face. It was an okay face. Kind of like my mum's. I had naturally pink lips, and naturally flushed cheeks—probably from the adrenaline of almost dying all the time. My eyes were a brown that seemed strangely translucent in most lights. The kind of brown that reflected other colours. It wasn't at all odd for a person with blue eyes to think that mine were slate-brown, or a person with green eyes to think that mine were mossy-brown.

I didn't really see all those different shades and highlights that other people mentioned. I thought they were *tawny*. Tawny brown eyes. Plain and simple. I also had tawny skin, a golden-brown from having spent far too much time outdoors. I was lucky that I didn't also have tawny brown hair, or else I'd probably be blending into walls and trees. My hair was similar to Emmy's—a white-blond, with a scruffy curl to oppose her sleek locks. It was also a little darker, with less silver. I pulled all of my hair back from my face now, slapping a hand over my forehead to see what I'd look like in a cap.

"Not bad," I muttered. "But there's still the boobs."

"Okay, we're leaving, before you start talking about that again." Emmy led the way, taking us through the many corridors and back into the dining hall.

The sols were already seated at their tables, indicating that we were probably late, but I was really good at being late, so I took Emmy's arm, dragging *her* for once. We plastered ourselves to the wall, moving along the line of other dwellers toward the middle of the room, where it would be easier to see all the tables. It wasn't until we were properly stationed that I noticed the group of dwellers hovering out in front of the kitchens, a few sols standing in front of them. I recognised most of their faces, because they were the other dweller recruits.

Crap. We were standing with the resident dwellers.

"Welcome, dirt-dwellers!" One of the sols shouted, even though he was only standing a few feet away from the first line of recruits. "Welcome to our city, welcome to our academy, and welcome to the commencement ceremony! Now ... *strip!*"

Wait ... what?

The demon-sol laughed, his head thrown back, his dark, golden-onyx hair tousled perfectly around his face. *Was that ...?* He looked exactly like Siret, except that I could *see* Siret standing right beside him, wearing the same clothes as this morning. The trickery-gifted sol had a twin? I could tell them apart, but the twin thing was clear. That wasn't good. That definitely wasn't good. But what was *worse* was the fact that the recruits actually appeared to be ... stripping.

The seated sols started laughing, a few of them jeering rudely, and one of the resident dwellers next to me sighed.

"Why do the sols find this so funny, anyway? Why can't Yael think of anything better to use his Persuasion gift for?"

I had no idea who the guy was talking to, but I decided it wouldn't hurt to let out a matching sigh, lean back against the wall, and fold my arms casually.

"I know, right? It's getting old. And don't even get me started on the twin thing. One of them is enough, am I right?"

The guy snorted. "Yeah, and five is overdoing it, just a little bit."

Five? Five! Holy fu—

"I feel sorry for whoever's assigned to their dorm rooms," I whispered back, applauding my even tone.

"It'll be one of the recruits," my new friend informed me, lowering his voice even further and leaning my way. "You know it's been absolute chaos in here since they turned up a few moon-cycles ago. They've had twenty resident dwellers assigned to them already, but they dismiss them like it's in their schedule to get a dweller fired every few weeks. After the last one, Elowin announced that she'd start assigning them recruits. You wouldn't know that because you aren't one of the slaves attending the dweller-relations committee—I know, because I *am*. Anyway, I guess she thought that if she gave them someone 'fresh,' they'd be able to mould them however they wanted."

"Sounds creepy. So is Elowin giving them special privileges?"

"They're the most powerful sols here. You didn't know that? They're our future gods—"

"And on *that* note," Emmy broke into our conversation, leaning over me to glare at the guy, "you two should really stop gossiping about them."

"Sorry," I muttered to the guy, after pushing Emmy back. "She hasn't eaten yet."

He chuckled. "No problem. I'm Atti, by the way."

"I'm Willa, and my grumpy friend here is Emmy."

Atti shook his head, his short curls jumping around a little like they were trying to escape his head. "Why haven't I seen you two around before? I know Elowin keeps us locked down in service to her, but I thought I'd crossed paths with most resident dwellers by now."

Before I could fess up to my mistake and our recruit status, a commotion across the room stole all our attentions. The recruits—who were now wearing no more than underclothes—were dragging themselves out to stand in the centre of the room. They were being paraded around. The two almost-identical demon-sols—Siret and Yael—remained standing at their table. Just *standing*. Smug, arrogant, assholes. They had these half-smirks on their faces, like they were enjoying the discomfort of the dwellers—*feeding* on it, even. Their huge bodies seemed to grow even larger, the perfect planes of their faces deepening. The shimmers of gold which tinted the darkness of their hair was stronger, almost as if they had this inner light which was shining brighter.

I was starting to see the gods-in-training thing, to really *see* it. There was nothing dweller in these sols, no matter what the history said of the origins of the gods and sols.

"Why does no one stop them?" I murmured, my

feet shifting. I had to force myself to remain against the wall, I couldn't stand to see others humiliated like this.

It was different when *I* was humiliated. I was used to it; I could handle it. They couldn't. They had once been the brightest, the smartest, the most honoured amongst their own people ... *and now*? All of a sudden, they were less than garbage.

Atti answered. "The teachers tend to leave sols to deal with things themselves. They don't monitor them outside of lessons. They say the gods are always watching, and that usually keeps most of them in line."

Except for the Abcurse brothers. Clearly they weren't worried about the gods and their spying eyes. I tilted my head to the right, my gaze catching on Emmy. She started shaking her head frantically at me.

"Don't you move, Will. Don't move a freaking muscle or I will kill you. Drawing the attention of any sol is a bad thing; drawing the attention of those five sounds like it'll be catastrophic."

She had a point, but I was a pro at catastrophic. With that in mind, I took a deep breath and stepped off the wall.

FOUR

No one noticed.
No one!

Where was my clumsy curse when I needed to make a scene? I had no idea what to do short of stripping off my own clothes and running naked through the gaps in the tables. But how could that help the shaking recruits out there? Just as my hands went to my shirt, fists clenching the sides, another short, tinkling bell rang out, and the scent of food drifted in through a set of now-open doors.

Siret waved a hand then, and the room shifted. I blinked twice to make sure I was seeing things clearly. *How in the hell?* All of the recruits were back against the wall, fully dressed. It was as if none of the last few clicks had even happened. My mouth was open, like right open. A damn flying mantis could have walked right in there with no problem.

"He tricked us," I muttered, managing to speak around my shock. As if he had heard my words, Siret shifted his body in my direction, and those shimmery golden-green eyes slammed against me. Hard.

Now someone noticed me?

I was grabbed from behind; either Emmy or Atti yanked me back against the wall, probably trying to save my life. If Siret or his brothers retaliated to my tiny attempt at making a stand against dweller-abuse ... well, it would probably be the second time this sun-cycle those bullsen balls would try to kill me. How many times would it take for them to succeed?

A line of resident dwellers brought forth the sols' dinner, looking completely oblivious and unaffected. I braved a glance from under my lashes, and managed to breathe deeply when there were no jewel-like eyes staring in my direction. Like most men, the Abcurse demons had one true love.

Food.

Emmy kept two eyes on me for the rest of the dining time. No other humiliation was dished out for the dwellers, if you discounted the normal shitty way they were treated. Trays thrown at them when the sols were done eating, barked orders for more drinks and food, mutterings about dirt-dwellers and their ineptitude at all things. *All things.*

The recruits were supposed to observe this first dinner, learning everything it was possible to learn before being expected to dive right in for the next dinner. Thankfully, there were plenty of other resident dwellers who stood with me and Emmy, waiting for a summons. Not all of them had active duties in here, so we didn't stand out.

Right up until I heard a shout.

"Hey, Rocks, we're going to need some help over here!"

I froze, before slowly defrosting enough to face Emmy.

"What should I do? If I ignore them will they come over here and kill me?" I was whispering frantically under my breath, trying to make myself as small as possible against the wall.

"Are they talking to you?" Atti asked, his voice going a bit high-pitched at the end. "What is 'rocks?' Why are they singling you out?"

Great freaking question. What the hell did they want with me? *Come on, gods, this just isn't funny anymore.*

"Are you deaf, Rocks?"

I let out a little shriek, before plunging forward and head-butting the hard chest of a sol that had appeared to stand before me.

I hit him with a solid thud, but his body didn't even shift an inch. I, on the other hand, was shot back against the wall where I crumbled like a bag of ... you guessed it ... *rocks*. Looking up through messy hair, I knew I was staring at one of the Abcurse brothers, but not one I had seen before. He was golden. There was no other way to describe him. Rich, golden hair, the colour of the sun as it crests the sky in the early morning. His skin was also sun-kissed, his eyes like newly-cut topazes, the yellow jewel which was mined in the fourth ring. He was prettier than his brothers. Like really freaking gorgeous. No shiny sol would ever compare to this one; and that made me very wary.

He grinned at me, displaying his perfect white teeth, and there were suddenly all these warm feelings around my heart. Like happiness had sprouted throughout my body and was spreading like a weed.

He offered me his hand, and I knew from the gasps along the line of resident-dwellers that he was paying far more attention to me than a sol normally did to a dweller. Ignoring it—sure it was a trap—I pulled myself up and pressed back against the wall. The sol reached out then, dropping one of his hands against the wall. "No need to throw yourself at me, sweetheart." His low, lilting words drifted into my ear. "If you ask nicely, I'm sure we could sort something out … Why don't you give it a try? My name is Aros … go ahead, say *please, Aros*—"

Before I could stutter out some asinine reply, a voice cut across the room. "Hey, Seduction, get your ass back over here! We don't need Rocks anymore."

Siret dismissed me as the rest of the sols laughed like it was the funniest thing any Minatsol inhabitant had ever said. Aros drew back, his smile dimming to a half-smirk. "Guess I'll see you around, dweller."

Then he was gone, taking all his warmth and energy with him. I sagged against the wall, chest heaving in and out as I fought for air. Atti turned sympathetic eyes on me, his brow creased as he dropped a hand briefly on my shoulder. "I'm really sorry, Willa. Those five are trouble and any dweller who catches their eye hasn't lasted very long in Blesswood. As soon as they turn their attention to one of us, they make it their mission to destroy ..." He trailed off, seeing the look of horror on my face, and then tried for something a little more supportive. "If you can manage it, stay as far from them as you can. Don't let them see you, and they'll eventually get bored and turn their attention to someone else."

I didn't reply. I was still trying to catch my breath. His advice was great, someone just needed to tell my clumsy curse and the gods, because they clearly weren't done amusing themselves with my misfortunes yet. Emmy remained quiet, choosing not to mention the encounter as we dragged ourselves back to our dingy little dweller cave. She was trying to be considerate, because she knew me well enough to know that I definitely didn't want to analyse what had happened. She asked me once if I was okay, and I grunted out a reply. That was the extent of our conversation for the night, and I quickly fell onto the second bed in her room, even though I was pretty sure there was a room in the male dweller section with *Will Knight* written above the door. I pulled the blankets over my head, screwed my eyes closed, and forbade the Abcurse brothers from haunting me until sunrise.

The next morning, all dweller recruits were up with the sound of bells, indicating first light—which of course we couldn't see from our concrete tomb.

"When do we pull night duty?" I asked Emmy as we quickly dressed. We didn't exactly have uniforms, but the requirement was plain colours, and a *modest* amount of coverage, so as not to offend the sols with our dirt-dweller-ness.

"You're on call for your dorm rooms at all times," she said, pulling on her black top, which had long sleeves, and hung almost to mid-thigh.

She took off before I could demand to know how they planned on *finding* me at 'all times,' and I tried not to take it personally. Emmy didn't deal with stress very well, and whenever I got into too much trouble, she always went silent, drawn into a private little crisis on my behalf.

Wait ... at all times? Were there restrictions? What if they needed me when I was in the bathroom? What if more than one of the rooms needed me at the same time?

"Deal with it later," I murmured to myself, slipping on my flat boots.

They were the only pair I owned, but they were of the highest quality. They had been handcrafted by my mother, before she decided that leather work was a waste of her time, and that it'd be more productive for her to spend her sun-cycles exploring the tavern instead. I had expected Leader Graham to pull her up many life-cycles ago, since there was no room for those who were without skills to exist in the village. *Everyone must pay their way. Everyone must provide.* She managed to get away with it though, and I hated to think about what she might have exchanged for her special privileges.

Still, I wondered how she was doing without Emmy and me. I wondered if she'd even noticed yet. A yearning for home sank into my body, filtering through my blood and into my bones. Settling in with permanence. I had to accept that I'd never go back. I knew that, logically; but emotionally, being at Blesswood still didn't feel real. If Emmy hadn't been there, I'd have probably started thinking about escape by now. I'd have taken my chances on the road through the nine rings, and made my way back to the village.

"Will! Hurry up! The next bell is about to ring and you haven't eaten yet!"

Emmy's voice cut through my moment of sadness, indicating that she was actually waiting for me at the end of the hallway. I sprang into action, my feet tangling in the bedsheets I hadn't bothered to put back up on my rock-hard bed. It had been so narrow and uncomfortable that early this morning I'd ended up on the floor. Which was why I was now tripping over the sheets and flying through the air.

I tumbled out of the open doorway, the stone floor

biting into my skin. I heard a deep sigh above me, and by the time I stared up, a bandage had appeared in Emmy's hand. It took her a click to patch up my elbows, and quickly stitch the hole in the knee of my black pants. A new record, for her.

The bells tolled again then, and we started running. I managed to snatch up two pieces of hard bread from the almost empty tray of food which sat on the table in the main recruits' room, shovelling the tasteless cardboard into my mouth as I hurried after my friend.

"You need to attend to your dorms first," Emmy breathlessly informed me, as we ran up the stairs, taking them two at a time.

It was a miracle that I didn't crack my skull open at any point.

Which reminded me ... "I forgot the cap to hide my hair," I mumbled around my breakfast.

Swallowing it, I took a moment to run my hands over my head. *Shit*. My hair wasn't even pulled back, instead hanging in a mass of scruffy, white-blond curls. "My hair is out, and the *boobs*, Emmy. I didn't wear a top to hide the boobs!" My top was white for freak's sake. White *and* fitted. It was actually my usual sleep-shirt—I'd been too busy agonising to change properly. I might as well have just stepped out naked.

Emmy grabbed my hands, pulling them from my hair, before she started dragging me in her now-familiar way. "Don't worry about it. The sols have early training in the arena, so none of them will be in their rooms. If you pass any, just keep your head down and hopefully they won't notice you."

Before I could protest again, she was gone. Dashing across the domed room, heading east toward the female dorms. We knew the layout from our basic tour the previous sun-cycle, but it was easy to lose direction—everything looked so similar. I did at least remember where the male dorms were. The path lay to the west, on the opposite side to where I was supposed to be cleaning. Supply carts were located at the beginning of the sleeping quarters, which meant that I had nothing to hide behind until I got there. Wrapping my hair up in my hands, I quickly swirled it around, and then tucked it into the back of my shirt. This was the best I had. I took off with my head lowered, my eyes constantly moving to make sure no sol crossed my path.

The long hallway I traversed had massive floor-to-ceiling windows on one side, which gave me an uninterrupted view of Blesswood. It was a huge estate with multiple buildings. There were also all the trees, plants, and water features—which, to be honest, still kind of freaked me out. So much water everywhere. What did they do with it all? Why couldn't they share with the villages who were desperate for more? A male dweller pushed a cart past me, and I could see his double take at a female on this side of the building, but he didn't stop to ask me what I was doing. Luck was on my side, for once. *The sols in my assigned dorms better request a dweller change.* The tension would kill me otherwise.

The long hallway opened to a room that jutted out over the grounds, giving an uninterrupted view of the Sacred Sand arena—a massive, circular, open-topped stadium. I paused for a beat, taking in the grandeur of it all. I knew a lot about that building now. I knew that sols with gifts for barricades would put a roof over it in inclement weather, I knew that it could seat twenty thousand and that there was a special boxed area up high for the gods, I even knew that on occasion, Original Gods would grace the sols with their presence and watch the battles. There were always some secondary and minor gods there, of course, but the Originals were the big draw card. So yeah, I now knew more than I'd ever expected to know about the training stadium, courtesy of the over-achiever who always slept next to me. What I *didn't* know was the point. How did battling—sometimes to the death—show the gods anything of real worth?

Why would the Original Gods want to recruit the strongest sols in Topia?

It always struck me as odd, that they would invite in the very beings who might be strong enough to overthrow their positions. The very beings who might end up more powerful than they were themselves. What evidence did the sols even have that they would go to Topia when they died? There was so much faith going on in that scenario, and frankly, the gods didn't seem the type to throw all your hopes at.

Footsteps shook me from my thoughts, and I turned from the view and continued toward my dorms. There was a cart sitting outside the storage facility, and it looked to be well stocked, so I grabbed it. It would save me having to waste more time when I was already late. Eventually, the dorms came into view: a door on either side of the wide and well-lit hall.

The numbers started at 500, and started working down. Of course they did. I would expect nothing less than to be assigned the furthest possible rooms. I sucked in my sigh, tucking my chin to my chest while I pushed ahead with my cart. If there was anyone in my path, they were going down. They'd have to get their asses out of the way, or else. Luckily, I didn't encounter anyone, and I made it to Room Number 5 without incident. I didn't bother to pause and check the name. I didn't care which spoiled, sacred sol resided within. Not unless they were going to write me into their will and leave me a bunch of tokens when they died so that my mother wouldn't have to …

Best not think about sex-for-token favours so early in the sun-cycle. Save the hard thoughts for after lunch.

I knocked on the door, waiting a few moments without an answer before pushing inside. *Wow*, these rooms were even nicer than I had expected. Tall, rippled glass windows displayed a warped mirage of the mountainside past the arena, to the back of

Blesswood. I didn't actually know what was beyond the academy, beyond the mountain. I left the cart at the door, stepping over scattered clothing and dropped books, passing by the massive bed, with ornately carved, matching bedside tables. I passed it all without blinking, reaching the glass and walking alongside the windows, my fingers tracing the rippled surface. It followed along the entire length of the room, ending in a small, attached sitting room, separated from the bedroom by a stone archway. Shelves lined the walls, two stuffed armchairs facing the glass. Glass which wasn't rippled anymore. I gasped, stepping into the room and pressing both hands against the window.

Beyond the mountain ... was nothing.

Miles and miles of *nothing*. More mountains, tipping and reaching, piercing the skies with uneven peaks, some of them even appearing white-capped. There wasn't even a discernible road weaving through the mountains. I felt my nose bump against the glass, and knew that my breath was fogging it up, just the same way the mist was fogging up the base of the mountains in the distance. I'd never seen anything like it. Anything so vast and empty all at once. It was *technically* nothing; no more towns, cities, settlements. But it was everything; it was beautiful and proudly formidable.

That was where I belonged. In that place of unforgiving, empty terrain.

But for now ... there were beds to be made. I pulled

away from the window, rushing back to my cart. I actually had no idea what to do. We'd been given our assignments, but no real instruction to go along with the assignments. I supposed most dwellers knew how to clean properly, though, because most dwellers weren't me. I hurriedly made the bed, punched the shape back into the pillows, and picked everything up off the floor. I didn't know where to put any of it, so I just tossed it all onto the freshly-made bed. There were a bunch of big, cloth bags in my cart, with labels for me to put on each bag, so that made laundry easy. There was even a list stuck to the top of the cart—something that I only noticed after moving the basket of supplies that had been covering it. The locations of the laundry-rooms assigned to each hallway of dorms were listed, along with room numbers of resident dwellers tasked with ordering new supplies.

I finished with the first three rooms in record-time, but I was slowing down by the time I got to the fourth. I'd suffered three stubbed toes, one near-concussion, and an accidental rag to the face, because apparently jumping up and down and tossing a wet rag at the glass wasn't the best way to clean a window. My shirt was damp with sweat and soap, my hair kept dragging into my eyes, and the hole in my pants had reopened. I was starting to wonder how I was going to survive a full sun-cycle of this, let alone a lifetime career of it.

I didn't bother to knock on the door this time, because Emmy had been right, the dorms had all been empty so far—the sols obviously having arena practise. I pulled down the handle and turned around, pushing the door open with my butt while I walked backwards, dragging the cart, since I'd lost most of the strength to push it in front of me like a normal person.

"No, it's fine, come right in," a deep voice drawled, making me freeze.

I had a moment where I thought it would be a good idea to *pretend* that I hadn't just waltzed into someone's dorm, to *pretend* that I hadn't heard them clearly admonishing me, and to *pretend* that I'd had a sudden, unexplained change of heart. I slowly started pushing the cart forward, instead of pulling it backwards. I didn't stop until the door closed behind me, and then I just stood there, my internal organs threatening to explode with panic.

The door swung open behind me, a hand landed on my shoulder, an arm shooting out beside me to grasp the handle of the cart, and before I knew it, both myself and my cart were back inside the room, and the door was shutting behind us.

"Wrong room," I squeaked, keeping my eyes fixed on the door. Maybe if I didn't look at him, he wouldn't look at me, and then he'd just forget my face and I'd never be punished for this.

"You mean wrong *hall*, maybe?" he asked, walking away from me.

I still didn't turn. Instead, I just listened *really* hard. I couldn't tell where he was standing anymore, but I could sense that he was still there somewhere. Well *obviously* ... because he didn't exactly jump out of the window.

"Dweller?"

"Will you reassign me?" I blurted, spinning around, and *immediately* wishing that I hadn't.

He was sitting on the end of his bed, and he appeared all-too familiar, with glittery green eyes smoking to black around the very edge of the iris, and messy, textured hair, coloured in a meld of blood and ochre.

"Reassign you?" he asked, with an arch to one single, dark brow. He wasn't quite smiling, but he was obviously amused.

Why me? That was all I could think. *Why? Why!*

I swallowed carefully. Another Abcurse brother. The last one. He looked just like Coen, the pain-gifted sol who had tried to kill me. They both appeared slightly older than the other three: Yael, the persuasion-gifted one; Siret, the trickery-gifted one; and Aros, the one who apparently had some kind of seduction gift.

I didn't even want to imagine what kind of sol I was now standing alone with. It was too much for my minuscule little mind. I was going to have a breakdown and start screaming obscenities at any moment. He stood then, because I obviously wasn't uncomfortable enough. I stumbled back a step, my eyes stretching even wider. He was huge. Massive. Like a freaking giant. Or a mini-giant, at least. Coen had been big, too, but this was something else. Coen looked like he tossed trees around for fun, but Room Number 2 looked like he *ate trees for breakfast.*

"You don't happen to have a real happy-sunshine gift, do you?" I stammered, falling back yet another step. "Like flowers or butterflies?"

I was forced to let go of the cart—the cart was on its own now.

"You mean like Nature or Bestiary?" he corrected. "Because *flowers and butterflies* aren't a real gift."

"Yeah, right. Nature or Bestiary—except Bestiary still sounds scary, so scrap that one. Just nature. Is your gift nature-related?"

"No." He grinned, his teeth flashing, his cheeks dimpling.

Mind momentarily blown.

"Aren't you supposed to be at the arena?" I was mostly just keeping him talking now, so that he wouldn't notice me backing toward the door.

"They don't let me train with the others. I keep crushing them."

"So that's your gift, then?" I squeaked. "*Crushing?*" I couldn't really believe I was having this conversation with a sol alone in his bedroom, let alone having this conversation at *all* without a whip cutting across my back.

His smile disappeared and he jumped into motion,

backing me into the door much faster than I had been backing myself into the door.

"Strength," he whispered, pressing a body against me that kind of felt like a giant boulder. Or a brick house. Or maybe a stone mountain. "Strength is my gift, dweller, and I'm not going to reassign you, so start cleaning."

He was off me instantly, pulling open the door hard enough to send me sprawling on the ground. He then slammed it shut hard enough to knock the broom off my cart. It hit me in the back, of course.

"Strength," I mocked, picking myself up off the floor and kicking the broom away. "Clean my room, slave! Or I'll crush you like a bug because I'm a *big strong sol!*"

I was working myself up a bit. I realised that ... I just couldn't seem to prevent it. Yanking the door open, I leaned out and peered down the corridor. I was pretty happy to see that Number Two was nowhere in sight, because I definitely would have tried to kick his ass, and definitely would have ended up in someone's soup come morning. I glanced to the top of the door, on the outside, reading his name.

Room 2: Rome Abcurse.

I pulled the rest of the way out of the room and moved to Room Number 3.

Aros Abcurse.

With a feral-sounding growl catching in the back of

my throat, I glanced at the other two rooms that I had already cleaned.

Yael Abcurse and *Siret Abcurse*.

I didn't even bother looking at Room Number 1. I knew what it would say. My luck was just that bad.

Coen Abcurse. A.k.a., Pain Master of Blesswood. The guy with the crossbow.

"Motherf—" I paused, my tantrum on the verge of spilling out, when a dweller pushed out of Room Number 8, his cart pulled behind him.

He blinked at me, his mouth falling open, and I recognised Atti.

"You're a recruit!" he accused, his voice a hiss as he moved closer.

"You're a boy!" I returned, a dose of horror shot into my tone, my finger raised in a point. "What are you doing in the girl's area?"

He had a moment. He totally had a moment. I could see it all over his face—before he realised that he'd just finished cleaning the rooms that he always cleaned, and then confusion descended.

"What are *you* doing in the *male* dorm?"

"Exploring my sexuality." I leaned against the cart, propping my elbow, wiping my expression into something neutral. "How am I doing?"

"I can see your nipples. Your shirt's wet."

My elbow slipped, and I almost toppled over, but my chin caught me against the edge of the cart. "I knew the boobs would be a problem," I groused, rubbing the pain out of my jaw. "I knew it. I tried to tell her, but she wouldn't listen to me."

"Who?"

"Emmy. Remember? Grumpy Emmy?"

"Oh yeah, she looked kinda uptight."

"She's not."

"Really?"

"Okay, maybe a little. Do you have a shirt I can borrow? Maybe a cap? Maybe some pants? And a fake moustache?"

He laughed, glancing down the hall before looking back to me. "You seriously got assigned to their dorms?"

"Yeah, the leader of our village gave me a boy's name on the form. Think they'll reassign me?"

"Probably." He stroked his chin, trying to hide his growing smile. "With those five, you can expect a reassignment at some stage."

"Like *when*, exactly?"

"When they're done playing with you, given that you're still alive. I'm in room 17, in the dweller residence. Come and find me once you're done. I'll lend you some clothes."

"Thanks, Atti. I'll put in a good word for you with the big boys," I promised, jerking a finger over my shoulder to the doors behind me.

His smile stretched, taking over his whole face. "Try not to get yourself sacrificed," he warned, pushing his cart away.

FIVE

After I finished the Abcurse rooms, rushing through the last two like my life depended on it—which it almost definitely did—I found myself sneaking into the dweller residence with Atti. He'd finished his dorms at the same time as me and decided it was safer to show me where to go, rather than leave me to my own devices.

How did he know me so well already? Maybe he was just smart like that. Smart like Emmy. Smart like every other damned dweller in Blesswood.

Maybe I was the only stupid person there.

Their permanent dweller residence was set out much the same as the recruit side, but they had one window, and a few squishy-looking day beds. I paused at a small structure filled with games and books.

"Books?" I laughed. "For all your free time, I guess?"

Atti gave me a sympathetic smile. "Once you're promoted to resident you'll get one sun-cycle off per moon-cycle. We're expected to spend that time learning of the gods, and the gifts of the sols, so that we may increase their chances of success."

"Wouldn't it just be easier for us to plot all of their deaths? Since they have to die to get to Topia. They'll know their exact chances ..." I trailed off as his face went a sickly white colour. "What?" I looked around, afraid that someone had busted me in their residence.

Atti shook his head in this manic back and forth motion. "Don't even joke about that, Willa. The gods are always *listening* here in Blesswood, and the sols would take any threat against their person seriously. You never know when a dweller might be acting under the influence of a powerful sol. Sometimes they're happy to act as spies and saboteurs—even if it will get them killed—because they think they're serving a future god."

I forced my face into sober lines. "No worries. I'll keep all plans for mass execution to myself from now on."

He swallowed hard, seeming unsure if I was kidding or not. That made two of us. With a shake of his head, he hurried off toward dorm 17, rushing inside and throwing things around to find me some clothes. I waited in the doorway with my arms out as he piled things into them. He was a lot taller than me, and really skinny, so Emmy was going to have to work her needle magic and fix a lot of these up. But at least I was going to attempt to look male.

"And finally this cap will work to cover all your hair. You have a lot of hair."

Well, thank you. I was taking that as a compliment. Not very much hair seemed like an insult. My arms closed around the pile of dark clothing and I hugged it closer to my body.

"Run now, Willa," he said, giving me a shove out of his door. "You have to be at breakfast shift in five clicks."

Did they ever stop *rushing?* We barely ever used our timepieces in the village. Our schedule ran on shouts from Leader Graham's advisors out into the centre, where our old statue and well were located. But here it was all *bells* this, and *clicks* that. The sun was a pain in my ass. It never stopped moving; always making me late.

I took off, clipped my elbow on the side of his door, and shot-putted all of the clothes and my own body across the room and into the wall of the dorm next to Atti's. My head hit with a decent thud and my vision was a wash of colour and then darkness, all at the same time.

"Willa! Holy hell. You ... can't even walk? How in the gods did you get chosen for Blesswood?"

Rolling over with a groan, I ran my hand across my forehead. Pain sprang back at me, sending another burst of light and darkness through my mind.

"Long story," I managed, releasing another groan. "I'm totally a secret genius ... just shove me in the corner and throw a sheet over me."

Atti, who was going to end up on the same shit-list as the Abcurse brothers if he didn't stop chuckling, ignored my words and hauled me to my feet. "There are no sick days here, no matter the size of the lump on your head, so you'd better get moving."

By the time I'd prodded the already-raised side of my head, Atti was back with all his clothes, and I was again stumbling out of the room.

"Remember, dining hall in ... now four clicks."

I compartmentalised his words, placing them away for when I could think around the splitting pain in my brain. My natural healing would kick in soon—my body was good with injury—but until that time, I was in half-dead mode.

I somehow found my way back to the hall that led to the domed room, with double points for not falling again on my way, and then I was down the stairs and back in the dungeon.

"Holy crap, Will, you look like, well ... *crap*." Emmy was tugging on my foot. I was on my back, spread eagle across my bed. I'd made spread-eagling on the bed a priority, so I hadn't even bothered to look at her after barging into the room.

"You weren't at the dining hall," she continued. "I was worried you'd forgotten. Some teachers were there this morning, and Jerath. They're observing the recruits. You need to get up."

I propped one eye open in a tiny slit, sending forth all of my dark thoughts. "This is all your fault, Emmy. You made me come here."

She snorted before grasping my leg and hauling me off the bed. I landed hard on the rocks below and now I had a bump to my butt which would match the one on my head.

"Get up now before I make you get up," she ordered. *Damn, she was mean.* "Willa ..."

I glanced up, curious at the adjusted tone of her voice. She was clasping her hands in front of her, lines deepening between her brows. She was about to give me some shitty news.

"What?" I moaned.

"If they kick you out of here, you don't get to go back to the village. I don't know what happens to those dwellers, but trust me, it isn't anything great."

And there it was.

I was suddenly up, on my feet, and out the door, Emmy right behind me.

I had no idea what happened to those dwellers either, but I wasn't planning on participating in *crushing* practise with Rome, while Coen tried to pin me up against the main gate with a few crossbow bolts. *Not* getting kicked out was looking like my best option, even though it wasn't such a great option all on its own.

I only had to clean and serve one table at breakfast,

while Emmy took the table next to mine. Both tables had been—thankfully—filled with perfectly normal, sacred, spoiled, and slightly sadistic sols. Not the special demon-sols whose rooms I had cleaned. It felt like the five of them—who were all the way across the other side of the room—spent a lot of the morning locking their bright gem-like eyes on me, but I could have been wrong. I hoped I was wrong, because the only reason they were all paying attention to me, was because Rome had told them that I was their new dorm bitch. I'd be the first female they'd have had to deal with, and probably they were thinking up new tortures to suit me. *Specialised torture.*

"Where are you going now?" Emmy murmured to me as she dashed into the kitchen with an armful of plates. I was on my way out, heading toward the classroom.

"Classroom 346. We need to stand in attendance in case any of the sols need us to blow their noses or wipe their butts."

I was almost out the door when I said that, which meant my voice carried further than I intended. As I turned toward the dining hall, I froze. Every single sol within hearing distance was looking at me—*no, glaring at me. Holy baby gods.*

This was it. The moment I was kicked out of Blesswood to be churned into bullsen feed. As I slowly started backing up, toward the kitchen doors, one of the Abcurse brothers got to his feet. It took me a few beats to recognise which one, because terror had my eyes functioning at about half-sight.

Yael.

Maybe he was about to *persuade* me to take my clothes off and parade around as punishment.

He was the first to stand, but his brothers soon followed. One by one they stood, and somehow all the eyes in the room shifted to them. I was just about to make a run for it, since this was a golden opportunity, when Yael spoke.

"Nothing happened ... nothing to see here ..." His voice was low, hypnotic. It rolled out of his mouth and avalanched across the room and I found my mind fuzzing over as I tried to follow his words. "You have not heard or seen anything out of the ordinary, go back to your food."

Just like that, the room resumed its previous level of activity. A group of female sols to my right were squealing over their hair or something. *Oh no wait, one of them just had a spider on her head. Those weren't squeals of excitement.* A group of males to my left resumed bicep-curling one of the recruits.

Blinking rapidly, trying to clear my mind, I tentatively stepped into the room. I waited for the jeers. For the teachers to pounce on me. But no one noticed me. No one was paying attention at all.

I swivelled back to face the Abcurse table. It was the centre of everything, the entire hall, the entire academy populous. And it was empty. *Empty?*

Why had Yael used his persuasion to help me? Had they saved me just so that they could take me down themselves? I wasn't sure what was worse: knowing that I owed them one now, or that things were about to escalate like that one time I told a little lie to explain why I hadn't done the home-reading Teacher Harris had given me, only to accidently put the entire village into a state of lock-down. Turns out, 'my mother caught a plague' has a few holes in it, as far as excuses go. I stumbled out of the dining hall toward the classrooms and just as I crossed into the first hall, I could have sworn there was a whisper on the wind.

We're not done with you yet.

So now I was hallucinating. Like *actually* hallucinating. Hearing voices and crap. Hearing the voices from hell. Maybe they were calling me because the Abcurse brothers were about to *end* me. It was a given that I was going to go to hell—all dwellers did. The sols got to go to heaven, unless they were chosen to become a god, in which case, they went to Topia. They got more than a second-chance at life. They got a first chance at immortality, at a *living* heaven. Or actually … still a dead heaven, but a dead heaven that was still connected to the living world, somehow.

And here I was philosophising about a whole bunch of realms that had nothing to do with me. Because I was crazy now. I heard voices and everything.

I was screwed. So *very* screwed.

Well, no time to dwell on my fate. This dweller had work to do. My next shift was classroom duty and I actually arrived there early. For once. The teacher in room 346 was a woman. She was a sol, her gift was song, and she would randomly burst into a musical serenade whenever she felt like it. I'd already heard three different tunes and considering the class hadn't even started yet, I knew it was going to be a long lesson.

I stood against the side of the wall with six other dwellers. Three were recruits like me. I recognised the wide-eyed look of fatigue and despair. The other two were residents, wearing stoic, and mostly expressionless masks. They never even cracked a smile when the teacher's high notes rattled the windows, which told me that they were probably dead inside. They had to be; she was possibly the funniest, most annoying sol I'd met to date, and that was saying something.

"Hurry along, my lovelies," she sang, as a few more sols passed into the room.

Most of them looked to be my age, or even a little younger. All shiny and full of confidence. Must have been nice to be born all blessed and sacred and destined for great things. To know that you had all the rights. That no one would treat you like dirt, or make you scrub windows with your nipples showing. That you might someday become a god. Even if it didn't happen, the thought alone was worth something. Was worth *more.* A dweller's greatest hope was to make it to Blesswood, or one of the secondary academies.

And I mean ... *what* a life goal, right? What with all the cleaning and not-being-seen-or-smelt thing. And I mentioned the nipples, didn't I? *Life goals.*

The final bell rang and Teacher Sing-Song walked across to close the door of the room. She paused with her hand on it, before a beaming smile crossed her face. "I was worried you three wouldn't be joining us this sun-cycle. Come on in, boys."

Somehow I knew it would be them before they even stepped through the threshold. Something about the energy of the Abcurse brothers was distinct. Annoying. Frustrating. Arrogant. Superior. Soul-sucking.

Yael, Aros, and Siret dropped into seats at the back of the room, long legs sprawled out in front of them, not a book or writing device between them. Teacher Sing-Song made no comment on the fact that they looked like they were only there to darken the classroom a little, instead taking her place at the head of the room.

"Good morning, sols, and welcome to a brand-new life-cycle at Blesswood. I am Teacher Crest, and I will be in charge of this class: Original Gods, and The Beginning. I have been teaching at Blesswood for twenty life-cycles, and I have met two Original Gods in person, so I have as much hands-on experience to share with you as the best teachers in this academy. My gift is song; I'm aiming to become part of the entertainment branch of Topia, if I'm chosen by our wonderful deities."

A few sols looked impressed, some even clapped their hands. Siret yawned and ... *what the hell was I doing?* I needed to stop looking at those three, and focus on my duties. But I couldn't, because it was kind of like a solid kick to the gut, seeing the three younger brothers together. I'd clearly been wrong earlier about Siret and Yael being twins. Nope, not twins ... triplets. It made the most sense since they all looked to be the same age, were in the same class, and shared the same features. Coen and Rome were the twins. Which would mean that their poor, *poor* mother had given birth to one set of monster twins, and then—as if that wasn't bad enough—a set of monster triplets.

Just to make a complete little monster set.

They all had varying shades of the same colouring, so when they were sitting close together, it was actually very easy to tell them apart. Yael had eyes that were mostly green, with only a little gold in them. His hair was also darker, with more black than gold. His colours made him seem almost earthy: I could see the forest in his eyes, and was sure that I would be able to feel the soot in his hair—not that he'd ever let me touch him. There was something oddly, uncomfortably *real* about him. Siret had a little more of the gold: the dark of his hair was tainted by it, lighting almost to pure gold as it reached the tips of the strands falling around his eyes.

The green of his eyes was lighter, half of the pupil melded with yellow-gold. He had eyes like a cat. An evil cat.

And Aros ...

Golden Aros. I couldn't even make out the green in his iris from where I stood, or the black in his hair. He was a sun-blessed sol with shining, topaz eyes.

"Actually," he drawled, his eyes flicking to the side of the room and locking onto me, "that's wrong."

I thought that he was *answering* my *thoughts*, but when the rest of the classroom swivelled around in their seats to stare at him, he turned his head toward Teacher Sing-Song.

"The Bestiary God isn't as *nurturing* as you might think."

Teacher Sing-Song stuttered, unsure how to deal with her authority being undermined. I had no idea what she'd even been talking about, because I had been too busy staring at Aros. I wondered how much time had passed.

"The Bestiary God was created by the Original God to populate Topia with animal life-forms," Sing-Song replied. "In a way, that made him a creator in his own right. A lesser creator, maybe, but one all the same."

"You described him as a *nurturing*, *forgiving* god." Aros was smiling, his tone as smooth as silk, his posture relaxed.

I was sure that he was mocking her. I just didn't

understand why. She moved to her desk in the centre of the room, shuffling a few sheaths of parchment.

"Do you have information to the contrary, Aros?" she asked carefully.

There was so much tension in the air; even the sols were tense, their wide-eyed attention switching from Sing-Song to Aros, and back. *Was a sacred sol trying to say something bad about the gods? I never thought I'd see the day.*

"Yes." Aros sighed. He was acting like it was his job to inform us all differently, and he was sick of the task before it had even begun. "Terence—the Bestiary God, the Original Beaster, is also the Original Asshole—well, other than Rau, but I'm sure nobody here wants to talk about *him*."

Cue multiple brain explosions.

Sing-Song was shaking, her arm raised to direct a finger toward the door. "G-get out," she stuttered, her face now sheet-white. "I'll not have that talk in my classroom."

I guessed there were limits to the Abcurse rule on special privileges. Even if they were going to become future gods, they still weren't allowed to upset the *current* gods.

"Oh don't worry." Aros stood, but rolled his eyes. "The gods won't smite you for hearing my words ..." He paused, waiting as his brothers all rose to follow him out of the classroom, appearing completely unfazed. "And I have a feeling they won't smite me either." He winked at Sing-Song as he passed, leaving the rest of us standing around, mouths open, metaphorical pieces of our brain scattered all around the room.

I walked out of the classroom in a daze after class ended, not even paying attention to where I was going as two dwellers jostled my shoulders from either side. I was shocked when they quickly dashed away from me—when *everyone* quickly dashed away from me.

"Abcurse brothers," someone muttered, right before the hall completely cleared of people.

I blinked, still a little dazed, and found myself face-to-face with the triplets. Siret jumped forward, snatching the timetable out of my hand.

"She's in 2213 next," he told Yael, who stepped forward, grabbed the timetable, stuffed it into his pocket and then bent until he was on eye-level with me, his hands on his knees.

"Hey there, Rocks." He was grinning, the deep green hue of his eyes pulling me in, and *in* ... until the world was suddenly fuzzy and nothing existed beyond him. "You're going to skip your next class and come with us."

Of course I was. *Why would I do anything else?* I nodded.

His smile deepened and he turned suddenly, striding off with the other two. As soon as he broke eye-contact with me, I snapped back to myself, as though a frigid bucket of water had just been tossed over my head.

"What the hell was that?" I snapped, even though my legs were carrying me obediently after them.

One of them laughed, and Siret turned on his heel, walking backwards while I still walked forwards. "Aren't dirt-dwellers supposed to be *silent*?" he asked me, his expression painted in mocking question.

"If we were always silent, how would we be able to say *yes master, no master, everything you need master*, every time one of you sols—" I cut myself off, hearing a gasp to my left.

It was another of the dweller recruits. She had been scurrying along the corridor toward us, but now she was turning and going in the opposite direction. Apparently, she was so desperate not to be associated with me that she was willing to be late and feel the wrath of whatever teacher was in charge of her next classroom.

"Our new dweller is gonna die," Siret announced, snapping back around to walk normally. He sounded highly entertained. "I give her seven sun-cycles."

They were discussing me like I wasn't even there. *And* they were predicting my death. Lovely.

"Let's see how far we can push her first," replied Yael, a laugh in his voice. "I give her three sun-cycles."

"One sun-cycle!" Siret shot back.

"One rotation," Aros teased, glancing at me over his shoulder. "Teacher Christin is pretty lenient, so let's see which one of us can push enough of her buttons to get the dweller sacrificed by the end of this next lesson. It has to be a death sentence, too. Whoever manages it first will win a single favour from each of the rest of us."

Holy shit. "What if *I* win?" I quickened my steps, trying to walk right behind them.

I was pandering to their obviously competitive nature, and hoping that I lasted longer than a single rotation in the process. It was a dangerous game, but dangerous games were pretty much the only games I knew how to play, so at least I was in familiar territory.

"Well then I guess *you* win the favours," Siret returned thoughtfully. "Should we let her play?" he asked the others.

"She doesn't have a gift," Yael pointed out. "She's way out of her league."

They definitely underestimated the power of my clumsy-curse.

"So there's no harm in letting me play," I added gently. I was attempting to be coaxing. Siret snorted—he clearly wasn't buying it.

"Sure." He grinned, walking backwards again to show me the way his cat's eyes were crinkling at the corners. "You can play with the big boys, little dirt-dweller."

"But you guys can't use your gifts," I quickly added, now that he'd already agreed. "Because then it's no fun, no challenge. You want at least a *little* bit of a challenge, don't you?"

"Is the dweller trying to manipulate us?" Yael asked

the others. He sounded unimpressed and bemused all at once.

"Cute," Aros added, his silky voice doing funny things to me. "It manipulates."

Wow. Ouch.

We entered a classroom, and even though I knew it wasn't the classroom I was *supposed* to be in, I still attempted to move against the wall with all the other dwellers. It was Siret who stopped me, grabbing my arm with a chuckle and forcing me past a few rows of shocked sols toward the back row of seats. I suspected that people left the back row of each classroom purposefully empty, just for the Abcurse brothers. He dragged me into the row and forced me to take a seat beside him. Aros claimed the seat on my other side, and Yael lowered himself into the aisle seat, indicating that I'd have to fight past *two* of them if I wanted to escape. I stared back at the sea of faces all now staring at me. They weren't staring at the Abcurse brothers, even though they were *clearly* at fault for this. Nope. Apparently, I was going to be the one to take the fall, because nobody wanted to punish *them*.

Teacher Christin—or at least I assumed it was the same teacher that the guys had mentioned—strolled into the room, her nose stuck into a book, a mumbled, "Hello students," floating eerily over the still-staring room full of sols. She glanced up when she realised that nobody had answered, and her eyes traced all the attention back to me.

"Dweller?" She seemed too surprised to think of anything more to say.

And now I had a choice. I could get myself sentenced to death-by-sacrifice, and somehow use the favours I won to get myself out of the death-by-sacrifice, or I could ... *Run? Hide? Play dead? Ask to use the bathroom?* I really had no idea.

"Last I checked," I attempted to drawl nonchalantly. "That's me. I'm a dweller. Dirty, er, dirtiness and everything. What's it to you, woman?"

Her mouth dropped, her fingers loosening around the book. I watched as it fell—seemingly in slow motion—toward the floor, landing with a deafening *thump* that echoed off the walls. She looked toward the sols either side of me, probably hoping for some kind of explanation. The sols admittedly looked a little put-off, but I was sure it was only because they hadn't actually thought that I would try to get myself sentenced to death. *Pfft*. They clearly didn't know me.

"Now insult her again," Yael suggested, his persuasive voice washing over me.

He wasn't actually using his gift on me, but he was making it sound as though he was. Now I couldn't insult her again, otherwise it would be because of *him* that I got sentenced to death. I turned to glare at him, but he wasn't paying attention to me. He was leaning back, his arms crossed over his broad chest, his green eyes almost *shining*, because he was just that entertained by the rapidly reddening face of the teacher.

"I'll do what I *want*!" I exclaimed, surging to my feet and attempting to barge past Aros to poke a finger into Yael's face.

Unfortunately, Aros had only drawn back enough for me to get one leg past before slipping forward in his seat again. His knees closed around my other leg, trapping me solidly. He was *much* stronger than he looked. I froze, my eyes locked onto Yael's face. Whatever insult I had been mustering, ready to shout at him, died. I could feel it fizzle out, making way for shock. I didn't even know why I was so shocked, I really didn't. It had nothing to do with the fact that even sitting *next* to Aros had been making my head spin a little bit, and it definitely had nothing to do with the fact that him now touching me had scattered my brains to the far ends of the room. I was avoiding looking at him, but Yael was meeting my stare, and he had this *knowing* expression on his face that made me want to sucker-punch him in the face.

So ...

Yeah.

That's how I ended up sucker-punching a sacred sol on my second sun-cycle of being one of the Luckiest Dwellers in the World. He shot out of his seat, capturing my hand as I began to draw it back again. All three of the brothers were on their feet now, crowding around me. I had no idea what was about to happen, but the whole world froze when the teacher's voice rang out, loud and cold and shrill.

"DWELLER!"

I froze, my eyes on the ground. There were three sets of shoes, all pointed toward my boots, only a few inches away. The grip on my wrist tightened, and I felt one of them moving against my side.

"Forget ..." It was Yael, and the word had been whispered into my ear, though it rang around the room with the tenor of travelling magic. "Forget everything you just saw ..."

The room became still, and I finally glanced up, meeting the eyes of Aros, who stood directly before me.

"You win," he whispered, as the class began to stir back into motion.

"Yay," I mumbled, my tone flat.

I needed my head examined.

Emmy was going to *murder* me, which hardly made sense as a punishment for almost having gotten myself killed.

"Dweller?" The teacher again. She sounded confused, this time. "What are you doing?"

"H-he left his ... paper behind," I spoke up, edging past Yael and breaking into the aisle. "I—I'm in the wrong classroom. I'm so sorry!" I dove for the doorway, escaping through before any of them could grab me and question me.

I ran through the maze of corridors, trying to read

each of the numbers above the doors, even though I was moving too fast to read much of anything, let alone pay attention to where I was going. All I knew was that I had to get out of there; away from the Abcurse triplets. Away from the fear and the danger.

Away from the fact that I might have actually enjoyed it.

The rest of my second sun-cycle at Blesswood passed without incident. And by 'without incident,' I mean that I tripped three times, almost stabbed a dweller with a pencil, and accidentally started a tiny little fire in the kitchen. *Gods,* the way that Jerath had reacted you'd think I had burned the entire academy down. The fire had been barely two feet tall. Anyway, the point was that there were no more Abcurse sightings for the whole sun-cycle. They hadn't been in any more classes, or at dinner that night.

Rumours abounded about what those boys got up to when they disappeared, but all I could think was that the gods were finally giving me a break. I hoped that the break continued ... otherwise something told me that next time I crossed paths with one of those shiny, golden assholes, there wouldn't be any more contests to break the rules. The only breaking which would happen, would be me.

SIX

Early the next morning, Emmy was in lecture mode.

"You're playing a dangerous game, Will. Why did you have to challenge them? Why would you call attention to yourself? Sometimes I wonder how much of your curse is god-given, and how much is your insatiable need to stir up your sun-cycle. Your boredom is going to be the death of you!"

She'd been at it since just after the early bells. I'd spilled on the 'classroom incident' while we got ready, and now I wished I'd kept it to myself.

"How can you just take the abuse, Em? It's not in me to lie down and let them crush me. I'll stay out of their way as much as I can, but if they come at me, I'm going to fight back."

I was totally kidding. I couldn't 'fight back' against five massive sols even if my life depended on it, but I talked a good game. Talk was my thing, and I was working at perfecting it.

With a huff, Emmy pushed back her mass of silvery hair, artfully twirling it up into a neat knot on top of her head. I roughly gathered my own off my back and threw a few clips in there, hoping the curls would hold. No time for top-knots. I had some dorm rooms to sneak in and out of. Plus, I would only be covering it all in a cap.

I was fully decked out in Atti's old clothing; Emmy had done me a solid and stitched up the hem and waist on the pants last night, so they fit reasonably well. I took a quick look in the mirror: there was no pretty gloss, shadow or powder on my face; my hair was hidden beneath the cap; and a dark, baggy shirt attempted to hide my boobs. The outfit was paired with boy-pants and my usual boots. I was as male as I was going to get without any actual magic.

"I'm heading out now," I announced, interrupting Emmy as she started on her next lecture. "I want to make sure I'm done before any of them return." I hoped like hell that Rome wasn't in his room. He'd know that I was coming this time and with a little luck, he wouldn't be there.

Right. *Luck*. Because that was a thing I was totally familiar with.

"This sun-cycle we have to clean and set up the dining room before the sols get there. You can't skip cleaning duties!" She was all aghast and stuff.

Sometimes, I wondered if she knew me at all. I skipped my duties back in the village all the time. I literally couldn't seem to help from breaking rules. Maybe that was curse-induced too. Or maybe duties just sucked. I didn't believe what Emmy said; I didn't have a death wish. I had the opposite of a death-wish. I had a life-wish, where I actually wanted to *have a life* outside of serving and working and being told exactly how to serve and work.

I patted her arm quickly, before sprinting toward the door. She lurched out to grab me, missing by an inch.

"If I get to the dorms early, there's even less of a chance that one of those ... *sols* will be back from their training," I whisper-yelled as I left.

The words lingered behind me but I didn't stop moving, grabbing a few pieces of breakfast rock-bread as I passed the common dweller area. I took the stairs one at a time, even though I wanted to jump up as many as I could. It was safer this way. A broken nose would slow me down and I was on a mission. The Abcurse brothers would not get a jump on me this morning. Willa was going to get one over on them. Yes, I now spoke about myself in the third person. It was *that* kind of mission.

The domed room was reasonably empty; I noticed a few dwellers slipping into the dining area—they had the not-be-seen-or-smelt thing down. Eating my food as I ran, I took a sharp left and continued sprinting toward the male dorms. My disguise instilled me with a little more confidence this sun-cycle, but I kept my vigilant observations up. I hadn't roamed at this time before and had no idea who I might run into. The sols should be either at breakfast, or at training in the stadium, but it worried me that the Abcurse brothers had been missing for the second part of the previous sun-cycle. They were rule-breakers like me, apparently. Although, *unlike me*, it wasn't going to get them killed.

There were no cleaning carts conveniently waiting for me, so I had to barge through the storage room door, rip a poor defenceless cart free, and push it at super-dweller-speed toward dorms 1-5.

The hallway was empty and I had this amazing feeling inside. All warmth and life. I was totally killing it at being a dweller slave this sun-cycle.

Killing it!

When I was almost at the end, doorway five sprung open, and a huge body emerged. With an audible shriek, I skidded to a stop and hit the deck, hiding behind my cart. I was still a few feet from their rooms. If they didn't look this way, they hopefully wouldn't notice a rogue cart just sitting in the hall, all on its own.

I heard voices, and keeping my breathing as shallow as possible, I peered through the small gap in the towel area on the cart. Lots of goldenness, muscles, and arrogance came into sight. I couldn't quite tell, but judging from the glow, all five Abcurse brothers were leaving.

"We need to make sure D.O.D. knows that we're done with his bullshit. When we get back, I'm going to rip his ungodly head off."

Rome's voice was distinct—a low growl which tingled down my spine and settled somewhere low in my body. Which I was *so* not okay with.

"We need to figure out how to end this banishment." That was Yael, his velvety persuasive tone was enough to almost have me up and crawling toward him. He was *dangerous*. Affecting me way more than was safe. He continued: "I almost lost control of them the previous sun-cycle, it's starting earlier than usual this time."

They were moving away now; I could hear them still, but it was getting softer. Shifting my body forward a little, I decided to take a risk and see what was happening. Just as I got my head around the edge of the cart, blood red and ochre hair came into view.

"Well, well, well. What do we have here?" Coen reached out and wrapped his arms around me, and even though he wasn't as huge as his strength-gifted twin, he was still giant-size. He lifted me with ease, and I flinched, bracing for the pain. You weren't gifted to cause pain unless you were a sol who took pleasure in it.

"I'm not going to hurt you, Rocks," he said, whispering close to my ear. My eyes shuttered briefly as I fought for composure. I was potentially a click away from begging for my life, which was pretty uncool, considering my life hadn't been outwardly threatened. Yet. "I prefer my pain in a different outlet to what you're imagining," Coen continued. "If I cause you pain, you're probably going to like it."

What the ... holy gods of Topia, was he saying? I ... why was my brain trying to sign me up?

Aros.

It was his fault.

Blame the seduction-sol—even if he wasn't touching me. Seemed the simplest option.

"Let me go," I hissed, trying to wiggle out of Coen's grip. He still held me above the ground, my feet dangling below.

"What are you doing here, dweller? Don't you have rooms to clean, breakfasts to serve?" Siret stepped forward, his fitted black shirt had the green of his eyes darkening. His hair looked blacker than usual, like Yael's.

"Where were you the previous sun-cycle?" *What was wrong with me*? Why did I ask that? I didn't care where they were; as long as they weren't near me I was rejoicing. *Rejoicing*!

The four of them now stood in a circle around Coen and me, the intensity coming from them was enough to have my light-headedness increasing.

"You aren't like other dwellers." Siret ignored my question, stepping closer to me. His head was slightly tilted, his eyes locked onto mine. He stared at me like a bug he'd found in his food. Like I was strange and annoying. And yet ... there was a sort of curiosity there too.

Aros also stepped forward, and I turned my glare on him. Whatever I was feeling, it *had* to be his fault. My sanity depended on it.

"We never know what you're going to do next," he said. "You think for yourself, which in itself is rare on Minatsol." His summer glow was now seeping into me, warming up my blood. "We might be able to use someone like you, dweller. If you think you're up for it. The rewards could be great."

They were all close to me, towering over me despite the fact that I was being held off the ground. I'd never been surrounded like this. I'd never had so much beauty and magnetism directed toward me. It gave me both chills and nausea. I had no idea what they were going to do with me, but right now I felt like a little rabbit, completely surrounded by vicious predators, and that was *not* a great feeling.

Coen dipped his head forward, pulling me back into the trap of his gaze. "Will you help us, dweller? Remember, if you betray us ... well, the pain-pleasure thing can just become pain. I thrive on either. I'd just prefer it if I didn't have to go there."

Me too! I would definitely prefer that too.

He lowered me to the ground and my legs crumpled beneath me. They didn't seem to be capable of holding me up. I went down, my body collapsing as vertigo finally got me. Then, in a blink, I was somehow back on my feet.

"Follow us," Yael drawled.

The five of them strode off in the opposite direction of the domed room. None of them looked back. If they had, they would have seen a shell-shocked dweller trying to figure out how she wasn't on her ass right now. I'd been falling. Then I wasn't. And no one had touched me.

My breathing was all panty and shallow; my body couldn't seem to figure out whether to be excited or to fall apart. I really didn't want to follow them. I didn't want to find myself in another life-or-death situation, but I took Coen's warning very seriously. If I didn't help them, I was going to get hurt. *Dammit!* Why was this happening to me again? I was super-dweller this sun-cycle and then *boom*, back to sitting in bullsen shit.

The brothers were almost out of sight now and I couldn't delay any longer. Cursing under my breath, I scrambled after them, my weak legs not helping as I tried to catch up. Unsuccessfully. Those long-legged bastards were faster than me even though I was *running*. I was running badly, but that wasn't the point.

The hall reached an intersection, and the brothers went right, which was the general direction of the Sacred Sand arena. Why were we heading there? My shift to clean it wasn't for two more sun-cycles, so this could only mean one thing. *They were going to use me for fight practice.* No, couldn't be that. They might as well use a straw-stuffed dummy, I'd be as much use. So, there had to be another horrible activity waiting for me.

I was so busy freaking out about being dragged to the slaughter, that I didn't notice the stairs which led down into the outdoor grassed area. I hadn't actually been outdoors since we had arrived in Blesswood, and I'd have liked to enjoy the brush of the warm sun on my face, and the sound of a nearby trickling waterfall.

Instead, I took a one-way trip down the stairs.

I threw my hands out because a broken skull was much harder to heal than broken arms. I closed my eyes and braced for impact, preparing to roll like any good clumsy-cursed dweller knows how to do, but there was no impact. No thud as my hands followed by my head slammed into the grass below.

Two hard bands were wrapped across my torso, heat surrounding me as I was lifted against a firm body. The sunshine seemed to increase around us, and I knew without even looking up that it was Aros. My sunshine sol. I mean ... not mine or anything. That was weird, but you know ... *a* sunshine sol.

"You okay there, Willa?"

Golden eyes stole my breath. "You know my name?" I managed to ask.

He knows my name?

"Come on, Seduction, put her clumsy ass down

and let's go." Coen shouted his command, already moving toward the Sacred Sand arena.

Aros gave me a wink, and for the second time that sun-cycle, an Abcurse was dropping me onto shaky legs. He then strode off to catch his brothers, taking all the warmth and life with him. *Seduction.* Was it just me, or was it weird that they called each other by their gift? Like it was a name. I hadn't heard any other sols do that, so it wasn't like an 'in' thing. Not that it really mattered with my imminent death looming.

I picked up the pace, feeling like a super-dweller again because even though they were really good at dropping me, they had also seemed to be pretty good at catching me. The sols were useful for something, at least. Coen was striding ahead of the rest, appearing almost a speck from my vantage point as the straggling, weak-assed dweller. Rome was right behind him, followed by Aros—who had caught up to the others without a problem, despite the burn in *my* thighs and the pant on *my* breath—Yael was next, and then Siret. I laughed, almost causing myself to trip again because laughing and running weren't activities that should be carried out simultaneously. But it was funny. They were lined up in order of their dorm numbers, from one to five.

Pain-Master Coen was number one, *Crusher* Rome was number two, Golden Aros was number three, Hypnotic Yael was number four, and Evil Siret was number five. That was *one* way to differentiate between them.

"What are you laughing at?" Siret slowed until he was beside me, that mixture of curiosity and annoyance back in his eyes.

"Nothing, Five," I replied on another pant-laugh. I almost tripped again. Talking, running, *and* laughing was even less advisable.

"Five?" Yael called over his shoulder. "What the hell is she talking about?"

"Nothing, Four!" I yell-panted.

This time, I did trip, but I swung out a hand in natural reaction, catching a fist-full of Siret's shirt. He started to go down with me, but then he managed to catch us both, his arm quickly wrapping around my back.

"She's *ranking* us?" Aros stopped running altogether, turning to face us with an incredulous expression.

Yael also stopped, but the others continued, too far ahead to realise what was happening.

"Why do you keep *doing* that?" Siret asked, using his grip on me to shake me a little bit.

"Doing what?" I asked, pushing on his chest to indicate that he could put me down. He didn't. My stomach decided to flip.

"Falling. Tripping. Almost getting yourself killed."

"What does it matter?" I groused. "Aren't you taking me to get killed anyway?"

I spotted Rome and Coen up ahead; they weren't running anymore, but they weren't coming back to us. They were waiting. Rome had his hand raised to his eyes, trying to block out the sun.

Yael laughed. "We're not taking you to get killed."

"Maybe we are?" Siret seemed to be asking the others a question. He seemed to have forgotten that he was holding me. I looked down at my feet, kicking my boots back and forth a little, trying to reach the ground.

"You have a point," Yael returned. "She'll probably twist this around so that she finds a way to die, even if that's not our intention."

"Doesn't matter." Siret was shaking his head. "She still needs to stay alive until we're done with her. She can die pissing off D.O.D., but she can't die *getting* there. That's just inconvenient."

"Right here," I grumbled.

"Yeah you are." Aros stepped forward, grabbed my arm, and *yanked* me out of Siret's grip.

It hurt like a bitch, but I didn't complain, because they were talking about killing me again, and I figured complaining probably wouldn't help my situation very much. I rubbed my shoulder, trying to ignore the way Aros was twisting his fingers through mine, because it seemed to be tied directly to something inside me, twisting and twisting and twisting ...

"Don't get possessive, Seduction," Siret growled, stalking past us. "She's *our* dweller. Not yours."

"Still right here," I added. "I'd also like to have a say, if it's dweller claiming time."

"No." Yael was chuckling, moving past us with Siret. "You get no say."

Aros tugged me forward, his feet eating up the distance faster than I thought it would be possible for me to follow, and yet somehow I managed it. We were almost to the edges of the academy now, with only the mountains in the distance, separated from us by a short stretch of forest, where Coen and Rome were waiting.

"What happened?" Coen demanded, once we reached them. His eyes were on my hand. Specifically, the hand that Aros was holding.

His bright green eyes narrowed, luminous and dangerous, and I tried to tug my hand free, feeling a ball of panic lodge in my throat. Now was *not* the time for them all to start fighting over dweller-slave-claiming-rights or whatever. They could do that *after* I was dead. Aros tightened his grip, and I swallowed, my stomach lurching.

"She ranked us," Yael replied nonchalantly. He seemed to be the least concerned about the ranking, compared to the other two.

"She *what*?" That had been Rome. He looked confused.

"RIGHT HERE!" I shouted, my temper flaring and bursting before I even had the chance to realise that it had been building. I was panting again, but this time it wasn't from the exercise. It was because the five idiots were messing with my internal organs. Or my brain. Or something. They wouldn't stop making me dizzy. *Aros wouldn't stop holding my hand!*

Siret burst into sudden laughter just as I managed to finally tear my hand free from Aros. Everyone was staring at me as though I had just temporarily lost my mind, except for Siret.

"Well?" Coen crossed his arms, giving me a look. "If you're right there, go ahead and explain yourself."

"Nothing to explain." I shrugged.

"This is why we don't talk to her." He tossed his hands up, turning on Yael. "What ranking?"

"She ranked us," he repeated. "Four—" he jabbed a finger at his chest, and then turned it on Siret, "and five. Don't know what she gave you guys."

Rome's mouth dropped open, but Coen was all stony-faced, until I caught the edge of his eyebrow inching up. "Is this out of ten?"

"Maybe." I considered telling him that it was just their dorm numbers, but that wouldn't have been half as fun. It was nice to see him squirm. I considered it pay-back for the crossbow incident.

"What's my number?" he demanded.

"One."

He frowned, and I knew that he was considering the possibility that this might have been a *one-out-of-ten* situation.

"And him?" Coen jerked a finger in Aros's direction.

"Three."

"And him?" This time, the finger was jabbed in Rome's direction.

"Two," I said, cocking my head at Rome.

Rome was smiling, like he had figured it out. He didn't tell the others, though. He seemed content to allow them all to stand around, baffled. I would say that it made him a little bit evil, but what difference did it make? They were all evil anyway.

"Can we figure this out later, maybe?" Once again, Yael seemed unconcerned with the ranking.

The others nodded, Coen casting me one last look before they started moving again—this time, through the forest. Because the trees were so dense, we had to slow to a walk, and Yael dropped back to walk behind me. The others didn't seem to notice when he twisted a hand in my shirt and pulled me off my feet. This was just way too much yanking around for my poor cap, and it finally gave up trying to cling to my head. I tried to see through the spill of white-blond curls, feeling like the sudden colour was almost blinding after not having it swinging into my line of vision for most of the morning.

"What—"

A hand slapped over my mouth, cutting off the question before I could voice it. My back hit one of the trees and I quickly pushed the hair out of my eyes. Yael was only an inch away, leaning into me.

"Raise my ranking," he ordered softly. I felt the

heavy roll of his power rushing over me, carrying on the tenor of his voice.

Holy shit, were these five competitive or what?

I made a sound behind his hand. His eyes narrowed, and he lifted his hand almost suspiciously.

"Not a ranking!" I finally managed to get out. "It's just your dorm number."

He frowned. "Make me One, then."

"You have to be in the first room to be One."

He released me suddenly, stalking away.

"Hey, Pain!" he shouted, making his way through the trees again. "Switch rooms with me!"

"What?" I heard Coen shout back.

I was still leaning against the tree, my heart threatening to jump out of my chest and bury itself deep, *deep* underground, where it would be safe. Because I swear to the gods, those boys were going to give me a heart-attack. How was that for karma? A sexy sol was going to kill me by frightening me to death.

And I didn't just say sexy.

None of them were sexy. And their sexiness definitely wasn't the reason for my heart-pains. Not that they had sexiness. Because they didn't.

"Rocks?" Siret strode back into sight, a scowl twisting his lips. "You fall again?"

"Not sexy ..." It kind of slipped out. I wasn't sure how. I wanted to take it back immediately, but he had clearly already heard me.

He blinked. "Well ... I wouldn't put it that way. You go down like a pro. It's a little bit sexy."

My mouth dropped open, my eyebrows inching up. Somehow, that had sounded filthy. He seemed to realise it, too, or maybe he was just reading it on my face. *Oh, gods in hell. I need to never speak again.*

He started smiling, the flash in his eyes driving the heat further into my face. I pushed past him, ready to face my death. Maybe I could ask them to hurry up, and save myself from any more of ... whatever it was they were doing to me. Or maybe I could just trip on something and fall onto a nice, suicidal rock.

Yeah.

That'd be nice.

SEVEN

One moment we were picking a precarious path through the mountains about a mile from the boundary of the academy, and then, suddenly, we weren't even in Blesswood anymore. I gasped, my footsteps halting, my eyes going wide. The seemingly endless stretch of mountainous terrain before us had dissolved, and a dark, damp-smelling cave had loomed in around us, only a pinprick of light visible in the distance.

"What in the world of the gods ..." I spun around, trying to take in everything at once, even though it was too dark to take in even an inch of the 'everything'.

"Exactly." Rome had been the one to utter the reply, sounding right behind me.

He had dropped to the back of the procession after declaring to the group that I kept getting into *trouble* whenever he left me unsupervised, whatever that was supposed to mean. He had been the one to plant a hand on the centre of my spine and push me forward, initiating this trip through reality.

"What do you mean *exactly*?" I asked in the general direction of his voice.

"The world of the gods," he replied, making me realise that I was staring at the wrong patch of darkness.

I adjusted my eyes, and then it hit me.

No—it didn't hit me! Because that was impossible!

This cave couldn't be Topia. *The Abcurse brothers couldn't possibly know a secret passage into Topia!*

"Anything is possible, Rocks," Siret muttered, grabbing my wrist and drawing me through the darkness, toward the little pin-prick of light. I must have spoken out loud—or else they could read minds.

Knowing my luck, it was the latter.

As soon as Siret's skin touched mine, my head was flooded with conflicting images. Thoughts. Memories. I had no idea what they were, but the men and women pictured in my mind weren't anything like the sols I knew. They wore robes as they strolled past insanely gorgeous scenery; lakes, rivers, *oceans*. Some of them were sitting on floating marble platforms which looked down over miles and miles of sky. Siret was using his trickery gift to fill my head with nonsense, and yet ... I couldn't help the feeling that this particular nonsense was actually *real*.

Because I was in Topia. *Those demon-sols snuck me into fucking Topia!*

Emmy wasn't just going to kill me anymore. She was going to cut me up into tiny little pieces, put each piece of me into a tiny box, and feed each box to a single bullsen, which she would burn, and then she would separate the ashes of the burnt bullsen into tiny little piles, and then she would put each tiny pile of ash into a tiny box, and then—

"Welcome to the world of the gods," Rome drawled, as we stepped from the cave and into the glaring sunlight.

Siret let me go, only to grab me again as I pitched forward. My feet were trying to move before my mind had caught up to the world in front of me.

It was beauty. It had to be beauty personified in a land because there were no other words to explain what I was seeing. Everything glowed, like the sols, but a million times stronger. As if the gods lived on the sun and somehow they'd turned down the heat, but not the shine. The land spread out far beyond what I could see; it was all sparkling lakes, rolling mountains and everything that the tales of Topia had promised. Everything that the tales of Topia had promised *to the sols that were going to become gods.* It was more, too. More than the stories, and the lectures, and the songs. I was now staring at the same things that I had seen when Siret had dragged me through the cave and into paradise.

Floating marble structures, twenty feet in diameter, drifted lazily above our heads. I couldn't see beyond them to know if anyone was up there, but ... *who cared?* They were just floating there. It was magic, pure and simple. Powers beyond anything I had ever seen, and beauty beyond what I could understand.

"I finally get it." I must have murmured it out loud, because five sets of gem-like eyes were suddenly focusing on me, five massive bodies surrounding me.

"What do you finally get, Rocks?" Coen stepped into my space again. He wasn't the only one. I could feel another at my back, but I was too terrified to turn and find out who it was.

Trying to breathe around the panic, I stuttered out, "I get why you sols spend your lives trying to get here. It's perfect."

I heard a snort of laughter to my left, and somehow knew that it was Siret. "Don't let the beauty fool you," he said. "This world is filled with as many ugly assholes as Minatsol."

I found myself swivelling to see him better. To read as much as I could from those words. It always felt like the brothers were speaking in riddles. Half-truths. What they said and meant were definitely two different things, but that was hardly surprising from a trickery-gifted sol like Siret.

"How do you know so much about Topia? How are we even here?" I asked, glancing between the five of them. "How did you find the entrance and then ... not *die* getting here?" Because that was supposed to be the requirement for entry. You had to die and then hope that a God chose you for immortality. To rule with them here in paradise.

Silence greeted my question.

Somehow, though, they managed to exchange a single glance between the five of them. *Crazy.* These sols were a full range of crazy and powerful. Not to mention scary and gorgeous. And they'd brought me into Topia. Right in that moment, I couldn't figure out whether to hug them or run the hell away from them. They had taken me to the world of the gods. The one place a dweller would never, *ever* go. *Ever.*

It might have been crazy ... but it was still a gift.

I didn't even care if they killed me; right then I was happy. My joy spilled out, and in my usual *act-before-you-think* fashion, I dived forward. In the brief moment before impact, I saw raised eyebrows and wide-eyes, and then I landed against the brothers. I could only manage to get my arms across three of them, but that was enough. I hugged them as tightly as I could, their bodies solid against me.

"I don't even care how we got in here. Thank you! I can't believe this! *I'm in TOPIA!*"

I was muttering nonsense, my own happiness leaking out in random babble. Coen had been the one in the centre of my hug, next to him Siret, and on the other side was Aros. None of them moved; they just let me hold them for an awkward amount of time, and I couldn't believe that I wasn't being tossed across the world yet.

The silence washed over us, the peaceful nature of this land. It was almost like we were secured in the clear perfection of this immortal world for one click in time, and it was kind of nice. For that instant, I forgot that the Abcurse brothers were scary sols who would probably get me sacrificed to the very gods we were now in close proximity to, because they actually felt like friends.

A throat cleared behind us, and Yael said distinctly, "There better be a reason you're hugging them and not me. And you'd better start sharing it around."

Right, crazy competitive.

"I was going to, Four—" I started to say, before he cut me off.

"One! I'm number One!"

I pulled back and turned toward the persuasive sol, his eyes were so green in that moment that they didn't even remotely look natural. His hair shone more in Topia's light than it ever had in Minatsol. It was the colour of thick, dark ink, piled over gold—mixed just enough for the gold to rise up and peek through the darkness.

He was close, but he didn't step into me. I knew he wanted me to come to him, but something held my feet firm to the ground. Beside him was Rome, the other one to not fall victim to my enthusiasm before.

"We don't have time for this." Rome grunted out

the words, clearly annoyed by something. "Yael, go over and get your hug so you can feel equal and then we need to get to Luciu." Noting my confused expression, he added, "It's where the Original Gods reside."

Wait just one freaking click ...

"We can't go there! They'll kill all of us. You guys might be a big deal in Blesswood, but here you're just sols who snuck into their world. You haven't been chosen by the gods yet. This is suicide!"

Rome shook his head. "*We're* not going to Luciu. You are."

Say *what* now?

Coen sounded from over my shoulder. "The gifts of the sols are god-given, which means they can sense our energy. We can't get close without alerting one of them, but you ... you're a dweller. You have no gifts—unless we're counting your lack of common sense and general physiological imbalance as a gift. Dwellers can't even get into Topia without touching a gifted one. They'd never expect it; you're the perfect one to sneak in."

I was screwed. This was why dwellers and sols were not friends. Because of this. With a huff, since it didn't matter anymore, I shoved through the brothers, not even trying to be gentle. I strode a few feet from them, needing the space. I took another long look at the world. I wanted to imprint it in my mind, if this was the last thing I'd ever see. I was especially entranced by the huge ocean of water out in the distance, so vast that there was no way anyone could swim across it. I'd never seen anything like that before and I knew I never would again.

"I can't believe I hugged those assholes." Muttered curses spilled from me. "I hugged them. Stupid Abcurses. Should have known they'd be bad luck with a surname like that. Cursed. Just like my life."

Strong arms wrapped around me from behind, and I found my body lifted up off the ground and spun around until I was staring at Yael. His hugeness engulfed me, the strength in his grip almost too much for my poor little heart.

"No one ever hugs us for no reason." His voice was a whispered caress across my body. Like the sweetest, most seductive breeze ever. "No one gives themselves without expecting something in return. You honoured us, little dirt-dweller."

Wow. *Back-handed compliment much*?

He'd been waiting for me to hug him, and I hadn't. That kind of hurt my heart, and I had to lift my arms and loop them around his neck, even though he'd also half insulted me. I had to squeeze him toward me to try and ease some of the hardness in his cold gaze. My body softened against him, and I felt some of his anger ease.

This was all insanity. All of it. That I could be so forward with any boy, let alone a god-blessed sol, was crazy. But here we were.

Hugging.

In Topia.

Shit, maybe I was already dead, and this was hell. Note that I said hell there. Definitely not heaven. *Even if it felt a little bit like heaven ...*

Yael's huge body rumbled beneath me, and an energy drifted from him toward me. It was warm. Then, in a flash, I was back on my feet. I found myself feeling a little bereft. He strode away. I stared after him, not sure what had just happened.

"We won't let you die, Willa." Coen distracted me, and I flinched back at the look on his face. He wore his hard, carved-from-granite face, which was ten types of scary. I associated it with the trying-to-shoot-me-with-a-crossbow incident. "We need you to help us, and then we'll make sure that no one at Blesswood messes with you again."

Sucking in deeply, I tried to gather up every iota of bravery inside of me. I had like a teaspoon so far. The Abcurses weren't giving me much of a choice, but they were at least making it worth my while. If I managed to do this for them, I wouldn't be getting sentenced to death-by-sacrifice anytime soon by the Blesswood teachers. And I appreciated Coen's promise that they wouldn't let me die in Topia. It showed that they didn't think of me as being completely expendable, only a little bit expendable—maybe like fifty-percent expendable.

I nodded a few times, the lightest of breezes ruffling my curls. "Okay, I'll try my best. Just remember that even though they might not be able to sense my energy, I am still curs—clumsy. I mean ... things sometimes happen around me. Things that aren't very inconspicuous. Like bleeding injuries and shattered valuables. So, I can't promise anything." My bravery was almost at a tablespoon now, so I asked, "What do the gods have of yours? What am I getting back?"

The others all glanced at Yael, as though he had magically persuaded me to cooperate. He met their stares with a smirk twisting his lips, but Siret was the one who spoke.

"It's just a little cup, nothing serious. Well, nothing serious to D.O.D., but it's very serious to us. D.O.D. took it the last time he was in Minatsol for the moon-cycle tournament. He won't even realise it's gone if we take it now."

"And who the hell is D.O.D.?" I asked.

"He's a god," Siret replied, as though I should have already known. And, well, seeing as we were in Topia ...

"I gathered that much." I deadpanned. "But *which* god?"

"You wouldn't know even if I told you." Siret was suddenly in front of me, tapping against the side of my head. "You were getting stitches the sun-cycle they taught the dwellers about D.O.D."

I frowned, and not because he was insulting me again, but because he may have been right. There was every chance that I had no idea who D.O.D. was because of one of my many medical emergencies.

"So where's Luciu then?" I turned, looking up to one of the marble platforms. "And will we be done before dinner? I'm starving."

"She's starving," Siret repeated, shaking his head.

"You'll have to go through another pocket to get there." Coen stepped up behind me, his hand shaping to the curve of my spine, his softly-spoken words sounding just a little bit frightening. "I'm going to push you through, and then you'll be on Luciu's main platform. One of the gods hosts a feast there every sun-cycle, without fail—"

"Yay! Feast—"

"*And*," Coen cut across me, his hand pressing harder, "the cup is always at his side. You won't be able to miss him; he'll be wearing purple. It's his colour—"

"His *God*-colour?"

"One more thing." Coen completely ignored my question, stepping up so that the heat of his body hovered right behind me. He ducked his head, his words whispering over the sweep of my neck. "This is going to hurt."

And then he pushed.

The world around me shifted once again, closing in around me and then opening up, revealing open blue sky above me and smooth rose-tinted marble beneath me. I was on my knees, having landed hard against the marble. *Ouch. Totally not kidding about the hurting part.* I glanced over my shoulder and saw that I was on the very edge of one of the floating platforms. Below was miles and miles of sky, and below that was a snow-capped mountain with a pine-covered base. The mountain itself was some kind of onyx stone; nothing that I recognised. I gulped, crawling away from the edge and then pulling up to my feet. Those bastard sols.

"We won't let you die, Willa." I mimicked, brushing off my boy-clothes and shoving my hair out of my face. *"We'll just teleport you onto a platform in the sky, where you're definitely going to die, while we wait in our little safety-cave."*

"Excuse me?" A voice piped up to my left.

I turned my head and promptly shrieked. The thing wasn't entirely human, but it certainly wasn't a god. It was almost naked, except for some weird kind of skin-suit that covered about as much as ordinary underwear would cover, before stretching up over the stomach, over the chest, and then separating into straps to go over the shoulders. I could still see the general shape of *everything*. I wanted to cover my eyes, just to be polite, but the thing had a face that didn't really allow you to look away. There was a nose, but *it* didn't seem to be breathing. There was a mouth, but I couldn't see any teeth. It had eyes, but there was a strange, waxy texture to them.

"What the hell are you?" I hissed, before I could think of a more sensitive way to ask the question.

"I am a server," the thing replied. "My name is Jeffrey."

I blinked, my eyes moving to Jeffrey's strange covering. "No offence, Jeffrey, but I'm pretty sure you're a chick."

"A chick?" Jeffrey cocked her head to the side, blinking that waxy gaze. "I am sorry, Sacred One, I do not understand."

I spluttered out a laugh. "Sacred One?"

"Yes, Sacred One. I am a server and you are a Sacred One. I was made to serve the Sacred Ones of Topia by the Sacred Creator."

"Way too many Proper Titles in there," I muttered. "So you're like a servant? And you're not real? You can't push me off this platform if I do something stupid?"

Jeffrey made a mechanical gasping sound. I took it as a no.

"So why'd he name you Jeffrey?" I asked, trying to wipe the look of shock off her waxy face.

"The names are distributed at random," Jeffrey answered. "It does not matter, as long as they have a name to call when they require something."

"I require something."

"How may I assist you, Sacred One?"

I looked up to her head, noting that the Creator hadn't bothered to give her any hair at all. She was all smooth and bald and freaky.

"I need a cap. Something to cover my hair. And whatever the hell it is you're wearing. I need that."

Jeffrey let out another mechanical gasp. I sighed, rocking back on my heels to wait it out. Eventually, she jerked herself into a short bow, and then turned and walked away, presumably looking for a cap. I doubted that any of the other Jeffreys were wearing caps, but they could just assume that someone had put it on me as a joke. Because they definitely made jokes out of those things, right? Maybe that's what really happened to dwellers when they died. Maybe they turned into semi-naked, Topian serving robots. That was worse than the 'hell' we were all supposed to be going to.

I was still pondering the living-hell in front of me, and the promised hell-for-the-dead that I had always grown up believing in, when Jeffrey returned, a cap in her hand. I tucked my hair away while she pulled off her covering, handing it over to me. I pulled my boy-clothes off and changed into the skin thing, casting one very quick glance down.

"Motherfreaking gods," I grumbled. "Why am I always doing embarrassing things with my nipples showing?"

Cue mechanical gasp.

"Don't worry," I told Jeffrey, handing my clothes over to her. She stared at them, and then dropped them, evidently preferring to be naked. "I say stuff like that sometimes. I'm the God of Embarrassment."

She frowned. "Sacred Luke is the God of Shame, Sacred One."

"Did I say shame?" I shook my head at her.

"Honestly, Jeffrey, it's like your head is full of empty air and Proper Titles." I raised a hand, cutting off the mechanical gasp. "I need to find a cup now. Can you help me?"

"I will fetch a cup, Sacred One."

I caught her before she could disappear again. "Hold up. It's a specific cup. Is there someone here called D.O.D.? It's his cup."

Jeffrey shook her head. Her waxy face was twisting in a particular way. I thought it was concern.

"Well are there any special damn cups up here?"

"Sacred Abil has a cup. The Trophy of Staviti."

That name. *Staviti*. It was familiar to me, but I had no idea why. I also didn't particularly care. "Okay, great. Where's that?"

"Sacred Abil always has it with him, always by his side."

"And Sacred Abil is where?"

"Eating." Jeffrey pointed off to the side, through a maze of columns leading further into the centre of the platform.

I took off, weaving through the sky-high columns, toward the sound of tinkling music and conversation. There were mini-columns set beneath the taller ones, acting as plant-stands to cradle vine-like things that were snaking out to try and smother everything in their path. They had even spilled from the columns to spread over the marble beneath my feet. Eventually, I began to see other people: robot-servers in similar, bare coverings, and then ...

Gods.

They all seemed so *big*, wrapped in robes that dragged along the marble. Even the females seemed larger-than-life, with tall and willowy frames, their hair left free and flowing, dragging down their backs in a shining display of immaculate colour. Hopefully Coen hadn't lied to me, because there was only one man wearing purple that I could see. He stood right beside a massive buffet table, every dish of food imaginable spread over it, the purple robes draping over his massive shoulders to pool on the marble. There was a cord around his waist, and there was a cup hanging off the cord. It looked more like a trophy, complete with a golden sheen and everything. I made my way over to him, grabbing a knife from the buffet table as I passed, and then up-ending a basket of bread and pulling out the little cloth sack that the bread had been sitting in.

"Excuse me, Sacred One," I muttered, bumping into D.O.D., slicing the knife through the cord and catching the falling cup into my sack, which I quickly hid behind my back.

"Watch yourself," he growled, spinning around. "Or I'll push you off the damn platform, useless thing."

Wow. Rude much?

"Apologies, Sacred One," I muttered, bowing just like Jeffrey had, backing a few steps away.

I should have known better. 'Backing away without looking' was never a thing that had worked for me before. I backed right into one of the willowy god-women, who fell forward, also knocking over the man who had been standing next to her. I toppled toward the woman and she pushed me away, sending me sprawling onto the man, instead.

I tossed out my hands to catch myself, forgetting that I was holding the knife ...

And that was how I stabbed a God in Topia.

The man looked down at the knife protruding from his stomach, his eyes wide. I also stared at the knife protruding from his stomach, my own eyes wide. Nobody said anything. The whole platform had fallen into a heavy, shocked silence. Someone grabbed me by the back of my measly covering, hauling me to my feet and spinning me around.

D.O.D.

And he was pissed.

"Another faulty server," he muttered, planting a hand into the centre of my chest and pushing, *hard*.

The air closed in around me, the whole world turning black. I landed on my back, softly-packed soil breaking my fall. The darkness didn't lift, and it took me a moment to realise that I was in another cave. I pulled myself up onto my elbows, seeking out the light of the entrance. There were some splotchy shapes blocking out most of the light, but I could still see it, so I forced myself to my feet and began to struggle in that direction. I pulled my prize-trophy out of the bag, leaving the cloth behind in the cave while I ran my hands over the smooth metal surface.

This better be worth it.

Ahead of me, the shapes began to shift, forming into silhouettes.

Five silhouettes, to be exact.

"She's back." I recognised Rome's voice as I finally made it closer to the entrance of the cave. It hadn't been the same cave, but a new cave altogether. "You were right, Trickery. She did get sent to the banishment cave."

"I'm always right." Siret sounded like he was laughing, but it tapered off when I stepped out into the light and tossed my trophy into the dirt in front of them.

"What's with the blood?" Coen asked, his eyes on my left hand.

"Stabbed a god," I told him.

His expression went blank very quickly, but I was sure that he was hiding a laugh. "Don't go drowning in guilt or anything."

"Well he can't *die* from it; he's already dead, right?"

Coen smiled: a wide, crazy-disarming smile that caught my breath and wiped every thought out of my head. He was looking at me as though he'd only just seen me, but then his brows drew together and he flicked his eyes up to the cap on my head, and then down to my borrowed 'outfit'.

I tore my gaze away, almost immediately wishing that I hadn't, because four more sets of eyes were staring in the exact same way.

"Uh ..." I tried to drag an explanation out of my still-blank mind when Aros shook his head, drawing my full attention.

"What the fuck are you wearing?" he growled, the usual smoothness of his silken voice disappearing altogether.

EIGHT

My first instinct was to hide.

To try my best with stupidly tiny hands to cover my nakedness. Nakedness which was probably tinted a nice shade of pink right about now. But as five sets of eyes continued to bore into me—eyes belonging to the sol-shits who had dragged me into *Topia* to *steal* from the *gods*—I realised something. I realised that I didn't care. They could just deal with it.

I dropped my hands to my hips, and with a voice as firm as possible, I said, "Would have thought you boys would have seen more than your fair share of boobs and vag—"

A snort of laughter from Siret cut me off mid-sentence, but they got the point. Before anyone said another word, Aros whipped his far-too-valuable-for-me-to-ever-dream-of-owning shirt over his head. He then reached out a hand and curved it around my shoulder, pulling me across to stand before him. In a blink, the warm length of material was being pulled over my head, falling past my thighs. It had clearly been hand-made for someone his size.

I would have spent some time enjoying the soft material—it was woven from magic, or at least some form of special, extra-silky blend reserved for extra-special sols—but I couldn't enjoy it. I couldn't because Aros was now shirtless. *Holy dweller babies.* Could I have his dweller-sol babies?

Wait ... no. Not what I meant. What I meant to say was *put your damn shirt back on*. All of that golden sunshine skin, draped tightly over hard muscle was horrible to look at. I was not going to spend any more than the next thirty to forty clicks staring at him. Before my tongue could actually fall out of my mouth, Siret swept me up, throwing me with ease over his shoulder.

"Come on, Rocks," he said, as he started to move. *What the crap?* Why did they keep doing that? I struggled against his hold, and even though I knew it was a bad idea, I kicked out as hard as I could at him. Aiming to hurt.

Of course, he didn't even seem to care, his strong arms tightened across me, halting my kicks. "Stop fighting me. You know you can't leave without touching one of us, and frankly I don't trust you to make it without a concussion or more of your ass showing."

TRICKERY

I knew I was bright red, partly from the blood rushing to my upside-down head as it hung down his back, but also from his words. *When did this become my life?* Upside down and naked, except for some weird skin-suit and a borrowed shirt. Once she heard about my escapades, Emmy would either have a heart attack and become the first person to die from the simple act of me speaking, or most probably would refuse to believe any of it.

The journey back from the banishment cave was a little rockier than the initial journey into Topia. Apparently, they didn't like their rejected beings having an easy escape route. A few times I thought I caught sight of something in the darkness—at least from what I could make out by lifting my head up from its hard resting place.

"Can you let me down now?" I asked, my demand the twelfth since we'd entered the cave. "I can't feel my fingertips; they're going to fall off, and then who will make your beds? Seriously, making beds without fingers is pretty difficult. Not that making beds with fingers isn't difficult either, because it is. You guys should really try it some time."

The screechy tone of my voice should have gone a long way to endearing me to the five sols. Surely they loved a screechy woman. Didn't all men?

I was just opening my mouth again when a hand wrapped around it. It was Coen. "If you think you can manage it, shut up for a little bit and we'll be out of this cave. The only reason they aren't attacking us is because we hold this cup." From the corner of my eye, I could see him brandishing the stolen cup.

Narrowing my gaze on him, I was about to let him know exactly what I thought about being handled like that, when his words registered. Who were *they*? In that moment, the flickering shadows I'd been noticing around us started to become clear. Well ... clear enough for me to see what was surrounding us.

Creatures.

Living creatures.

Hundreds of them. Grotesque, ghost-like, wraith-figures. Coen must have seen the wide-eyed fear I was suddenly channelling, because he slowly removed his hand, and leaned in closer to whisper to me.

"When you are rejected by the gods, there is no escaping. You remain here until your physical form fades away, and then only the shadow creature is left."

I swallowed hard, trying not to either throw up or cry. *Damn the gods.* They sentenced the very beings who had already spent their sun-cycles serving them to this kind of eternal torture.

"Can we free them?" My voice was very low; I was afraid to draw their attention. There were so many of them, and even with this magic-cup-deterrent, it was scary.

Rome slipped in next to his twin, and even though Siret was walking pretty fast, none of them looked uncomfortable walking and whispering to me like this.

"There's nothing left but anger and vengeance," the most giant of the Abcurse brothers said. "If we free the spirits, they will wreak destruction across Minatsol, destroying the nine rings in no time. They can never be freed."

I shut up after that, trying my best not to stare at the scary surrounding us. Scary and sad. I wished that I could un-see them, but no such luck. Thankfully, Coen hadn't been lying about us being close to the exit; the brightness we'd been moving toward was increasing, and I sucked in a deep breath at the junction between cave and outside. The blood rushed through my body as Siret dropped me to my feet, keeping a tight hold on my shoulder, which was helpful against the weakness in my body. I was barely keeping myself up, but after all my carry on, I needed to prove that I could stand on my own two legs. The other Abcurses stepped in beside us, forming a single line of sols.

Their expressions varied from grim to stoic. I wasn't sure what to expect judging by that, but something told me it was going to be a bit of a rough journey to get out of this banishment cave.

"Just take a deep breath, Willa," Aros instructed from my right side, and then the six of us stepped through to the other side.

Well, sort of. The actual transition between the worlds, this time, was akin to having my skin torn from my body by means of grating it off. The cave did not want to let us go, and right now I was biting my lip hard enough to taste blood so that I wouldn't scream out in pain. The agony felt like it lasted entire sun-cycles, and when we finally found ourselves outside, with tall, thick trees surrounding us, I all but collapsed to my stomach.

My hands ripped into soft, green grass, my breathing ragged as I fought against the last tendril of pain. I pushed myself partly up so that I could run my hands from my shoulders to wrists, obsessively checking to make sure that my skin was still intact.

Fancy shoes appeared in my line of sight, a shadow blocking the light above me. "You doing okay, Rocks? It's a real bitch getting in and out of the banishment zone."

I knew it was Coen. The pain-gifted sol had predictably been the first to recover. Hands fitted in under my arms and lifted me to my feet. I found myself staring into his dark green eyes, a storm of darkness hovering just around the edges. He was smiling, right until he focused on my face. The darkness in his eyes expanded outward then, shading over his features like a roiling storm cloud.

Reaching up, I tried to figure out what had happened to bring on that expression. Knowing me, it could have been anything. There could have even been a sleeper on my head. Those bugs hung above you, hidden in sticky white nets, and then when you were least prepared, they dropped into your hair. Most of the time you didn't know about it, so they were able to burrow in and create a nest. They lived in your head, had their babies, and then when all their young were born, they would bite and kill you. Just so you wouldn't be able to tell anyone that they were there.

My hands started frantically patting now. I'd seen a few sleeper-deaths in the seventh ring, and I was not going out that way. Not a freaking chance in hell. Coen's eyebrows slowly drew together as he watched me jump around, shaking my hair out, flipping my head upside down and everything.

"Is it out?" I was shouting. Panic had me in its hold.

I didn't fear much, but the creepy, multi-legged, weird-looking bug was high on my list. Almost right at the top. Only a few rungs below the recurring dream I sometimes had about someone dying and making me queen. Luckily, we no longer had monarchies, because it pissed the gods off too much to see us worshipping anyone other than them. So yeah, it was an irrational fear ... but I still couldn't seem to shake it.

"What is the dweller doing?" Siret stood next to his brother, both of them staring at me. "Has she lost her tiny mind? That was fast."

Aros joined them on the other side and the slightest of smiles was visible at the corners of his full lips. "Pretty sure she's trying to get a bug off her, I've seen this before in Blesswood."

"Help me!" I shouted. *What was wrong with them*? Were they hoping I'd die from sneak-sleeper-attack?

Coen grabbed me then, huge hands wrapping around my biceps as he held me in place. I struggled for a click, before realising that it was fruitless. I was never escaping his grip.

"There is no bug on you," he said slowly, like he was speaking to an idiot.

"Well ..." I spluttered out. "Why were you staring at me like that? You went all dark and gloomy and I thought it was a sleeper."

The corner of his mouth twitched, which felt like amusement, although the corner of his eye did the same, and that was more like anger. Before I could try to salvage the relationship I thought I'd been building with these sols, Coen freed my right bicep and traced a thumb over my lip. "You have blood on your face," he said. "Were you hurt in the crossing?"

I stared at him as his thumb shifted, rubbing back and forth along the slope of my bottom lip. If there really was blood on my face, he was only spreading it around—which was hardly surprising, because he wasn't watching what he was doing. He was staring right into my eyes, an intensely focussed look in his.

Before I could answer, Aros was in my face. "How could she get hurt? We were assured it was the same for dwellers and us to cross. And we were touching her!"

I found myself reaching out to comfort him, before deciding at the last moment that it was a bad idea. "I bit my lip, that's all. I'm fine."

I heard a snort from someone behind. Fair point. *Fine* might have been an exaggeration, but I wasn't hurt from the crossing to Minatsol. I should have been more specific.

Yael, who'd been silent and distant, didn't hang around any longer. He turned and started pushing his way through the thicker growth to the east. The rest of the Abcurses gave me one more look over, before following their brother. Siret nudged me, indicating I should go in front of him. Pretty sure I heard him mutter something about stopping me from breaking my neck, but I could have been wrong.

As soon as I stumbled free of the alcove of trees and bushes we'd been in, I realised that nothing in the hilly area we were in was familiar. Siret nudged me again; his brothers were already quite a few feet in front of us, so I picked up the pace.

"Where are we?" I asked, leaves and debris kicking up under my feet as I jogged to keep up with their pace. "This isn't where we entered Topia from."

He didn't answer at first, and I wondered if he was just going to completely ignore me. *Seriously?* I was here because of their need to procure an item which probably did not originally belong to them, no matter what their story had been. Why would the gods care about anything a sol had? Instinct told me it had been stolen from the gods by the Abcurses in the first place, and the gods had wanted it back. I was the only sucker they could rope into helping them and now I was going to face a certain, painful death-by-angry-deity.

"The banishment cave is across the other side of Minatsol." Siret's voice was lazily drawled, like he could barely be bothered to answer. "We have a couple of sun-cycles walk to get home."

"*What*?" I screeched, grinding to a halt. "But I was in Topia for like one rotation. I was with the Gods for like half a rotation. How could you five get to the cave in half a rotation if it's going to take us *a couple of sun-cycles* to walk back?"

Siret nudged me again, clearly not liking my refusal to walk. "Those sun-cycles are going to turn into moon-cycles if you don't start walking, dweller. Don't make me carry you again, it'll be far less pleasant this time."

A red haze kind of washed over my eyes. I was so furious that when I opened my mouth, it actually surprised me that steam didn't emerge. "You dragged me into this, how the hell am I going to explain being away from Blesswood for this long?"

Siret must have realised that I wasn't going to move; he leaned down closer and spoke in fast, clipped tones. "To reach the banishment cave within Topia is fast, which is why we were able to get there so quickly. We are in Minatsol now, so there's no quick way back to the academy. We could have gone through Topia, but the risk was too great with you having stolen something from the gods. They tend to take those things seriously; they would have been searching for you very quickly. Add on the fact that you stabbed one of them, and, well … It's much safer on this side."

Okay, that all made sense. With a sigh, I turned and started walking again.

"Oh, and, Rocks?" Siret added. I swivelled my head around to see him. "We'll make sure no one at Blesswood punishes you for your absence. We have more than a little pull there, which is something you should remember."

Whatever. Arrogant sol.

Emmy was going to be out of her freaking mind with worry. She was probably going to start asking a whole bunch of questions, until every damned living *thing* in the academy had been notified of my absence. There was no way that Yael was going to be able to *persuade* every single one of them to forget. That would require more power than it was really possible for a sol to possess. That would require the power of a god. I knew that there was nothing I could do right then to change the situation, but that didn't stop me from losing my mind with worry. *Damn those sols!*

We walked for the better part of the sun-cycle, picking our way through forests and winding trails that dipped through the mountains. My feet started aching far too soon to complain aloud about it without embarrassing myself, and slowly, the ache began to travel up my legs. Coen was leading us, with Rome two steps behind him, me stuck in the middle, and the triplets bringing up the rear of our procession as they talked quietly amongst themselves.

"So ... your mother ..." I tossed the words over my shoulder, trying to speak through the ache in my ribs. "Is she still alive?"

"Is it normal for dwellers to ask each other that?" Siret shot back, sounding amused.

"Sorry." I didn't sound sorry at all, but that was because of the wheezing. "I just meant ... there's three of you ... and two of them." I paused, notching my hands on my knees and bending over to catch my breath. "And those two are like the size of monsters. How'd she live through all of that? Does she have some kind of fertility gift or something? Do you have another bunch of brothers tucked away? More Abcurses? A few unlucky sisters?"

"Beauty. Her gift is beauty," Aros answered, ignoring my other questions.

"Oh. Cool." *Made total sense.* Those boys had magical genetics. "But that doesn't really explain the whole twin-triplet thing."

"The whole twin-triplet thing?" Yael gave me a look that seemed to be part inquisition, part annoyance.

"Well it's not really normal or common," I hedged, starting to walk again as he loomed closer. "I mean ... to have a set of twins *and* a set of triplets. That's pretty rare."

I could feel him behind me. Hovering. I'd obviously hit a touchy subject. Apparently, the twin-triplet thing wasn't something they wanted to talk about. I stubbornly focussed my eyes on the ground ahead of me, pumping my little dweller legs as fast as they would go without actually breaking into a run. Because that would be obvious. It was much less obvious to power-walk as fast as possible, even if it made me certain that my legs were about to snap in half from over-exertion.

"We aren't normal *or* common," Yael finally muttered, his hands gripping my hips and lifting me from the ground midway through a power-stride.

He pulled me up and then tossed me behind him. I thought I was going to land on my ass and probably break a few things, but I only landed against a hard chest, arms easily plucking me from the air. Aros. I could actually smell him; that faint combination of something addictive and sweet, and a hint of burning. I realised after a moment that it was the smell of smoking sugar-plants. A very familiar smell to me, since the sugar-plants had been one of our main export goods back at home. I blinked up at him, but he wasn't even looking at me. He was just striding on, as though I hadn't been tossed at him, and he hadn't caught me. As though girls flying through the air at him happened every single sun-cycle.

It probably did.

"So how often do you guys sneak into Topia?" I directed the question to Aros, since he was now much closer to me than the others.

His golden eyes flicked down to me, switching between my eyes before moving over the rest of my face. "Every now and then. How often do you fall on your ass?"

"Every now and then."

He shook his head, shifting me closer. One of his arms was hooked beneath my knees, the other banded across my back. He was cradling me like a baby. "You should be more careful."

"Says the guy who sneaks into Topia."

"You concerned about us, Rocks?" Siret turned his head, his eyebrows lifting, his teeth flashing.

"No." I crossed my arms.

It was hard to look impassive and intimidating while being cradled like a baby, so I settled on pouting. Aros smirked, taking in my expression before lifting me up. The world around me dropped away as the gold in his eyes became more prominent, almost shifting with energy as his face loomed above mine. Very suddenly, and completely without warning, his lips were pressing against the very corner of my mouth. I was simply too shocked to react. The kiss was barely even a kiss, but my body didn't seem to know that. The simple brush of his lips had sent spiralling heat all the way through me, locking down the air that should have been flooding in and out of my lungs. He pulled his head up, the smirk back in place, and continued walking.

Meanwhile, I was pretty sure that he had just

reached into my chest and pulled out my poor little dweller heart. Now it was laying somewhere behind us. In the dirt. Beating pathetically.

"Seduction is using his *talent* to change his rank!" Siret shouted, his voice carrying with enough force to make me flinch.

Up ahead, I could see Coen and Rome stopping, the setting sun turning them into huge silhouettes as they spun around, threads of yellow and gold weaving over their bodies and highlighting the fact that I really shouldn't be encouraging them to compete over an imaginary ranking, because they were *far* too powerful-looking to mess with, just for the fun of it.

"That's cheating!" Coen shouted back.

"You cheat, you die!" Rome added, in an equally booming voice. Why the hell was he playing into this when he already seemed to know that it wasn't a *real* ranking?

I told myself to come clean; to open up that mouth of mine that was always getting me into trouble and tell them all what Yael and Rome were obviously keeping to themselves. Or maybe they weren't keeping it to themselves. Maybe they had completely disregarded the fact that the ranking had nothing to do with them and everything to do with their dorm numbers, because they didn't care. Because it *was* a competition. Because they were making it a competition. Because they clearly wanted one of their brothers to murder me.

I had to come clean. *As soon as possible.*

We had reached the others by now, and they all seemed to be staring at Aros, waiting for an explanation. It was annoying me, because they couldn't just turn it into a competition without me agreeing. The whole thing was my idea. They couldn't just steal it. Plus, Aros was still cradling me like a baby, and for some reason, it was making my temper bubble. I wanted to be standing on my own feet, preferably towering over all of them.

"My ranks, my rules," I blurted.

"So we *can* use our—" Rome began, but I held my hand up, palm facing outward, hoping that it would cut him off. *Hell no*, Crusher couldn't use his 'talent' on me.

He stared at my extended hand for a moment. He seemed confused. It was possible that nobody had ever tried to cut him off before.

"No, you can't!" I twisted out of Aros's arms, landing on my hands and knees in the grass, pain shimmering up my body. I quickly pulled to my feet, brushing off my knees. "Nobody is allowed to use their talent on me to change their rank. Because that would be cheating. And like I said: my ranks, my rules." I realised that I was doing the exact *opposite* of what I was supposed to be doing, but it seemed like a pretty promising way to prevent the Abcurses from using their talents on me, period.

"We might as well stop here for the night," Coen

muttered, breaking up the stare-off that I had going on with his brothers. "The dweller is getting cranky. She needs to be fed and watered and rested, or whatever dwellers need."

"You're getting us confused with bullsen." I shook my head, insulted at the comparison.

"You don't need to be fed?" he prompted, his expression blank.

"Food would be nice."

"And you don't need to be watered?"

"As in watered-down, like showered? Or *given* water?"

His blank mask cracked, just barely, but it was enough for me to glimpse the surprise beneath. He didn't answer me, trading a look with Rome. The others were similarly silent, their faces quickly morphing into the same, locked-down expression.

"You need help showering?" Siret finally asked, evidently the first of them to cave and ask the question that had held them all up. "Dwellers don't shower on their own?"

"What? No. *What*? I meant—"

"We're getting nowhere with this." Rome cut across me, raising his hand in my face. So, they were competitive *and* vengeful. I should never have taught him that trick. "The dweller needs to tend to herself. They need regular breaks and sustenance, just like the bullsen."

"You guys don't need regular breaks and

sustenance?" I asked, folding my arms, and attempting to look down my nose at them.

I knew all too well how much tending they needed. I knew, because I watched people fetch them food, and I collected their laundry.

"We don't need *regular* anything," Rome returned, a laugh in his voice.

"Exactly," Yael added, his smile matching his brother's. "Our breaks are never normal, and our food is never normal. That's how we stand apart from the bullsen and the dwellers. Everything about us is extraordinary."

"Especially your egos," I sneered.

"I said 'everything', didn't I?"

NINE

I shook my head, storming right past Yael, hitting him hard in the shoulder as I went. It hurt the way you'd expect bashing your shoulder into a boulder to hurt, but I didn't just have plenty of experience in feeling pain ... I also had a decent amount of experience in stalking away from people angrily. I was in familiar and comfortable territory—or at least I *had been*, until the sky started to darken, drawing tight and heavy, the clouds swelling as night-time accelerated across the horizon. I stopped walking, my head drawn back, panic building somewhere at the base of my spine.

"What the actual f—" the words were barely even out of my mouth before the Abcurses were suddenly all around me.

They were standing in a circle, their backs to me,

and they were completely ignoring the doomsday sky, peering around us at the land instead.

"Which god did you stab, dweller?" Rome growled, his eyes roving over the slope of a nearby hill. He was turned just enough for me to see half of his face.

"I didn't catch his name," I replied automatically.

I found myself drawing closer to Rome, even though he appeared to be pissed at me. I couldn't help it. His was the broadest back. My shoulder bumped against his spine and his arm suddenly twisted around, pulling me fully into him. I pressed my forehead to his shirt, keeping my hands tucked beneath my chin and my eyes closed.

"Please don't let me die right now," I started whispering, as the world darkened further, the ground starting to rumble beneath our feet. "I'm not ready to die, yet. I still don't know how to cook, and I'd like to punch someone in the face *not* by accident. Just once."

"Shh," Aros interrupted. He was standing beside Rome, evidently close enough to hear my panicked prayers. "You stabbed one of them. They aren't going to do what you say just because you ask nicely."

"They're not here for her," Yael spoke up, his words dark. "Trickery? You would know better than us ... is it D.O.D.?"

"No. It's not a trick." Siret seemed to be speaking through clenched teeth. "He has no idea we stole the cup."

"Show yourself!" Coen suddenly shouted, his voice

carrying all the way to the cluster of trees we had left behind, almost seeming to shake their leaves.

From the darkness caused by the stormy sky and the shelter of the short forest, a man suddenly materialised, walking toward us. He was cloaked in a blood-red robe which swept over the ground, collecting sticks and dust as he swooped in toward us.

"Rau." A collective growl announced the name from five different directions. I could even feel the name as it vibrated the entire way through Rome's body.

"What's with the nightmare illusion, Rau? What do you want?" Yael demanded, stepping away from the circle.

I craned my head away from Rome, trying to see the man better. It was difficult, because as soon as Yael moved, so did the others. They tightened the circle around me, Aros and Coen spinning around to face the man called Rau, though Coen still had one eye on the rolling hills behind us.

"It's not an illusion," Rau answered, his voice oddly high-pitched for his imposing stature. It made him sound more than a little unhinged, as though he would break out into a maniacal laugh at any moment. "It's just a bit of fun. Who are you hiding back there?"

"Coen's current plaything. He seems to like this one so we're trying not to scare her off."

"I thought fear was a big part of Coen's playtime." This time, Rau *did* laugh manically.

I shivered, huddling back into Rome. I was pretty sure that Rau was a god, since he was wearing one of those flowing, coloured robes, and he would have been considered massive, standing next to a normal sol. He just looked average standing next to Yael. Either way, I didn't want to look anymore. I didn't even care that they were making me sound like a dim-witted, dweller toy. I just wanted the sky to go back to normal and for Rau to stop talking because his voice was creepy as hell.

"Let's get to the point where you tell us why you're here," Rome said, probably well aware of the way I was trembling against his back.

"I think you all know why I'm here," Rau shot back, his laugh fading away. "There hasn't been another Chaos god in hundreds of life-cycles. Whenever one gets close, Staviti finds a way to kill them. I need someone to help me. Someone who has access to Blesswood. Someone to find the Chaos student and protect them until they finally reach the threshold of power. After that, they are free to die. Staviti can kill them all he likes. It won't stop them from joining me."

"*Tiny* problem with this plan," Yael replied, a smirk in his voice. "We don't really *want* another Chaos. I mean, no offence, Rau, but it's pretty fucking exhausting."

The god's already dark features hit black-out level then. I counted my loud heartbeat as I waited for whatever horrible thing was about to come from his fury.

One ... two ... three ... four ...

His next words burst out in a swarm of whispers, trickling through the air and somehow filling the wide spaces around us. "I'm sure you all know that I don't take kindly to my *suggestions* being denied. You five have ignored our rules for far too long. Don't forget that you stand here among the dirt-dwellers, growing weaker by the sun-cycle. You wouldn't want one of the gods to take advantage of that now, would you? I can make sure that you have no more trouble here, all you have to do is find my Beta."

Rome's arm tightened minutely around me. I wouldn't have noticed if I wasn't completely aware of every single part of my body pressed against his. Of course, that was far less worrying than the fact that his *arm had tightened!* Was he worried? Shit, of course he was worried. This was a god, even if there were five Abcurses, it wouldn't matter. One god could annihilate them in an instant.

No! That was not okay, I ... what the hell was I going to do?

In my panic, I had missed some of the boys' reply to the veiled threat from Rau. I caught the tail-end of Siret saying, "... would be a mistake to try us. We take orders from no one, not even you."

Rau grinned then, and somehow that was even more sinister than the previous dark scowl. "We'll see, boy, we'll see. Stay safe out here tonight, looks like a storm is coming."

With that not-at-all-creepy parting line, he turned, and in a flash of red robes, he was striding back into the trees. I felt it, the moment he left Minatsol. The air around us thinned-out somewhat, even though the storm above seemed to be growing in ferocity. Which said nothing for the five sols still surrounding me. Their bodies seemed to swell as their muscles tensed. I struggled against Rome, needing to get down so I could see them all better. So that I could ask them what the hell had just happened.

The strength-gifted sol released me, keeping one hand on me as I stumbled. Somehow, he knew that I was going to stumble. Okay, let's be real here ... everyone knew that I was going to stumble, I just wasn't used to anyone knowing this fact and preparing for it. *Don't get used to it,* I forcefully told myself. The Abcurses weren't going to be there to pick me up forever, I had to remember that. I had to step back from all the confusing emotions they instilled in me. Sometimes, they almost treated me like an equal; like when they saved me from being sentenced to death-by-sacrifice, just because of a stupid competition. Or just before, when they had formed a circle around me to protect me, as though I was someone worthy of protection. A dweller that actually meant something to them. A dweller that meant something ... period. And then there were the other times. The times when they treated me like dirt beneath their feet. The way they were supposed to treat me.

I needed to make sure I never forgot my place—dwellers who did that ended up with a fate worse than death. They became Jeffrey. Or something. I didn't really know. I was just assuming that becoming a Jeffrey was the worst thing that could happen to our kind.

Time to remind them all I was an emotional dweller.

"Which one of you sols is going to tell me what the freaking hell just happened right then?" Going on the attack felt natural. "How in the hell did a god just walk out of Topia and talk to us? What the hell is this weather—storm—thingy? What the hell are you five hiding that means you can walk into Topia ... and you know about the god's colours ... and what the HELL?"

I might have been yelling toward the end there, which might have caused lots of huffing and puffing when I finished. Damn, I needed to get into shape. Clearly making beds was not enough to build stamina.

As I heaved, five sets of eyes observed me, each sparkling unnaturally in the darkness around us. Was it possible that these sols were extra-special? Sure, they had told me that they were, but I figured that it was just their arrogance speaking. I hadn't really taken them that seriously.

Maybe I wasn't paying close enough attention.

And why wasn't anyone answering me?

I was about to go crazy-dweller on them again when the sky opened above us and Rau followed through on his storm promise. I was scooped up by someone, and then we were running. It was only the hint of gold and the summery scent of burning sugar wrapping around me that told me it was Aros. He tucked me close to his body so that no trees smashed into my limbs, and then they were full-on sprinting.

"We need to get to higher ground!" Siret shouted. He looked to be out the front, leading the way. "I know a spot!"

Higher ground? It never rained enough in Minatsol to worry about water rising above the ground. I was starting to think that I knew nothing about this world, or the gods. I probably should have paid better attention in class; Emmy surely knew all of this.

It was almost pitch black around us now, and since we were running at a full sprint, through a tightly knit forest, it was pretty scary. I could barely even focus on the trees flashing past us, and the knowledge that I was probably going to be smashed against one soon was enough to have my face pressing into Aros's chest. A girl could get used to being pressed against an Abcurse chest whenever the world decided to go insane. One benefit to all the shitty drama they brought into my life. I sensed they were talking above my head, but by this stage, I was too tired and cold to even listen. I had been walking for almost a full sun-cycle, which was something I was sure I had never done before, and now my body was punishing me for it. My ears refused to work, so I let my mind drift off.

I must have dozed off fully, because *obviously* a crazy storm and being lost in Minatsol was the perfect situation to get comfortable enough in to have a little nap. I was going to blame the exaggerated forty million miles we'd walked that sun-cycle. It had nothing to do with Aros and the comfort of his strong arms.

As I opened my eyes, I realised that it was still dark and cold outside, but the cave we were in was awash with warmth from a huge fire right in the centre of the round area. A rock wall was on my right side, warmth pressing along my left. Shifting my head, I saw the silky strands of golden-black hair: Siret. From what I could see over his huge body, next to him were his brothers—well the other two parts to the trio anyway. It didn't look as if Coen and Rome were in the cave with us. Hopefully they hadn't been abducted by angry gods, or smashed against a tree.

As I shifted slightly, I realised that I needed a bathroom break. *Immediately*. My bladder was at the bursting point. I wiggled around to get my hands on the rough ground—my head was pillowed on a shirt, which thankfully was not mine. I still wore Aros' shirt, and it was now dry and toasty warm. Realising there was not enough space on either side of me to get up without using Siret for leverage, I attempted to use my stomach muscles to pull myself up. Of course, I didn't really have any stomach muscles, so all I managed to do was flap around like an idiot.

A heavy arm draped across me and I almost peed myself. *Come on, gods. This is so not funny.* A flash of light from outside drew my attention and before I could say anything, the three sols around me were up on their feet and standing in front of me. I understood why the moment the red robes came into view.

Rau stood there, no expression on his face, just the tiniest of fires burning in his eyes. "I will have my Beta," was all he said, and as Aros, Yael, and Siret started for him, he shot out a blast of energy that materialised in front of him as a sphere of loosely-held smoke. It rose above us all, circling around the top of the cave, lit from within the sphere by some kind of milky, glowing light. My eyes took a while to adjust to the glare, and even though I was terrified, I stumbled forward in the hope that I could help the Abcurses if they were in trouble. This glow couldn't kill them, right? What was it even doing? Their huge shadows were all I had to aim for, so I headed toward the one shaped like Siret, since he was the closest.

The intensity of the glow shot up again, and I was worried that my current blindness was moments from becoming permanent. I continued pushing my way forward, hoping that I wasn't about to stumble into the fire.

There was a roar in the direction of the doorway, and this one I recognised as Rome. The giant sol was not happy, and I would not like to be in his way when he lost it. I kind of hoped that Rau got crushed. Deciding I needed to get to Siret sooner, I started to sprint, which of course had my feet tripping up against some of the spare firewood, propelling my body forward and sending me flying into the darkness. Because of the momentum I had built up sprinting to get to Siret, I managed to launch impressively high into the air, my body sailing across the cave, the glare of light becoming so intense that even with my eyes squeezed tightly closed, I was still blinded. My mind reacted by trying to repel the force, shutting down all of my senses. I had only half a click to see Siret's horrified face. He was reaching for me, but it was too late.

A surge of something hot pierced my heart, branding me painfully as my breath was cut off. I tried to choke back some air as I began losing height, plummeting toward the ground, but there was no air to be had. I prepared myself for impact; I should have hit the ground long ago, but for some reason my fall continued on.

Why couldn't I breathe? And why did my chest feel like something had sliced it in two, and now a hot branding iron was slowly burning a path through my heart? Had I been hit with a god-bolt or something? Was there such a thing as a god-bolt?

"*Willa!*"

Someone was shouting my name, but it scarcely

registered as I continued to slowly die, or whatever was happening to me. When my body finally hit the ground, I was barely conscious enough to even feel the impact. It didn't even feel that rocky, and it smelled good. Like summer sun-cycles.

Aros ...

Well, at least if I was going to die, I was going to do it in the arms of a golden sol. With that thought, my heart stuttered one last time and then everything went dark.

♡♡♡♡♡

Shouting was the first thing my subconscious registered. "How did Rau even make it past you two?" Yael was angrier than I had ever heard before, his voice thundering around the room.

I was afraid to open my eyes and bring attention to myself. *What happened?* Had I fallen asleep again? Why did my chest ache and *crap* ... Rau had been there! And a weird, glowing smoke-ball. The Abcurses had been about to fight him, and I had ... tripped? Fallen? Did I *fly?*

My eyes snapped open and I was up on my feet in an instant. Everything spun around me but that didn't stop me from scanning my surroundings, my heart rate only settling when I realised there were five sols standing in a wall of muscle across the front of the cave. Rau had not hurt any of them. *Safe.* My Abcurses were safe. I mean—someone else's Abcurses. Their mother's Abcurses.

They all had their backs to me, forming a line of defence between me and the outside world. Aros, Yael, and Coen were shirtless now, and I realised I had been laid across the soft surface of their clothing. Looking down at myself, I blinked a few times as I tried to remember what had happened after I had tripped over the firewood.

My hand dropped to rest against my chest, right above my heart. The pain had been excruciating, I wasn't surprised that my mind had blocked it out. Right then, as the memories crashed back into me, my stomach heaved and I leaned over to dispel whatever small amounts of food had been left in my body. Thankfully it had been awhile between meals, so there wasn't much for me to lose.

I felt the five Abcurses as they moved toward me ... *what the crap?* I literally could feel them. In my chest, their energy moved closer and I had no idea how that was possible. As soon as they were around me, the pain stopped. One moment I was suffering, and the next, I was standing confusedly, feeling completely normal.

"Rocks?" Siret's hand was on the back of my neck, turning me around to face him. "You okay?"

He was holding out one of the shirts from the ground and a hollowed-out rock filled with water. I didn't ask about the rock. It held the perfect imprint of a pair of knuckles. So I wasn't getting into a fight with Rome anytime soon.

"Thanks," I muttered, taking the rock and the shirt.

I wasn't sure what the shirt was for, but I made good use of the water to wash out my mouth, before walking past them to the entrance of the cave. I needed fresh air. I needed to see that the world was still whole and beautiful, and not burning to the ground in a fit of godly rage. I took a few steps and then stopped as a small thrum of pain fissured through my chest. I frowned, dropping the shirt and curling all of my fingers around the rock, as though I needed something to brace myself with. I took another step, and it happened again. I sucked in a deep breath and shook my head, hurrying to the mouth of the cave. The pain grew worse, and then it suddenly disappeared. Aros was at my side.

"Do you feel any different?" he asked me, his stunning features dark with emotion.

Maybe he was concerned, or suspicious. Maybe he was trying to determine whether Rau's ball of smoke and light had altered me in a dangerous way. The question was ... if it *had*, what were they going to do about it? Would they put me down, like a rogue bullsen?

"I'm sore," I admitted, shaking my head and turning away from him.

I should have known that blocking him out wasn't a thing that would happen. He simply plucked me from my feet, pulling me against his body, and turned his face back to the inside of the cave.

"Let's go," he announced. "We should get her back to Blesswood and have someone look at her."

"We can't involve anyone else in this," Coen returned, appearing in my line of sight and taking the lead. "No one can know about Rau and ... and what happened."

Aros fell into step behind him. "I wasn't talking about that. She might have bruised ribs or something. She might get sick. We have no idea what he hit her with."

Coen didn't reply, but I wasn't even listening anymore. I was facing Aros, my chin tucked against his shoulder, my hands looped behind his neck. The knuckle-imprinted rock was banging lightly between his shoulder blades with every step. I didn't want to let it go for some reason. He was holding me with one arm, his hand settling into my waist as he stuck me against his front, a little off to the side so that he could walk easily. My legs were just kind of dangling. I considered wrapping them around his waist, just to be a little more comfortable, but decided against it. I was too numb to do anything. Too numb to ask questions. Not that it stopped them from springing up inside my head.

What the hell was that ball of light and smoke?
I ran into it, didn't I?
It hit me in the chest, didn't it?

Am I going to die now?

"No, you're not going to die," Yael growled.

My eyes flew open, connecting with his. He was walking behind Aros, his expression as dark as everyone else's seemed to be.

Shit, was I asking those questions out loud?

"Yeah," Siret answered.

I frowned, moving to clap a hand over my mouth. Only problem was, the knuckle-imprinted stone was still in my hand. Yael jumped forward, plucking the stone out of my hand when it was less than an inch away from smashing into my nose.

"Try not to make it *worse*," he begged.

"That's mine." I pointed to the stone.

He looked down at the stone, his eyebrows arching. "Sure, Rocks. I won't steal your rock. I'll just keep it safe until it no longer presents a danger to your face."

I nodded, once, satisfied. Aros's chest rumbled a little, a laugh barely audible as we walked. I rested my chin against his shoulder again, snuggling closer. Blame the exhaustion. His free hand landed on the back of my thigh, holding me a little more securely. I fought the urge to wrap my legs around him yet again, but then decided that there wasn't much point in fighting it. I was already growing attached to these sols. Maybe it was because I secretly wanted to be one of them. I wanted to be badass and superior too. I wanted to take on the gods and have a super-power. I wanted them to give me a nickname based on my super-power, instead of based on the fact that I was always falling over.

Or ...

Or maybe it was all the near-death experiences. I supposed that could form an attachment of sorts. Whatever it was, I was giving up fighting it. They could kick me out of the group if they wanted to. They could push me onto my ass and leave me behind. But maybe they wouldn't. Maybe they would keep me and teach me how to be badass while saving me from getting killed by all the other sols out there who definitely wouldn't appreciate my newfound badass persona.

I locked my arms tighter around Aros's neck, pulling my legs up around his waist. The hand on my thigh helped automatically, slipping further down, near my ass, to hold me up. He stopped walking, his chest rumbling again. This time, it wasn't a laugh. It was a growl.

I was wrenched away from him suddenly, passed into another set of arms. I wasn't even sure if I had been stolen, or if Aros had handed me off.

"Not a good idea, Rocks, pushing a guy with a seduction gift." Coen's voice shot through me, pooling heat into places that heat had no right pooling into. *Okay, what the hell was going on?*

"He's a big boy," I grumbled. "He can handle it."

That was probably the truth, but it wasn't *really* the issue in that moment. The issue was ... could *I* handle it?

TEN

I was trying to ignore a very big problem. It took us another sun-cycle to get back to Blesswood, and in that time, there was always one of the Abcurse brothers by my side. Usually it was because they were carrying me, since it was faster to travel that way and they wouldn't need to stop for too many breaks. I had ventured off on my own for a few clicks, though. We had stopped for a few rotations to rest, and I had been busting for the bathroom again. Since all hell had broken loose the last time I had been busting for the bathroom, I was understandably wary as I made my way through the trees, trying to find a private spot. The problem was, the further I travelled, the more my chest began to throb. Very soon, it was too painful for me to go any further. The pain wasn't as bad as it had been the previous sun-cycle, but as soon as I finished my business and made my way back to the others, it lessened.

When I touched one of them, resting my arm against Siret's as I curled back onto the ground, it disappeared completely. I stored the information away, turning it over and over in my mind.

I didn't want to tell them on the off-chance that they used it against me, but the need to say something was becoming increasingly more and more urgent as we fought through the trees back into Blesswood. It went completely against my nature not to push out of Coen's arms and stalk away from them. I wanted to find Emmy and get my lecture out of the way before delivering myself to the healer, *if* dwellers were even allowed to see the Blesswood healers. But I couldn't, because I knew, on some level, that the pain of being away from them would cripple me.

Which *definitely was not normal*. That went beyond the bond formed between people who saved each other's lives. That had everything to do with Rau and his creepy smoke-ball of light. Still, Coen apparently knew me well enough to know that the *normal* me would soon demand to be set on her feet, and so he let me down. I ignored the small pinch in my chest and started to stride ahead of them. It didn't last long, because my dweller legs were super short. They had overtaken me in about three clicks and then I was jogging to keep up with them.

We passed into the back building of Blesswood, the

Abcurses barging past other sols as though they owned the whole property, and me hurrying to dodge the stunned people who turned to watch them go. I didn't know where they were going, so it surprised me when they burst right into the dining hall. It was completely empty, but the kitchens were bustling with activity, so it must have been close to dinner time. They sat around their table and I hovered behind, absolutely *despising* this new dynamic where I was just forced to follow them around like a lost little cub.

Siret noticed me still standing there and moved over a seat, holding out the chair between him and Aros. I shook my head. He reached over to me, gripping my forearm and dragging me into the chair. I landed heavily, a sighing grumble sounding in the back of my throat. I needed to convince one of them to take me to a healer. Something needed to be done about this forced co-dependency.

"You going to enrol me in classes, too?" I asked Siret, my tone dry and slightly annoyed.

He smirked, turning on me. "What? You don't want to be one of us, dirt-dweller?"

I scowled, narrowing my eyes at him. "No." *Yes.*

He shook his head at me. "Make up your mind."

"I said no."

"You also said yes."

"No, I didn't!"

Aros leaned over, his breath against my cheek. "You did," he confirmed. "But it's okay. You're one of us now.

We said we'd protect you if you stole us the cup, and now we will. You becoming an Abcurse is the only way that's going to happen."

"What?" I turned on him, and then on the others. None of them looked shocked. Maybe they had discussed it while I slept. "Are you going to *adopt me*?" I screeched.

Coen leapt out of his chair, looking disgusted. A few mouths dropped open.

"What?" choked Siret.

"Am I supposed to be your sister?" I was still speaking in that voice that was part-screech. "Are your parents going to adopt me? Are you going to *marry me*? Isn't that illegal? No, wait, it's just procreation between sols and dwellers that's illegal. I remember now, Emmy told me." I was clearly rambling at this point, but I couldn't stop myself. "So I guess ... technically, marriage is legal ... but I don't want to get married! I'm too young to get married! I still need to learn how to cook! And ... and I—"

"Calm down." Yael's voice washed over me, stealing the bubble of words from my mouth. "Sit down."

I looked down at my chair. I hadn't even realised that I'd jumped out of it. Had it been when Coen jumped out of his? Maybe I had reflexively copied him. Which was weird. I sank back down.

"Take a deep breath, Willa," Yael continued, the smallest of smiles spreading across his face. "There's no way in hell that you're going to be related to us." He paused, meeting Coen's stare. Coen had arched a brow at him. He turned back to me, his expression darkening. "Because you're a dweller," he needlessly added. "But you *are* going to stick with us from now on, and we *will* protect you. We will send the message to this academy that anyone messing with you is messing with us."

I nodded, my eyes falling to the table. That could work. It would also help with the pain I felt whenever they weren't near me, but what would happen when classes ended for the sun-cycle and everyone went back to their dorms? I would still need to be near them. The realisation hit me with a heavy, sickening clarity.

Shit. *Shit! I can't sleep alone!*

"Why not?" Siret blinked at me, forcing me to reel in my thoughts.

"What?" Either I had lost my damned mind, or I kept accidently saying my thoughts out loud.

"Why can't you sleep alone?"

Okay, maybe both. I had lost my mind *and* I kept speaking my thoughts out loud. But ... I knew I hadn't actually said that last part out loud. There was no way, unless ...

"I ... I'm scared," I lied, trying to deflect.

Rome was suddenly in my face and all air seemed to be sucked from the vicinity of my lungs.

"What aren't you telling us?" he demanded, his eyes narrowing. "There's *something*."

Damn. Damn. Triple damn. I couldn't hide things from them now. Apparently, I was not only required to be attached at the hip with the five of them, but they could also hear my thoughts. Some of my thoughts. I was pretty sure that was what was happening. But *how*?

Yael is a competitive bastard. I directed that thought as loudly as I could and, sure enough, darkness descended over his features. Before he could react, though, Siret spoke: "You didn't move your lips. We all heard you say that, but you ... you didn't fucking *speak*."

I swallowed, my breathing shallow as it rushed in and out of my mouth. "Apparently ... you five can read some of my thoughts now."

There might not have been many other sols in the room with us, but it seemed that right then silence reigned through the entire dining space. The Abcurses just stared at me, not moving or blinking until finally Aros's hand landed on my shoulder, demanding my attention. His golden eyes had turned a dark bronze colour.

"How is that even possible?" he asked. "Rau's power doesn't work like that. He can't have done this. Can you hear our thoughts?"

As if they'd just wondered the same thing, Yael, Siret, and Coen were on their feet in an instant, their fury now crowding the space.

Damn the stupid gods. I wished I could run away from all the crazy right now. How far would I get before the pain killed me? It was probably an experiment I would have to try very soon.

Since none of them were backing down, I decided to put them out of their misery. "I can't hear your thoughts. This seems to be a one-way thing. And it doesn't appear that you are hearing everything from me either, otherwise you'd all have clicked on ages ago that something weird was happening."

Coen smirked. "Doubtful, Rocks. Something tells me there isn't a lot going on up in that mind, and around you, something weird is *always* happening."

Screw you, asshole.

His mouth dropped slightly, and now it was time for a smirk to cross my face. Before he could form any kind of a reply, Rome shoved his twin.

"Get a grip," he demanded roughly. "You *are* acting like an asshole. We're wasting time and energy. We should be figuring out what happened to her. What did Rau hit her with?"

I slumped back into my chair, burying my head in my hands as I tried to sort through the mess of emotions and thoughts I had going on.

"Dweller!"

I knew I should react. That feminine voice held a harsh bark of command, but I was so tired that I could barely lift my face again. By the time I did, there were three of them. The dweller-relations committee.

Elowin stood with her usual grace and perfection; her willowy body was wrapped in a flowing white robe, her golden curls perfectly arranged around her angelic face. The only thing to mar her perfection was her slightly open mouth, wide eyes, and creased brow. She was angry and confused. Henchman Number One and Henchman Number Two closed in on either side, and I knew this was the point where shit was about to get real. I had been living for the past few sun-cycles in a bubble, not in the real world. I was *not* a sol. I was *not* equal to these people, and I was definitely overdue for some knocking down from my imaginary pedestal.

Elowin recovered her composure, closing the distance between us. Her hands were trembling minutely—somehow I could see that, along with the fine beading of sweat across her brow. Why was she nervous?

The two Abcurses who had still been sitting, stood now, and the five of them did their wall of protection thing. Elowin and the two men halted. Like ground to halt, and suddenly I understood the sweat on her brow. She was afraid of them.

Trying her best to hide her fear, she cleared her throat. "We received word of a dweller who was seated at a table in the dining area. The same dweller who was reported missing to us several sun-cycles ago. She needs to come with us now for questioning and reassignment."

Reassignment. Yeah, right! Just sign me up to be kicked-to-death-by-bullsen.

Yael was the first to speak, which was no surprise to me.

"Elowin, you should not concern yourself with this dweller. She has been assisting us for the past few sun-cycles, and she is going to continue to assist us for the foreseeable future."

"You assigned her to us," Rome stated from beside him.

"So she's ours now," Aros concluded, his golden eyes catching mine for a brief moment.

Ignoring the emotions that stirred inside my chest, I remained sitting, pretending to be an invisible, stupid dweller.

A torrent of words burst from Elowin then, as though she couldn't keep them inside. "We have rules for a reason. You change them for one dweller and the rest of them are going to start wondering why they aren't allowed to sit with the sols at dinner. Or go to class and learn with them. Our world works because everyone knows their place. The natural order. What would the gods think about this?"

The Abcurses took one look at each other, and then each of them lost their shit. Like doubled-over-almost-on-the-floor kind of laughing. I bit my lip to stop myself joining them, but it was probably the hardest thing that I had ever done.

Finally, Coen straightened. He rubbed a hand across his still broadly grinning face, and said, "Those gods don't give a single shit what you do here. As long as you keep the worship and the sols coming, they wouldn't care if you all decided to strip naked and have mass sol-dweller sex parties."

Elowin turned a shade of green which had all of the Abcurses leaning back from her, and then, with a huff, she spun on her heel and stormed out of the dining room, her henchmen trailing behind her.

Siret's eyes were sparkling when he turned back in my direction, their gem-like nature very prominent. "Never liked that committee, think we should make it our aim to bring it down."

His brothers laughed and chimed in with their suggestions, and for a moment it was as if all of them had forgotten that I was in their midst. Until suddenly they didn't.

Chairs scraped as the five of them sat around me, and I had to admit: being the centre of all their attention had me squirming in my seat. *So intense.* Just so freaking intense.

Aros must have mistaken my unease for upset. He leaned in closer to me. "Don't worry about the dweller-committee, Willa. We'll make sure they don't bother you. She knows that you're under our order now, and they rarely ever mess with us."

I had seen the dark look on Elowin's face as she stormed off—well, dark and queasy—she would not be letting this rest. She was going to wait until they let their guard down and then she was going to destroy me.

"Do you think it's safe for us to leave Rocks with the other dwellers?" Aros asked the others. "She's the clumsiest one I've ever seen, even by their usual low standards."

Yael didn't miss a beat. "She'll be fine, no one will hurt her in the dweller dungeons, it's only above ground where the sols are that we need to keep an eye on her."

Sitting right here, Assholes.

Five sets of eyes. Five identical smirks. In that moment, there was no mistaking that they were brothers, and that their mother was blessed with the gift of beauty.

"Double bonus that she can just project her thoughts and we can hear them," Siret said. "If anyone bothers you, just call for us, Rocks, okay?"

Yep, sure, no problem. I nodded, and worked very hard to conceal my next thoughts. I wasn't ready for them to know about the tiny problem of me not being able to be too far away from them. They would most likely regret taking me into their protection if they knew that I was going to be stuck to them like glue. Maybe I could sneak and hide in the supply closet near their rooms.

Dwellers appeared around us then, each holding a plate of food. Somehow, even though it wasn't quite dinner time yet, they were feeding us ... well, the Abcurses anyway. I saw more than one set of confused eyes and dropped jaws. No one quite knew what to make of me sitting right in the centre of a pile of sols.

"Stop." Rome's deep voice thundered around the room. "You didn't serve Willa, she'll have the same, and some fresh water."

Some of the confusion turned to anger, and I could see that more than one dweller wanted to question Rome, but they knew better. They knew their place, and they probably didn't want to get crushed. I was the only one stupid enough to end up in a situation like this, one which could tear apart the very fabric of the world we lived in. Elowin hadn't been wrong ... this could change everything. *Damn Rau.* Was this exactly what he was hoping for when he bound me to the boys? He was the god of chaos after all, and this was bound to get chaotic.

As we ate, I was trying my best to breathe and somehow still stuff as much of the delicious food into my mouth as I could. Top of my list for hating sols was that they got all the best food. Freshest produce, meat from fine cuts, even regular berries and sweet ice. I glared at Coen— who was on my right side—and hooked my arm around my small cup of pink ice as a barrier.

"What?" he asked, lifting one eyebrow with a sardonic stare. "Do you really think I'm going to steal your dessert?"

My eyes flicked between all of them briefly, and I tucked the small dish even closer to my chest. "I won't let you have it, this is my crushed ice. I will end anyone who touches it."

There was a gasp from behind me, and I spun with ice in hand to find Emmy standing there. Her normally golden features were pale and she looked tired and a touch thinner than the last time I had seen her.

"Willa ..." it was a whisper of my name, but it still drew the attention of the sols who were around us. Dinner time was starting now, so the room was slowly filling. "*Willa!*" she screeched this time, and now every single face was turned in our direction.

My best friend glanced around, her eyes darting frantically. She knew she shouldn't draw attention to us like this, but she couldn't seem to stop herself from reaching out and latching on to my arm. *Here we go again.* I was hauled out of the room by her super muscles, and as soon as we were outside and the doors closed again, she let me have it.

"I have been going out of my mind with worry. Two full sun-cycles, Will! *TWO!* You just vanished. I thought you were dead, that the Abcurses took off with you and dumped your body in the forest. How could you do this to me? I thought we were best friends. I thought we were *family.*"

I was trying to listen to her while also hoping an explanation would come to me. One which would make sense to her. I needed to comfort her because it was killing me to see her so distraught, but I could scarcely concentrate around the pain in my chest. It was okay, not at dying level yet, but it was making it hard to focus.

"Emmy," I finally started, cutting her off mid-rant. "I'm so sorry for disappearing on you, and trust me, it was not my decision. I would never have left without telling you first, if I'd had a choice. Something happened with the Abcurses ... well, we ended up a long way from the centre ring and had to walk back. It ..."

What else could I tell her? I had no idea who was listening, and there was no safe place to talk about the gods and what had happened in Topia.

She opened and closed her mouth, looking like she was gulping for air, but maybe she was trying to speak and couldn't get around her shock. I waited patiently, my hand now on my chest as I rubbed it in slow circles. It didn't ease the pain.

If anything, the pain was getting worse.

Crap. The Abcurses had finished their meal and were leaving the dining area. Which meant that they were probably going to their rooms. It looked like we were about to test out the distance I could handle.

My head spun as the sharp stabbing sensation in my chest increased. It was almost like my heart was being pulled through my ribs, shredding it in the process.

"Willa, are you even listening to me?" Emmy must have started talking again, but I missed what she said. Her eyes were narrowed on me now, the colour darkening. "Are you okay, Will? You don't look good."

I crouched forward and narrowly missed vomiting on her shoes. All of my delicious dinner was exiting my body and that was about the worst thing to have happened to me this week. Including being hit with a god-bolt.

"*Willa*! What can I do? We need to get you to a healer."

I shook my head, stumbling away from her, my hands raised, like I could keep her back. I didn't want her making a grab for me. She'd use her super-muscles to drag me off to the nearest healer, and unless it was in the direction of the Abcurses, there was a good chance that it would actually kill me.

"I ... I'm sorry, Emmy," I choked out through the pain, stumbling back into the dining room.

They were moving fast. I could feel them now, drawing further and further away. I spun on my feet, narrowly missing a passing dweller, and sprinted through the dining hall toward the back doors. People jumped out of my way, but the furniture wasn't so intuitive. I smacked hard into the side of a table, which sent me spinning in the opposite direction. I went over a chair, and then my face was slamming into the ground. Dark spots flashed over my eyes, the pain seizing up my body into small convulsions. I could hear Emmy screaming my name. She was getting closer.

I forced my head to clear, forced my body to stop shaking as I drew myself to my feet, and then I was struggling toward the door again. There was a cut on my leg, blood dripping down my calf. It reminded me that I wasn't wearing pants, only Rome's shirt, which admittedly looked like a dress, but still ...

"Will." It was only a statement. Not a question. An acknowledgement. I needed help, and my best friend was going to give it to me.

She linked her arm through mine and I leaned a good deal of my weight on her, raising a shaky finger to point toward the back door. She started to drag me that way, her head tucked down and her stride purposeful, as though she would be able to trick the surrounding sols and dwellers into thinking that there was nothing out-of-the-ordinary going on. It almost seemed to work, too. Some of them turned away from us, going back to their meals.

We cleared the dining room and I pointed again, showing Emmy the way to the Abcurses dorm rooms. It was much faster with her than it was to walk on my own. I gained strength with each step, which meant that we were moving in the right direction, if nothing else. When we were in the hall outside their rooms, I tugged on Emmy's arm, and we stopped moving. I drew her to one of the supply closets, able to walk on my own now, and gently pushed her inside. We sent two of the cleaning carts into the hallway to make room and then closed the door, sitting against it in the darkness.

"Will ..." she started again.

"I'm okay." I sighed, dragging my hands over my face. "I need a bath, and something to wash out my mouth, but I'm okay."

"You can tell me what's going on, or I can sing Leader Graham's stupid Settlement Anthem until your ears bleed. Your choice."

"Harsh." I cringed, but followed it with a laugh. It was almost nice to think about Leader Graham and all of his hair-brained plots to make the dwellers more like the sols. Life had been much simpler then. "I snuck into Topia, and then one of the gods, specifically the god of Chaos—Rau—hit me with this weird smoke ball of light, and I think it did something to me. Also, I stabbed someone, but it was an accident. And I met this cool slave named Jeffrey. You would have liked her. She was a stickler for rules. I'm pretty sure we become Jeffreys when we die. Just saying. I mean, it makes sense. They're only half of what we are. It's like the Creator plucked them on their way to death and then set them in Topia, where they would have to continue to serve. For eternity. So when Teacher Marcks told us that dwellers are destined to be slaves, and have no further purpose outside of their slavery, he really wasn't kidding. You know what happens when a Jeffrey does something bad? They get sent to a banishment cave. They're bound to it. They turn into these creepy, twisted, shadowy things, and they just ... amass. There must be thousands of them in there. Maybe more. Holy shit. I didn't have time to think about that until now—"

"You can stop rambling; I've processed the first thing you said. Mind telling me why you snuck into Topia?" Emmy's tone was dry, almost sarcastic, but there was a hint of hysteria to it.

"Well, technically, I didn't *want* to. The Abcurses made me. They wanted me to steal a cup."

"Who did the cup belong to?"

"Someone called D.O.D.?"

It was too dark to see Emmy's face, but she was frowning so hard now that I could almost *sense* it.

"There isn't a god by that name, Will."

"Yeah, that's what Jeffrey said too. Oh, wait ... Jeffrey said something about a Sacred Abil and the Trophy of Stavlini, or Stavriti, or Stav ... something."

"Staviti?" The hysteria in Emmy's voice was definitely becoming prominent now. "The Trophy of *Staviti? You stole the Trophy of Staviti?*"

I clapped a hand over her mouth, trying to muffle her shriek. "No!" I answered reflexively. "Or yes. Kind of. Maybe. Why?"

She gave a muffled answer, and I realised that I was still holding my hand over her mouth. I pulled away, allowing her to speak again.

"You don't know who Staviti is, Willa? Seriously? You couldn't pay attention in class even for *that* much?"

"I knew it sounded familiar," I grumbled, feeling defensive. "Is it the god of ... um ... food or something?"

Emmy groaned, her head making a *thudding* sound as she knocked it back against the door. "It's the Creator. The Original Creator. Staviti. And *Sacred Abil?* He's the god of Trickery. *Definitely not someone you want to be messing with.*"

"I didn't want to mess with any of them."

"And yet ... you stole from the Creator. Tricked the god of Trickery. Stabbed someone. Probably someone important. Probably the god of Vengeance."

"Do you think they know it was me?"

"Of course not. You're a dweller from the seventh ring of Minatsol." Emmy suddenly launched herself onto me, hugging me tightly. "I'm so relieved. You're alive. You're ... what was happening back there in the dining hall? And why the hell are we in a supply closet?" She drew back from the hug, a hand still on my arm. She shook me slightly, as though she'd be able to dislodge the answers from me by force.

"Rau's magic. It knocked me out, and then when I woke up, there was this pain ..." I touched my chest, rubbing my fingers over the muted thud of pain that was still present, even now, though it was no longer trying to rip me apart. "The further away from the Abcurses I go ... the more it hurts me. If I'm touching one of them, I don't feel it at all."

"You need to tell them," she hissed out, panic riding her tone. "Maybe they know—"

"They were there. They saw it happen. I don't want to tell them about this; it's enough that they can hear some of my thoughts, and that I have to follow them around during the daylight hours. I don't want them to find out that I need to be around them *for the entire sun-cycle*. I don't even want to be around them all the time. I'm sick of them. I never want to see them again. Except Aros; he smells nice. And Rome, because he's so strong I'm pretty sure not even Rau can get past him. I don't need the others. Except Siret. I'm pretty sure he hates me, but he's really good at catching me like just before I face-plant into something. But the *others*, I don't need them. Not at all." I paused, my brow furrowing, my mouth pursing, and then I quickly blurted, "Except Coen and Yael. Coen is really good at making decisions, and if I leave out Yael he'll probably hunt me the hell down and haunt me—"

"That's all of them," Emmy interrupted smoothly. She didn't sound panicked anymore. Now she sounded like she was trying not to laugh.

ELEVEN

After Emmy snuck some food into my closet, she disappeared to finish her chores. Chores which I had no chance of doing, unless one of the Abcurse brothers decided to help me out with them. Instead, I sat in the dark, picking at a plate of normal dweller rock-bread, my chest thumping painfully. When the world grew so quiet that I would have been able to hear a bird squawk from the forest, I knew that night had fallen.

I opened the door a crack, peering out. I looked one way, and then the other.

All clear, Soldier! The stress was reversing my mental development back to the games I used to play with Emmy when I was only seven life-cycles old. I'd had some kind of sick fascination with the Minateur patrols, and I'd pretended to be one of them for a full life-cycle, constantly arresting Emmy for walking too fast, or too slow, or too normally.

Slipping down the corridor was difficult. It felt as though I had left my internal organs back in the closet, but just before the pain became unbearable, I reached the bathing chambers for that floor of dorms. I ran inside and slammed the door behind me, locking it securely. The faint drip of condensation echoed all around me, and steam assaulted my face, driving me back against the door for a moment. My senses were on overload, screaming out against the pain of being so far from the Abcurses. I fought my way past it, pushing off the door and heading into the steam. The wooden boards beneath my feet were damp and warm, sending comforting heat right up to my belly, somewhat easing the way the rock bread was now turning around, threatening to come back up.

I had no idea what to expect from the bathing chamber, since the dweller chambers were in the dungeon, and the water ran cold. Up here, there seemed to be a series of rooms to walk through. A bathing *experience*. I entered the first room by passing beneath a wooden archway. There were several wooden cubes, all empty. I stared beyond the room, through the next wooden archway. All that was visible was a fine mist, a spray of water that rained softly down from the ceiling. I guessed that the cubes were for the sols' clothes. I quickly whipped off Rome's shirt, stuffing it into the cube, and then I lost my boots, using one cube for each boot, because ... *why the hell not?* Next, I tore off Jeffrey's slave garb, flicking that onto the floor, because I broke into a sol bathing chamber and therefore I was a rebel of the worst kind. Might as well start acting like it. I stepped through the next archway, passing into the fine mist of water. It caressed my skin so softly, dripping condensation over my body.

The water was very lightly scented, almost too lightly to detect. It must have had some kind of magical property, because I could *feel* it stripping me of dirt and stress. I pulled my hand up before my face, squinting at it in the dim light of a few wall sconces. The grime was running out from beneath my fingernails, dripping right off my hand. I blinked, bending over to check my feet. I was sure I had never been so damn clean in my entire life. I was pretty sure I had been *born* dirtier than this shower was now making me. Maybe it was taking a layer of skin off. Was that healthy? I had no idea.

Also ... I probably needed to re-think that last thing that I just thought, because babies weren't all that clean right after birth.

I was just beginning to wonder if I should move on when the spray turned off. The next archway was now visible to me, and I stepped toward it, dripping along the ridged, wooden floorboards. The steam assaulted me again, but stronger this time. It crept along my skin, making me break out into an immediate sweat. But it was nice. A nice kind of sweat. Almost like the magical bathing chamber was now cleansing me from the *inside*. There were a few more wooden cubes stuck along one of the walls, piles of cloth stacked within. I wandered over, grabbing what looked like a hem of fabric and extracting what appeared to be a robe, without sleeves of any kind. I pulled it up over my chest, marvelling at the whisper of cloud-like material. It barely seemed to weigh on my skin at all. It did stick to the sweat, though, forming a second skin around my chest, stomach, and thighs as I wrapped it around, tying it off beneath my arms. It ended around my knees, so I supposed that on the male sols, it would be fairly short. And that was when I realised that I was wearing it wrong. It clearly wasn't supposed to be tied off at the chest. It was supposed to be tied off at the waist, because male sols didn't have boobs.

Eh, whatever. Innovation, Soldier! Leader Graham would be so proud of me.

I sank down into the wooden bench that ran along the back of the room, my head thumping back against the wall. The steam was making me sleepy. I could almost ignore the pain. It had dulled so much that I barely even noticed it anymore. And it was getting better by the moment. It was almost ...

Crap! Take cover, Soldier!

I scrambled up off the bench, but it was too late. Siret spilled into the room, looking wet, clean, and pissed. His clothes were soaked through, his medley gold-black hair was now mostly black, sticking to his head and running rivulets of water over his face.

"Er, hey there, Five," I muttered.

"Hey, Soldier."

I jumped to my feet, my face and body heating—no doubt as red as a berry, which he hopefully wouldn't notice through all the steam. "You've been listening to me!"

Siret's eyes darkened as he took a moment to run them over my body. A *really* long moment. No doubt the white wrap hid about the same amount as Jeffrey's outfit. Still, for the same reason as last time, I didn't cover myself. Part of me sort of felt like I didn't have to with the Abcurses. They wouldn't take advantage. They wouldn't judge me. I wasn't sure I had ever felt acceptance like that before. Then again, maybe it wasn't acceptance. Maybe it was apathy.

Siret stepped closer to me. My eyes were glued to the rivulets of water running through his dark hair.

"Why did you come through the bathing rooms in your clothes?" I asked, because the silence was getting uncomfortable.

He still wasn't saying anything, and I had no idea what I was supposed to do. He reached out then and wrapped his hand around the back of my neck, pulling me closer to his body before pushing me back down on to the seat and settling in next to me.

His hardness pressed along one side of my fairly naked body, and together we remained like that, for a long while. Both of us leaning back against the wooden slats, staring out into the steam room.

His voice was a rumbling whisper when he finally spoke. "I felt your pain. You were hurting before I got here."

I had actually gotten pretty used to the chest-shredding thing that went on when I wasn't with them. Of course, now that Siret was touching me, my body was able to relax in a way it couldn't when I was away from them.

"You felt me?" Why was my voice all breathy and low? What was Siret doing to me right now? This had to be some sort of sol gift, right? His trickery was messing with me.

"I felt you." He confirmed, his hand raising subconsciously, rubbing against a spot on his chest. "You were hurting and now you're not. I told the others we couldn't leave you alone."

"I'm fine. Well ... I mean, I did trip and hurt my leg, and then I was dirty and needed to be clean ... you know, the usual stuff."

I had no idea why I was resistant to telling them about the painful co-dependence Rau had created. Part of me wanted to try and figure out how to fix it before they realised what a thorn-in-the-ass I was.

Vibrations ran along my side and I realised that Siret was laughing. For some reason, this made me smile. I liked Siret's laugh, and hearing it did things to me. Hot, swirly things. Finally, he stood and hauled me up to my feet. "Come on, Soldier, let's check out your leg. And make sure you're clean."

Sweet gods of Topia.

His voice did that growly thing again. "I heard that, Rocks. I'd prefer it if you didn't offer any sort of exclamations to those assholes."

"Why do you hate them?" I asked as he led me from the steamy room. "I still don't understand how you five even figured out how to get into Topia." And why weren't they afraid of Rau? At no point during the entire threat-and-attack thing Rau had going on, did any of the Abcurses show one ounce of concern that he would smite them into dust. Their confidence was pretty amazing. And annoying.

I hadn't actually expected Siret to answer, but oddly enough, he did spill something. "The gods are not as deserving of worship as you people like to think. They have weaknesses. Fears. They fight and bicker amongst themselves about the stupidest things. Rau doesn't scare us, he's powerful of course—all of the Originals are—but he has one big problem. He's one of the only Original Gods without a Beta and no one really knows why there has never been a sol to step into the role."

His pause was heavy and I had to ask, "Are you sure you don't know why?"

Siret glanced down at me, a flash of white teeth shining in my direction. "Personally, I believe that someone is manipulating things so that Chaos doesn't get out of hand. Rau does enough damage on his own. Of course, having no Beta leaves him weaker and more vulnerable. The only thing ensuring his dominance is the fact that chaos is the natural order of the worlds. His power grows by the simple act of you all living."

"So if he got a 'Beta' then ..."

I trailed off as the horror of what the world might look like washed over me.

"Yes, complete and utter destruction of everything you're used to. He would burn this world to the ground in a bid to gather enough power to take down the other Original Gods."

"So that's what he wants? To destroy the other Originals?"

We were back in the first room now; Siret grabbed something from a small shelf before leading me out into the hallway. I shivered slightly as a cool breeze caressed my mostly naked and damp skin, before jumping when the sol draped a warm towel across my shoulders. "You have got to stop walking around naked, Rocks. You'll catch a cold and die. Dwellers are delicate like that."

Yeah, right. I'd ended up naked and freezing more times in my life than was even possible to count. It was almost my state of natural being at this point. "So ... Rau ... end game? Destroy the OGs?"

Siret shook his head at me. "No, his end-game isn't to destroy the *OGs*. He wants to take out the big daddy."

Staviti!

Thank you, Emmy, for making sure that I knew things.

"You know Staviti?" Siret suddenly looked darker and a hell of a lot more menacing than he had two clicks before the conversation had started. "That's not possible ... no dweller has seen him in several hundred life-cycles."

He was half muttering to himself, but I wasn't paying that much attention because there was suddenly a mountain in the hallway.

Rome strode up to us and, in a move which completely stunned the crap out of me, dropped to his knees right before me. *What the actual freak?*

I was about to hyperventilate, or faint, or do something stupidly inappropriate when his hand gently prodded the graze on my leg. "What happened to you, Rocks?" With him on his knees, we were basically at eye-level. His eyes were so green it was hard to stare directly at them. "Did someone hurt you?"

I shook my head frantically. It seemed to be the only movement I was currently capable of. "No, nope, no ... no."

Siret laughed. "You should scribe a book. You're so good with words."

I recovered some of myself, enough to be able to turn and glare at him, before turning back to Rome. Only to find he was already on his feet, towering over me again.

"I'm fine," I said, managing to get those two words out without stuttering or repeating myself. "I should get back to my room."

I knew it was stupid. I literally couldn't leave their sides, but the small part of me which had always been alone—independent ... a misfit—needed to prove to myself that I could make it without the Abcurses. Like I needed to know when they decided to turf me out like trash, that I'd be okay. Shredded heart and all.

Turning, I stomped off down the hallway, half dreading that someone was going to stop me. I had no idea what I was going to do once I reached the end of the hall. There was no way to jump into the supply closet while they were watching me.

Were they still watching me?

I turned my head as minutely as I could to see behind me. Five figures. Everyone was there for the show this time. Damn them. Since I hadn't been watching where I was going, and the agony in my chest was increasing, I missed seeing the small cart which was waiting in the hallway for the morning shift of room-cleaning dwellers to grab it.

I tripped. Of course I did. Right onto my face.

I heard some snorts of laughter from behind, and the distinct sound of Yael saying. "Half a click. Told you ... you owe me a hundred tokens."

It didn't surprise me that Yael had found a way to turn that into a competition. As I lay there, breathing in the dirty floor smell—some dweller was really letting the team down in this hall. Probably that dweller was me, but whatever—I heard their steps as the five of them closed in on me.

I groaned and lifted my head just enough to thump it back against the floor. *It's going to be impossible to hide this from them any longer.* Resigning myself to the fact, I rolled over onto my back. Aros wrapped his golden hands around my biceps and hauled me to my feet.

"What can't you hide from us any longer?" he asked when I was standing again.

The quiet and semi-darkness of the hall enveloped our group, and I could have been mistaken, but it seemed like the boys were looking a little wary of me, standoffish almost. Which was good. I needed them to be cold because otherwise I got flustered and forgot that they were leagues above me, members of the blessed sol realm.

"Rocks ..." Yael prompted. "Don't make me use my persuasion on you, I've been going easy with you but I *can* make you tell me."

Oh hell to the no ... he did not just say that, right?

My rage must have been clearly reflected across my face because I saw a few of them exchange a nervous glance before they took a step away from me. Not even a sacred sol was immune to the effects of a pissed-off woman. Lifting my finger, I jabbed it right into Yael's hard chest. It hurt like hell, and he even caught my wince, so I decided to use their own tactics of intimidation against them. I drew myself to my full, miserable height, and pushed myself closer to him.

"Don't ever use your gift on me, sol," I growled. "Dwellers are *not* play things. We might have drawn the unlucky hand on this piece-of-crap world, but we are not nothing." I jabbed him harder, hoping like hell his rock-chest didn't break my finger. "Not nothing."

His face was like stone, stone which had been carved and moulded by the very gods themselves. I knew I couldn't blink, that I had to maintain my serious stare or I would fail at this competition which had arisen. *Competitive shit-sol.* Yael was such a pain with this stuff, and yet I sort of thought it was awesome at the same time. My left eye started to twitch, my fingertip aching from being pressed so hard.

"You sure you don't want to step back, Rocks?" Yael's hypnotic voice rolled over me, and I knew he wasn't hitting me with the full force of his power, yet he still affected my will.

Gritting my teeth hard enough to crack them, I didn't blink, or move, or speak. I continued with the battle of wills that I was determined to win.

Then he kissed me.

Before I even saw him coming ... his lips were on mine, and I was pulled tightly against his body. I lost all time and space, my breathing cut off as my head spun. Before the pressure could deepen, Yael stepped away from me and I barely managed to remain on my feet.

"I win," he said, turning and strolling away. All casual. Like he hadn't just ... kissed the hell out of me.

"You cheated," I shouted after him. My eyes flicked between the other four. "He cheated!"

Siret shook his head. "What did you expect? He fights dirty. We all do."

I was breathing really deeply. Almost embarrassingly deeply. *Just a kiss.* My body was reacting like I'd just run up and down the steps to Blesswood a few hundred times. I wanted to go after Yael, probably to smack him in the face, since the chest-poking had done nothing. I should use a knife or something next time. Get all badass and sol-like.

Coen distracted me by stepping in at my back, his giant form crowding over me and wiping all Yael-revenge-thoughts from my mind. I could see flickers of fire and the promise of pain in his eyes, but maybe I was just hallucinating because Yael's kiss had fried my mind. His hand dragged along my arm and with it came these strange little sparks of energy. They hurt ... sort of, but they also felt good. Like he was igniting all of the receptors along my skin, bringing my body to life. I almost missed his words, my eyes glued to the hand trailing my arm.

"Willa," his deep voice caught my attention. "We have to be up early tomorrow for the moon-cycle trials in the arena. The gods will be sitting on their pampered asses expecting us to perform like street monkeys, which means you have exactly one click to tell us what you're hiding from us."

I looked down at my feet, trying to block him out. His hand moved again, drawing those strange, aching sparks over my skin, and my breath shuddered out, my eyes closing. His grip suddenly shifted, the light brushing motion disappearing as his fingers curled around my arm, just above my elbow. He pulled roughly, forcing me against his chest. His free-hand fell to the back of my head.

Is he ... hugging me right now?

Someone snorted, and Coen's chest vibrated with a laugh that he quickly cut off.

"Talk, Willa," he demanded.

Maybe it was the hug, or maybe it was the small spark of pain that accompanied his words, flashing low against the base of my spine, but I suddenly wanted to tell them everything. I twitched a little bit, but mostly clamped down on my reaction to Coen's 'gift,' because my reaction was to jump him, and that was hardly appropriate.

"Did you guys do something?" My voice was muffled against Coen's chest, but I refused to turn my head and look at the other three.

"What was that?" Aros asked, moving behind me, seeming almost to gravitate toward me.

I suspected that he was attracted to the desire swirling through me right now. Yael had lit the match, Coen was *deliberately* stoking the fire, and Aros was the moth, drawn to the flame. I could feel him pressing against my back, his chest brushing my shoulders, his hand curving around the front of my neck. My eyes drew closed before I could stop them, and my legs were suddenly weak, my head spinning dizzily.

"She's going to drop," I heard Siret drawl.

Coen's chest rumbled again, and this time, the spark of pain was somewhere in the vicinity of my chest, forcing my eyes back open and my breath to catch.

"Don't start acting like a dweller now, Willa," Coen mumbled.

Aros's hand moved against my neck, applying just enough pressure to pull my head back against his chest, and then I was staring right up into Coen's face. The green in his eyes had disappeared completely, leaving only darkness and violence. It was pitch black, closing in around me, drawing me away from the world.

"Did you all do something to save me back at the cave?" I heard my own voice, but it didn't even feel like it was *me* speaking. I had drifted out of my body and into the darkness of Coen's soul.

"No," someone answered. Siret, I thought. "Why? What happened, Rocks?"

"Now ... I need you all," I muttered. Dual growls vibrated through me, and I quickly amended the statement. "I need to be near at least one of you. Ever since the cave. It hurts me, here ..." I tried to raise my hand to my chest, but Coen and Aros must have pushed closer. Every inch of my body seemed to be plastered up against hard muscle. When I raised my arm, it only bumped against Coen's massive chest. He refused to back up.

"Where?" Siret asked, sounding frustrated. "Guys? *Seduction! Pain!* Get the fuck off her so that I can concentrate."

Aros pulled away so fast that I almost suspected him to have been yanked off by Siret, but when Coen spun me around so that I was facing the other way, Siret was still standing in the same place and Aros was striding down the hall toward his dorm room. He disappeared inside, the door slamming violently behind him.

"And then there were two." Siret rolled his eyes.

"Two?" I muttered, looking around for Rome, who also seemed to have disappeared.

Coen's hands were wrapping around my arms from behind, still holding me close to him.

"I'm taking her to my room," Coen announced, ignoring my question. "Tell the others to get their shit together and meet us there. If we put some clothes on the dweller, we might actually be able to have a full conversation."

I snorted. "The *dweller* can speak just fine, thanks." Okay. I lied. That was a lie.

Coen knew it, too. He only shook his head at me, marching me toward the last door at the end of the hallway. He didn't release me until we were inside, the door clicking shut softly behind us. I watched as he hunted through drawers, pulling out a shirt and a pair of male sleep-pants. They had been cut short for the summer season. I suspected they would have ended above the knee on Coen, but for me, they were almost a full set of pants. He handed everything to me and then jerked his head in the direction of the alcove at the other end of his bedroom. Siret's had been full of books, but Coen's was mostly empty. Just a rug and a chair, facing the windows. It had a door, too. I stripped off and pulled on the fresh clothes, chuckling at how ridiculous I now looked, before moving back into the main room.

"What's so funny?" Rome asked me, his eyes flicking over me once before settling on my face. He was probably just making sure that I was finally clothed.

The others had all gathered, too. Silently and rapidly, like smoke beneath the door. It was a little bit scary.

"Nothing," I muttered, wandering over to their group.

None of them were sitting down, but I was exhausted, so I sat on the edge of Coen's bed, facing them all, and then I just blurted it out.

"So I feel sick and my chest hurts whenever I move away from you all. It's really painful, like my chest is being ripped apart. When I move closer again, it gets better. With one of you touching me, it disappears altogether."

I paused, drawing in a breath and passing my eyes from one of them to another. They were all doing that scary, blank-expression thing.

"Allrighttt," I drew out the word, twisting my hands together nervously. "I'm going to go sleep now. I'm tired. See you all tomorrow."

I jumped up, heading for the door.

"Trickery," someone muttered, and a moment later, there was a sol behind me.

I glanced over my shoulder, catching the side of Siret's profile, and then turned back to the door. *Eh, whatever.* Siret could follow me to the closet if he wanted to.

Unless ... unless this was the moment that they killed me.

"Overreact, much?" Siret laughed, pulling me toward his dorm room. "You're staying with me tonight. The others ... they need a bit of time to process."

"Are they angry?" I asked, as Siret pushed me gently from one room to another.

"Very," he answered cheerily.

"Why aren't you angry?" I scowled, spinning around to face him as he started pulling items off the only couch in his room.

"Rocks ... my gift is *trickery*. I love surprises. Especially surprises that annoy people. Especially surprises that annoy my brothers. Especially surprises that spend half of their time naked. A naked surprise is always a good surprise."

I didn't really know what to say to that. He kind of had a point. He swept me up, mid-yawn, carrying me over to the bed and dumping me right into the middle of it, before leaning over me to steal one of the pillows.

"See you in the morning, Soldier," he said with a wink.

TWELVE

As soon as my eyes drifted closed, sleep claimed me. I was wrenched immediately into a dream, in which I managed to grow into something twice my size, with massive limbs and hands the size of my face. Manly hands. *What the hell?*

"That can't have been Rau's intention," my voice growled out, sounding far too much like Rome's voice for comfort.

My eyes rose, meeting the eyes of three others. Yael, Aros, and Coen.

Holy freak! I'm inside Rome's head!

No. That was impossible. *Calm down*, Willa! It was just a dream. A harmless dream …

"There's only one explanation." Coen was shaking his head, looking angrier, darker, than I had ever seen him. "Whatever his magic was, it was meant for one of us. Not a dweller. You know that they react differently to magic. They're so *fragile*."

"It should have killed her." Yael said the words like an accusation, but there was confusion riding his tone, too.

"I think it ripped her soul apart," Coen returned.

Whoa, I wanted to interrupt. *What? Excuse me? WHAT!*

"I think so, too." Rome's voice carried seemingly from my mouth. "And all of those pieces ... they latched onto us. We somehow assimilated her. It shouldn't have been possible. Maybe it had something to do with Rau's magic. If it was designed specifically for us, it would have sent the pieces of her soul toward us. It still would have tried to seek us out, even after it had shredded her."

Shredded.

Ripped.

Assimilated.

Pieces.

It was hard to believe that they were talking about me. It sounded like they were talking about a rag-doll.

"I don't like this," Yael snarled, beginning to pace.

Try being me, buddy!

"None of us do," Coen snapped back. "And I bet she hates it even more than we do."

Correct, for once!

Rome laughed. "No shit. She doesn't even seem to

realise that she's a dweller. There's not an ounce of accepting or obedience in her."

The others smiled, momentarily, before the stormy expressions rolled back over their faces.

"We need to do something." Aros spoke up, his silky voice thoughtful. "Maybe we can sneak her back into Topia."

"It's too risky." Coen shook his head.

Aros grunted out an agreement. "Well, maybe we can get a message to Brina. If anyone is going to be able to reverse this curse, it'll be her."

The others nodded, and then they all seemed to fall into a thoughtful silence.

"Have you hidden the cup?" Yael finally asked, looking over at Coen.

"Of course," was the bland reply.

"Think he's noticed it missing, yet?" Aros asked.

"Of course." This time, the reply was delivered with a flashing smile. Coen's eyes glinted dangerously, a laugh falling from his lips. "If he could curse us again, he'd do it. But you know D.O.D." He laughed again, shaking his head. "He's probably trying not to be proud, because we finally managed to beat his sneaky ass at something."

Their laughter slowly faded away, and no matter how tightly I tried to hang onto it, it evaded my grasp, dwindling into soundless night as sleep dragged me further away. After that, my dreams were normal. I dreamt about sleeper bugs the size of my face, and tables piled high with delicious sol food. I even dreamt about Rome's bare chest, for a little bit. I tried not to judge myself as I then moved on to think about the others and the various images that they had planted into my poor little dweller brain.

When I woke up in the morning, it was almost a relief, and I didn't feel rested *at all*.

I supposed that there was another way that Rau's curse had changed me. *Another* truth that I was hiding from the Abcurses. But they didn't need to know about the way my body misbehaved every time they touched me. I mean ... nobody really needed to know about that. I shot up in bed, trying to wipe the guilty look off my face. *Please don't have heard my thoughts.* Luckily, Siret was still asleep on the couch. I swung my feet to the ground and padded over to him, poking him in the shoulder.

He didn't stir.

I huffed out a nervous breath, sitting down on the low table beside the couch, notching my chin in my hand and poking him again, although the movement was pretty lazy this time. His gold-tipped hair was swept to the side, curling slightly against the pale pillow beneath his head. He was actually kind of beautiful, when he wasn't insulting me. He cracked one eye open, the cat-like irises flashing with warring green and yellow-gold. His other eye cracked open while I just stared at him, trying to dredge up the words to explain that I hadn't just been sitting there, watching him sleep, like a creep.

His arms shot out, curving around me and pulling me off the table and onto his chest.

"Go back to sleep," he muttered, his voice gravelly.

"Er." I turned my head to the side, so that his chest wasn't smothering me. "No."

He reached around my face, holding his hand over my mouth. "Yes. Shh."

I tried to wiggle out of his arms, but Rome decided to choose that moment to barge into the room. Siret cracked one of his eyes open again, and I twisted around just enough to see Rome's eyebrows inching up, his massive arms crossing over his chest.

"At least you're not naked," he said to me, before turning his eyes on Siret, his expression melting into a glare. "Let's go, we need to be at the arena in three clicks."

"*Three*?" Siret launched off the couch, sending me tumbling. And of course, since the clothing I wore was about five sizes too large, most of my butt managed to fall out of the pants.

Rome grinned. "I spoke too soon."

Coen, Yael, and Aros chose that moment to barge through the door of Siret's room; I frantically scrambled to get my pants up and shirt down. Why do these things always happen to me? *Why?* Aros crossed over to me, leaning over to offer me a hand up. I froze as the full length of his body came into view. *Whoa.* His goldenness was extra-blinding; he was dressed in some sort of battle gear which consisted of a gold-tinted breastplate, arm bands, and braces over the front of his thighs. I knew my jaw had fallen open, but he looked like a warrior, or a god. A really hot warrior-god.

Wrenching my gaze from his, I placed my hand into his outstretched one. My eyes catching on each of the other Abcurses. They all wore similar armour, in shades which complimented their natural colouring.

They're going to be gods. I had absolutely no doubt that these five were on the path to Topia.

But ... *how were they going to do that with me attached like an ugly sixth limb?*

"Don't you worry about it, Rocks," Aros said as he deposited me safely to my feet. "Our path to Topia was rocky long before Rau decided to add some chaos."

His words reminded me of the dream, and I found myself blurting without thought. "So speaking of souls ... what happened to mine?"

Siret shook his head. "No one was speaking of souls, and yours is the same speck of nothing that all dwellers carry around."

By the time I turned away from him, Yael was in my face. Well, his chest was in my face. "Why would you ask about your soul?" he demanded. "You wouldn't happen to be able to hear our thoughts now, would you, dweller?" It wasn't really a question. More of an accusation.

Clearing my throat and fighting for composure, I

shook my head a few times. "No, definitely not. I just kind of ... wentintoromesheadlastnight."

The last lot was one big word I spoke as fast as I possibly could. Silence reigned supreme, then Yael spun to face his crusher brother with one eyebrow raised and a snarl on his lips.

Rome didn't even flinch. I would totally have flinched. Maybe he could give me lessons. Something told me that I would need them. And by *something*, I meant the thousands of flinch-worthy glares that I'd already gotten since arriving in Blesswood.

"I would have told you if I had felt her there," he said, his tone drawling like that much should have been *obvious*.

"Two clicks to the trials," Siret reminded the room, and I was running out of time to get answers.

Stepping forward, I snapped my fingers a few times in Yael's direction. "Hey, can you seriously focus for like one click. What the hell happened to my soul?" If he answered my damn question, he'd have a much better idea of why I was in his brother's head. It was clearly all connected. "What did Rau do to me?"

The persuasive sol gracefully twisted in my direction, and part of me instantly regretted snapping my fingers at him. I'd seen some of the villagers do that to call the bullsen up and always thought it looked like a nifty trick. Possibly, Yael wasn't fond of being called up like a wild beast.

He stepped into me, and my eyes fell to his lips.

Lips which were kissing me only last night. *No, Willa. No more kissing sols.*

That was probably a mantra I would have to repeat a few times; couldn't quite get it to sink in.

"Rau hit you with a curse that was designed for one of us. A powerful curse which was most likely intended to cause chaos. He wanted to shake up the natural order even more, giving himself more power, and thereby gathering enough power to find his Beta." Yael spoke matter-of-factly, but his eyes were ice-cold.

"The more powerful you are, the more you can sense the sols with the gifts strong enough to ascend to Topia," Rome added.

"Or steal your godhood," Siret chimed in.

Yael growled low before picking up the conversation again. "Yes, as I said, it's important that gods can sense these sols, and Rau has had that power stripped from him by Staviti. He wants it back."

I tried to breathe around my confusion and panic. "So it was a curse meant for one of you guys and it hit me ... it splintered my soul and now you all carry it inside. Like in your heart pocket or some crap."

Heart pocket? Really, Willa?

Siret took pity on me. "Souls aren't like a bag of tokens. It's not like some got slipped into our pockets when we weren't looking. Your energy, the essence of what makes you *Willa*, is now woven with the energy of each of us."

So he was saying ...

"I'm never getting those parts of my soul back, am I?" I was not going to be able to demand that they simply empty their pockets and hand me my soul back. It was all mixed up with their messy-ass souls, getting tainted by the sol-ness of their stupid, superior selves.

A disembodied voice rang through Siret's room then, sounding entirely robotic and sexless. "Gods have arrived to the arena, all sols have one click to make it inside. This is mandatory."

The Abcurses started moving. I noticed that Siret was now dressed in his own pretty set of armour plates, black and gold to reflect his hair. "Come on, Rocks. We're going to the arena, you better haul ass to keep up."

I flapped around for a fraction of a click before wringing my hands. "Dwellers aren't allowed in the Sacred Sand arena like this. I haven't even done my first cleaning shift there because you have to be trained and cleansed before you step into the halls of the gods."

Siret fitted his hands under my arms and hauled me out of the room. The Abcurses were moving rapidly, ignoring my freak out.

"Guys!" I tried to drag my feet, especially when I realised that I was still dressed in Coen's huge clothes. "Stop right now. Now! I'm not wearing my own clothes and my ass is literally hanging out. I can't go before the gods like this."

"Close your eyes," Siret whispered in my ear and

for some reason, I obeyed him. I almost suspected that he was channelling some of Yael's persuasion.

Thankfully, he was still half carrying me down the hall because walking with eyes closed for someone like me was not advisable. I felt the warmth of something caress my body, and figured it was the sunshine as we stepped out the front door, but when I found my eyes flying open, we weren't quite there yet. Which meant …

I glanced down to find that my clothes had completely changed. The dress was a deep purple, moulding perfectly to my body, as though it had been made specifically for me. It even felt like I had underwear on and everything. I could even see that my hair had somehow been tamed, curling obediently over my shoulders, the strands looking silky and shiny. *Well wasn't I a bit fancy right now?* But how the heck had Siret done that to me? Was it a trick or an illusion?

"You shouldn't be wasting your energy like that, Trickery." Yael's face was expressionless, his voice flat. His brother didn't bother to answer; he was focused on getting to the arena.

A few more steps and we were outside. The massive arena rose up into the distance, the last straggling sols disappearing through the huge entrance. I'd only ever seen it from the outside, so I was looking forward to checking out the rest of it. This was the place where sols gathered every moon-cycle to perform for the gods. This was where they wanted to be noticed. This was the place where future gods were discovered.

The inside was as impressive as I had expected. A wide open circular space with a multitude of obstacles and different flooring was the centre and focal-point of the entire building. Around it, on all sides, were staggered rows of chairs, which were right now filled with sols. All five Abcurses paused to stare at the end furthest from us, where there was a raised and glassed-off platform. The reflecting sun through the open panes of the rooftop made it hard to see into that boxed area, but it had to be where the gods were.

"Come on, we need to take our seats," Coen muttered, leading us toward the empty seats that were very far away from the glassed box. Away from the gods. Which was totally not normal sol behaviour. From what I could see, the seats closest to the gods were packed with the students of Blesswood. Dwellers stood around the perimeter waiting to be called on for service, probably hoping that the gods would notice them too. They were all dressed in their absolute best: the females in dresses and the males in trousers and long shirts. I wondered if they'd still want the gods to notice them if they knew the uniform for the Jeffreys.

The end we were heading toward was practically empty, even though it was the row closest to the actual arena. Those sols who hadn't managed to get a place close to the glass box all seemed to prefer the middle ring of seats. I had only a moment to wonder why, before the first sols were called into the sands, and then I realised several things at once.

Firstly, sols were dangerous.

Secondly, a sand floor easily absorbed blood, and negated the need for a post-arena-demonstration cleaning crew.

And finally, the front row of seats was absolutely the *worst* row of seats.

More than once, a sol was tossed right up against the flimsy wooden barrier that I sat behind. I hadn't actually been paying much attention to the other sols of Blesswood until then. I hadn't bothered to even admire their slightly-better-than-dweller appearances, or their slightly-bigger-than-dweller statures, but now I was noticing it all, and my slightly-less-than-stellar coping mechanisms were kicking into gear, forcing my palms to sweat. In front of me, a male sol had a female sol pinned right up against the barrier. I could almost feel his snarling breath. I could almost feel the sharpness of the knife that he held up against her throat, and then I could *definitely* feel the blood that splattered right over my face.

"*What the fuck?*" I cried out, clamouring right over the back of my seat as the female sol's head lolled a little to the side, teetering as though it would fall right where my shoes had been tapping nervously against the ground.

The male sol … the one with the knife … the one who just almost beheaded his opponent right there in front of me—was now staring at me. I noted that he was still holding the bloody knife. That seemed important, but my frazzled brain couldn't seem to figure out *why* it was important.

"Dweller?" he sounded surprised. "Are you lost?"

"N-nope," I stammered. "Meant to be here." I looked down, at the boy whose lap I had basically scrambled into. He had been sitting right behind me. In the row of seats reserved for intelligent sols who didn't want to get covered in blood. "Totally did that deliberately," I told him—and Stabby, who was still staring at me.

A single gong sounded, signalling the end of the match, and Stabby shrugged, though there was a frown on his face as he spun around and walked to the other end of the arena. He bowed before the glass box, as the other victors had, and then disappeared through a door leading down below the arena.

"Dweller?" a male voice sounded, about a few inches away from my ear. "You're still sitting on me."

I glanced down at the guy. Now that I paid attention, I noticed that he was actually taking up two of the seats, he was *that* big. I couldn't even tell if it was fat, or muscle. He was just ... *huge*. Oh, and he was giving me a look. A 'what the hell are you sitting on me for?' look.

"I can explain," I managed, slowly standing up, my hands raised before me.

"We're waiting." This had come from Siret, who

had been sitting to my left in the blood row. He was now twisted around, as were the others.

He was smirking, clearly finding my awkward predicament funny. Even Aros was grinning, but the others weren't. A stormy expression had dropped over Rome's face. Maybe he didn't like other people being bigger than him.

"Stabby got blood on me." I frowned. "And he killed that girl." I pointed to said girl, who was now being carried away by two of the dweller attendants.

"That's what happens," Yael muttered, reaching over the seat and hauling me back to the front row, forcing me down between him and Siret. "In these games, you either surrender, or you die."

"So why didn't she *surrender*?" I crossed my arms over my chest, casting a quick look over my shoulder at Mountain Man. He was still frowning at me. I could feel it burning into the back of my head as I tried to ignore him.

He was probably waiting for a formal dweller-style apology, or for me to drop and kiss his feet. Problem was, Yael still had a hand on my shoulder, forcing me to stay in my seat, so kissing Mountain Man's feet was going to be a problem.

"Maybe she thought she was strong enough," Coen returned, from Yael's other side. "Maybe she thought that she would become a god." His voice was soft, but it had an edge of something malicious. It was almost like he *knew* that she wasn't strong enough. That she had died for nothing. And he liked that fact.

Coen was a little bit frightening.

"I'm next," Aros announced, jumping to his feet and launching himself over the wooden barrier without a backward glance.

I looked up at the Gamemaster—a sol male standing beside the gong that sounded the beginning and ending of each match. He was set right beneath the glass box, probably so that the gods could whisper down to him whenever they wanted to see a particular sol perform. Sure enough, Aros's name was now glittering in flame above the Gamemaster's head, along with *Tabatha*, whoever that was. I watched with increasing trepidation as Aros sauntered out into the center of the arena, standing there patiently. Pretending that poor sols didn't get beheaded there on a regular basis.

Speaking of ... "Uh, if you guys die, does that mean I'll die too?" I spoke rapidly, uncaring which one of my soul-stealers answered.

Siret laughed—loudly, as though he had just heard the funniest joke ever. This sort of weird red haze descended across my vision and I was about to launch myself head first into his face. I knew my head was hard, and it would hurt if I hit him with it.

Yael must have seen my intentions, because he wrapped an arm around my waist just as I launched. "Calm down, Rocks. Trickery is amused because there's no possible way a sol will ever take one of us down. None. So don't worry yourself about it."

Yeah, sure, don't worry your pretty head about it, Willa, it's just your life we are holding in our hands. My scowl swung to face Yael. "Don't think I didn't notice the deflection toward my actual question there, so either you know your death would kill me, or you have no idea. Neither of which are comforting."

Siret's laughter was dying off; lucky for him, because I was still calculating the best angle to head-charge him. Would totally be worth the headache. He spoke through the dying chuckles. "We aren't easily killed, don't you worry. And the simple fact is ... we don't know what this means for any of us. Maybe you can't be killed now either—as in until all six of us die, none of us can die. Or maybe there's still a piece of your soul inside you. It would make sense, seeing as you're able to feel emotions that are entirely your own, and you can easily make decisions for yourself."

Well, that would be a bonus, but knowing my luck, doubtful. If there was only a little piece of me left, I'd almost definitely turn into a Jeffrey when I died. My attention was distracted then when Tabatha entered the arena.

She was just a girl in simple fighting-gear striding out from the door leading below the arena. There was probably a dweller running down there to fetch sols when they were called. I couldn't see her properly from where I sat, but she looked beautiful and badass, her hair braided down her back, her scowl in place. She walked over to Aros, and then attacked, right when I thought that she was going to say *hi, how's it going?* or some other kind of casual greeting.

He flung out an arm as she pounced at him, so quickly that I would have missed it if the girl hadn't run right into it. He caught her right at her neck, sending her feet flying out from beneath her, sand spraying, and flipping her up. His other hand seemed to push against her face as she was falling, sending her toward the ground much faster than she would have fallen on her own. She collided with the sand so roughly that her body actually seemed to bounce, and then she wasn't moving at all.

Aros started walking back to us as the gong sounded. I supposed that an opponent falling unconscious would be considered a surrender, which was a good thing. I wasn't exactly spokesperson for the sols, but I was happy that there were alternatives to beheading. I knew both Yael and Siret had smug grins on their faces, like they were saying mentally *I told you so*.

Aros climbed over the barrier and sat down beside Siret, looking completely bored. I leaned over Siret, peering at him. "Why'd they pair you with a girl?"

He turned away from the sand, his eyes finding mine, his unease creasing fine lines between his brows. "The gods are always hoping that I'll use my gift to win a fight."

"How would that even work?" I was thoroughly confused, and a little too aware of the hand that Siret had dropped over my back.

Aros leaned forward, bringing his face close to mine. "I could have distracted her with desire," he muttered, his eyes flicking between mine. "And then she would have let me close to her." He reached out, his fingers winding around the back of my neck. "She would beg me to kiss her, because I would make her. I would make it all that she could think about." His power trickled through to me, nothing like the debilitating need that he was describing, but enough to convince me that he was telling the truth. I bit down on my lip, trying not to do something stupid, like moan.

"And then?" I couldn't help that my voice rasped a little bit.

"And then I would snap her neck," he said silkily, his fingers tightening on me.

I drew back, wrenching myself from his spell, and he allowed me. Siret's hand fell away from my back, and I turned to the arena numbly, my emotions running rampant.

Holy shit.

"Language," Siret chastised.

Fuck you. I narrowed my eyes at him.

He grinned. "You have a dirty mind, Soldier."

"I'm up." Yael's deep voice cut through the moment, drawing all of our eyes back to the

Gamemaster as the persuasive Abcurse launched himself over the barrier.

His name was there, in flame. I didn't even bother looking at the other name. *What did it matter?* They wouldn't last. Not against Yael. Not against *any* of the Abcurses. Part of me understood why Siret had laughed at me before. My guys weren't normal. They were something else.

Not my guys. Just guys. Some random guys. Some random, weird, annoying guys.

"Are you insulting us inside your head again, Rocks?" Rome asked through a yawn, standing and plonking himself into Yael's vacated seat, his massive hand falling to my knee.

I stared at his hand, and then at his face. He didn't even seem to be needing a response. He was watching his brother, who was standing out in the middle of the arena as Aros had.

"Nope," I lied. "I have other friends that I insult inside my head, you know."

He turned, finally focussing his full attention on me. The glittering, gem-like green of his irises darkened with his focus, making my seat a pretty frightening seat to be sitting in right then.

"We're not your friends," he told me blatantly.

"Your hand is on my leg," I shot back, not even missing a beat.

They were so my friends.

On my other side, Siret snorted on a laugh.

Rome didn't look at his hand—which apparently had a mind of its own—but I could feel his fingers tightening. They could reach all the way around my leg, his fingers brushing on the other side. If he squeezed, everything from the knee down would probably pop right off.

"Enemies don't put their hands on their enemies' legs," I pushed, holding his stare.

His jaw shifted, like he was grinding his teeth. I tried to edge my leg out from beneath his death-grip, but it only tightened further, pulling until I was dragged across the seat and pressed right up against his body.

"I never said that we were enemies," he finally answered. "We're just not friends."

Okay, so he was annoyed about the fact that my sneaky little soul had kind of chained itself to his. I could understand that. I mean, friends were supposed to have boundaries. That definitely crossed a line.

"Kay." I nodded, leaning my head against his arm—which was about as comfortable as a rock. If he was going to force me to sit on the edge of my seat, he might as well give me something to lean against.

He grumbled as I turned back to watch the other contestant finally emerge from the room below the arena. He was a big guy, dragging an even bigger sword behind him. When he drew near Yael, he looked pissed. Probably because they were forcing him to fight Yael. I'd be pissed too. He raised his sword as the gong sounded, and then tried to strike before Yael could speak, but it was no use. In half a click, he was laying the sword back down and stripping off his clothes. He ran toward the barrier, climbed over, and started running naked through the rows of laughing sols. Eventually, he ran right into a wooden post, and then fell down, unconscious. Apparently, Yael had grown tired of humiliating him.

The gathered sols cheered and laughed, louder than they had for any other fight, and Yael smirked, delivering them a bow before walking back to us.

"I'll be next," Siret predicted, as Yael pulled himself over the barrier and flopped carelessly down into Rome's old seat.

"How do you know that?" I asked.

"They always pick us like this. Aros first, to test the waters. If Aros doesn't use his gift, they pick Yael. If Yael takes too long to end his fight, they pick me. If my fight isn't a *real* fight, they pick Coen. If Coen doesn't kill his opponent, they pick Rome. If Rome doesn't draw blood, they do it all over again. One of us after another until they get what they want."

I blinked, looking from one of their faces to the other. They all looked kind of angry, but tired at the same time. Resigned to the fact. They couldn't disobey the gods on everything, it seemed. Otherwise they wouldn't have even walked into the arena that morning.

THIRTEEN

Siret was right. The gods were apparently the predictable sort of assholes in that they liked the same torture over and over again. Siret didn't bother with trickery in his fight. He smashed his fist through the face of a lean, dark-haired sol, rendering him unconscious with one blow. There was not an iota of expression on his face as he stared up at the glassed box of gods, and I wondered if he knew who was there this moon-cycle. Which god had bothered to come and view the arena battles. Which god was requesting him, and scowling when he didn't deliver what was expected.

I supposed it didn't really matter. Unless it was Rau. I would have liked to get my hands on him, except that he would probably hit me with another curse and I'd turn into a rodent, and then my little rodent soul would explode and attach onto a bunch more people.

It would be better if Rome got his hands on Rau. He had huge hands, hopefully he'd be able to just crush the god into dust.

"Heavy thoughts there, Rocks." I'd missed Siret making his way across the arena and back into the seat beside me.

"How do you kill a god?" I blurted out, and in a flash Siret's hand was across my mouth. He leaned in very close until his lips were almost touching the hand wrapped around my face.

"Don't provoke them, don't think about killing them. They'll destroy you without thought. You leave Rau to us; we'll deal with his chaos."

My reply was mumbled against his skin, my tongue flicking out to wet my lips before I remembered that was impossible. I kind of licked his hand instead. Siret's eyes went this stormy green colour as he slowly slid the hand from my mouth and let it curve around the back of my neck.

"How the hell have you stayed alive this long?" he asked.

I shrugged, trying to catch my breath. "No idea, it's been a rough road."

I heard his muttered, "I'll bet," before he turned back to watch the next round of battles. Coen's name flashed up in the fire sign. No surprise there. The real surprise was in the next name to flash up.

Willa Knight – dweller.

I always did want to see my name in lights, but not

exactly like this. I think it took me a few clicks to register that my name had appeared on the arena board. The Gamemaster, along with most of the crowd, were all staring at the fiery sign, completely dumbfounded.

"Well, looks like the gods decided to play a different game this moon-cycle," Siret noted. He looked like he didn't know whether to be angry, or amused. He settled on cringing.

Coen was sitting as still as anything in his chair. My frantic eyes searched him out, hoping he would have some answers about making this work. Finally, he turned to face me, and I wasn't sure what to make of his blank gaze. He got to his feet and in one leap was over the barrier, landing in the arena below.

I wanted to scream or cry. There was no plan, and I sure as hell couldn't fight Coen. He would destroy me. The gods were probably hoping that he would, that his need for pain would kick in and he would reduce me into nothing more than spilled blood and guts. Strong arms wrapped around me, and I half-shrieked when I was lifted from my seat.

Rome's arms were surprisingly gentle as he lifted me up over the barrier. My eyes sought out Siret, who was standing beside his brother. Actually, all of the Abcurses were on their feet. None of them looked happy.

"You have no choice but to go in there and do your

best," Siret told me, his voice projected so lowly that it barely carried to me.

Yael leaned close and added, "Coen will make sure that it ends quickly. Just don't fight him."

Before I could reply with the expletive they deserved, Rome let me go. I was too scared to scream as I fell to the arena below. I braced myself for impact, but instead of hitting the sand, I was caught by another set of strong arms and then set onto my feet.

I immediately stepped back to add some space between us, raising my fists hesitantly, just in case I needed to punch Coen or something.

"I got you, Willa." His deep voice wrapped around me, smooth and warm, like a silk-lined cloak.

He strode out into the centre of the arena, and I knew that I was supposed to follow him. The only problem was ... that would require my feet to move and right now they were glued to the spot. My body shook as the faces of so many sols and dwellers seemed to swell all around me, their stares bearing down on me. I couldn't stop myself from glancing up over my shoulder. All of the Abcurses remained standing, pressed close to the barrier. My eyes drifted around the stadium seating and I realised that a lot of the sols were standing. Some of them looked intrigued. Maybe this *was* just some elaborate way of poking fun at the sols who were all so desperate to please the gods.

Dweller-blood spilling on the super-absorbent,

sacred sol fighting sands ... that was the stuff of their nightmares. Mine too, if I were to be honest.

I glanced down at my fancy dress, cringing. I had loved the fact that it had the appearance of being made to fit me exactly, but that was before I had known that I would be fighting for my life in it. Or at least pretending to fight for my life.

We were pretending, weren't we?

Finally, I managed to stumble my way across to stand before Coen, grateful that Siret had given me boots and not heels. The pain-gifted sol was back to stoic, no emotions to clue me in on what he was going to do. Yael's words were painfully strong in my head. *Don't fight him.* Of course, that was easier said than done when a huge-ass sol was heading straight for you.

Coen moved fast, like the rest of the Abcurses, but I'd been around them constantly for almost half a dozen sun-cycles now. I had been expecting the strike, and somehow, on instinct, I dodged it. My mind swam at the realisation that I had moved almost as fast as Coen. And I didn't trip doing it.

He tilted his head to the side, and the slightest of sparks lit up his eyes, along with a smirk on his lips. *Great.* I'd just made this a fun game for him, which meant that it was going to be the very opposite of a fun game for me. *Time for Plan-B.* Before he could move, I ran. I *sprinted*. All the way across the arena, pulling up the skirt of the dress as I went. I aimed for the side that had a small step hopping up into the stands. I sensed him behind me but I didn't hesitate or glance back, since both actions would cost me precious time.

I reached the step first, and without even hesitating, I hit it hard and launched myself as high as I could onto the side of the barrier. There were slots in the higher sections, and I needed to reach those to be able to hold on. My fingers scrambled against the wood, I felt slivers cut into me, but I ignored the pain and managed to hook my hands into some holds and pull myself up so that my feet were resting on one of the slots. Turning, I held on with both hands above my head, not at all surprised to see Coen standing below. Waiting for me.

"You let me get away, didn't you?" My question was breathy and annoyance dripped from my tone. Running wasn't my thing.

He grinned, and this time it seemed real. He was either laughing at me or with me. Either way, I definitely amused him.

"Come on, dweller-baby. Where do you think you're going from there? You can't climb out, so get your ass back down here and submit to me."

I coughed a few times, my cheeks turning pink. It was definitely because of all the running.

"You mean surrender, right? Get my ass back down there and *surrender?*"

Coen's laughter was deep and rumbly; it managed to caress my body in places which should *not* have been reacting in a situation like this. "I always say what I mean. You should have figured that out by now."

Narrowing my eyes on him, I squeezed my hands even tighter on their holds, worried I was about to slip. "I will never submit to you, One! Never! So you might as well walk away now because I will literally hang here until nightfall if I have to!"

Yeah, *right*. Even as I spoke, my hands were losing their grip. I was such a liar. And an idiot. I needed to learn when to give up and cut my losses. Of course, none of that mattered when it came to those supersols. Coen leapt toward me, so quickly I barely even tracked his movements, and before I could open my mouth to shout, he was behind me, his hand grasping the top of the barrier, above my head.

"Love it when they run," he half-whispered, half-grunted beside my ear, and then his arm was winding around me and he was pulling me away from the barrier.

I would have screamed as my hands were wrenched out of their hold and we started falling backwards, but we fell much faster than I would have on my own, and Coen was landing square on his feet before the scream had a chance to gather up any momentum. I broke away from him as soon as our feet were on the ground, and we faced each other, both of us taking short, measured steps—him forwards and me backwards.

Until I stepped on the train of my dress and almost

fell on my ass.

"Wait," I pleaded, surprised when he actually stopped moving.

I bent over, grabbing the hem of the dress and attempting to rip it, needing a little more room to move. Typically, it didn't budge, and Coen grew tired of waiting. He was before me in a click, forcing me back to my feet as he leaned in close.

"Time's up," he announced, a small smirk in place.

His hands dropped onto my shoulders, sliding down to rest against my chest. The dress didn't have much of a covering above the bodice, so his palms almost seemed to slide against my bare skin through the thin, mesh-like material, raising goosebumps all along my body. I tried not to hyperventilate, but I knew that my breathing had changed. He didn't have his hands *on* my boobs, but I could still feel the swell of them—right above the top of the dress—pushing against his palms with each sudden, sharp breath. His massive fingers curled around my shoulders, digging in a little as his eyes darkened. The sparkling tendrils of weirdly addictive pain he'd used on me previously began running across my body again, only this time they were a million times stronger. It was like he was sticking hot needles into my skin, but the needles were coated in some kind of potion that just made me feel *good.* It was amazing that he could do that, but it seemed that the more he used his power, the more it began to resemble pain. The pleasure was still there, but the agony started to peek through, whispering against my bones and making me cringe.

I whimpered out a protest even as my body arched into him, reacting to the way his cloudy eyes were staring down at me. He dropped one of his hands to wrap tightly around my spine.

"Your fight is the thing which sets you apart from other dwellers," he whispered into my ear as he held my trembling body. "But you have to learn to recognise when you can't win."

Oh no he didn't.

I grabbed my skirt again, but I moved deliberately slowly this time, keeping myself pressed against him. I bunched it up into my hands, inch by inch, as his eyes flickered from my face, watching as the material climbed higher up my legs.

"Dweller..." he ground out.

For just a moment, unadulterated pain flashed through me, but as quickly as it happened, it was gone, leaving only an echo of it for me to react to. Coen blinked rapidly, once, twice, and then his gaze was back on my face. I had broken his concentration.

Willa for the win!

He frowned, obviously hearing that thought, but it was too late for him. My dress was up high enough now.

"What was that thing you said before?" I asked, as the gathered sols began to grow impatient, shouting things at us.

"You have to learn to recognise when you can't—"

I swung my knee up into his balls.

His breath rushed from him and he stumbled back, his hands falling away from me. *Whoops*. I *had* intended to knee him; I just hadn't intended to knee him *there*. I froze at the newly tinted green of his eyes, and in that moment, I was pretty sure that I was seeing death. Coen wasn't a pain-gifted sol at all. He was *death*.

I held both hands up. "Sorry, I didn't mean to …" I was backing up, my hands still above me. The crowds were noisy around us now, and even though I never planned on it, I decided to surrender.

Just as I opened my mouth to shout it out, a zap of energy shot through me, and no sound emerged from my mouth. I tried again as Coen stalked toward me. He had recovered in a mere moment, which didn't seem fair. I'd never get away with another underhanded shot like that again. It should have at least given me two clicks' reprieve. I tried for a third time to speak, and still no sound emerged.

My eyes flicked across to the glass box and I just knew one of those assholes had done something to me. They wanted to see what Coen would do. How far he would go. Whether he would hurt me or not. Whether he would *kill* me or not. I, on the other hand, didn't want to see what Coen would do at all. That wasn't the kind of knowledge that I required. I would have happily flounced right out of the arena, shaved off all my hair, and slipped into the unassuming role of Will Knight, sans obvious nipples, to hide from the gods. But I couldn't do that, because the guys felt some kind of obligation to the gods, or the gods had some kind of control over them. And I felt some kind of obligation to the Abcurses, or they had some kind of control over me. Really, obligation and control were becoming more or less synonymous to me.

And there was one more, tiny little thing.

The gods were cheating.

They were taking away my ability to surrender, and that was unfair. That made me mad. I stopped backing away from Coen, blinking as though I was about to start bawling like a little girl. He totally bought it. Idiot Abcurse. He frowned, some of the danger edging out of his walk as he approached me. I dropped to my knees, my hands tangling in the sand. I was really milking it.

"As much as I like this," Coen's voice rumbled, his hand in my hair. "You actually need to *say* that you surrender."

For a just a few, weak moments, I flirted with the fact that I didn't have the strength of will to resist Coen and his deep, rumbling voice. I considered that I wanted to be on my knees before him, and ...

But no.

Nope.

I was Willa Freaking Knight. Baddass Extraordinaire. Best Dweller in the World. And I was going to attempt to kick the ass of the massive Pain sol even if it was the last thing I did.

"Take this!" I shouted ... or *mouthed,* more like, but my point was still made.

I tossed the sand into his face, surging to my feet and running away from him.

Before I could figure out a plan, a huge body slammed into me and lifted me up to drive us across the arena, all the way to the barrier where the Abcurses still stood.

My back slammed against the wall. It was hard and hurt a little, but nothing like it would have if Coen had used all of his muscle.

His breath washed across my cheek, and I went a little dizzy at the woodsy, fresh-cut pine scent he had going on. I could feel his body trembling; he was on the brink of losing control and I couldn't even open my mouth to try and save myself. Instead, I tossed my arms around his neck, plastering myself to him in a fierce hug.

I might have been a terrible fighter, but I was a stellar hugger. One of the best.

When I drew back, Coen's stone-chip eyes locked onto mine like a predator to his prey, and I could feel the faint vibration of his growl as it passed from his chest to mine. Instinct took over and I leaned closer to snuggle my face into that spot between his shoulder and neck.

His body shuddered beneath mine, the hands on

my back tightening. "You have to surrender, Rocks. I can't stop until you do." There was pleading in his voice, and as I pulled back, I opened my mouth and closed it just as quickly, before shaking my head. I put my hand on my throat to tell him that I couldn't surrender, even if I wanted to.

Can't speak.

More than one growl sounded from around me then, and I knew that the other brothers had heard my thought. Coen swung us around so that he could glare up at the glass box, and then his voice slipped out into the air around us. "Close your eyes."

Our stare held for an eternity, and I was relieved to see that he was as unhappy about what was happening as I was. I gave him a quick head nod, and closed my eyes, mostly trusting that I would make it through this. My feet gently hit the sand as Coen took my face into both of his hands, the tingling pain started quickly, and increased to the point where I wanted to cry out, but thankfully, with a quick snap of energy, darkness took me.

♡♡♡♡♡♡

When I woke up, there was pain everywhere, but most of it was focussed around the area of my chest. I struggled to pull myself into a sitting position, peering cautiously around at the stone room. It looked kind of like a dungeon, with bare, stone benches and a barred door—which had thankfully been kept open. I groaned, doubling over and clutching my stomach. The Abcurses were near, but they were stretching me out, taking the distance right to the edge of what I could bear. I slipped off the bench, my head swimming dizzily, and padded toward the door on shaky legs.

"Fuck the gods," I muttered, just to make sure that my power of speech had returned.

It had. Check that off. I was also still in possession of every single one of my limbs, which I considered a feat, seeing as I had just jumped into the Sacred Sand Arena to face-off against Coen Abcurse, pain-master of Blesswood.

"Fuck the gods," I said again, a little louder this time. Just double-checking. "*Fuck the fucking gods!*" I screamed. I had no excuse for that one. It just felt good.

"We get it," a familiar voice noted dryly. "You're a little angry."

"Emmy?" I blinked at my best friend as she came into view, walking down the stone corridor toward me. "Am I in a dweller dungeon?"

"No." She reached me, pulling me into a fierce hug. "You're below the arena. Atti was attending this suncycle and he came and got me when they called you onto the sands. He said you might need some clothes."

"Are the gods still here?" I asked as she set me back, running her eyes over me critically before handing me a bundle of cloth.

I looked both ways down the hallway before

struggling out of the ruined dress and pulling on the clothes that she had brought for me. A pair of shorts and a shirt; they were the plain sort of clothing that I'd run around in back at the village. She must have found them in my backpack. The sols didn't wear these sorts of clothes—especially not the shorts—but the village dwellers often had to overcompensate for the heat and the lack of cooling methods with sparse clothing.

"I have no idea. They rarely ever show themselves anyway. What the hell have you done, Willa? Why the hell have they singled you out? Do they *know* that you snuck into Topia?" She lowered her voice for that last part, eyes darting around as if she expected some of the robed bullsen-balls to just pop into existence down here.

"I ..." I opened my mouth, closing it again. *I have no idea.* "Maybe this was Rau. He seemed to be really angry at the Abcurses, and they told him that I was Coen's plaything. That Coen was fond of me, or something weird like that. So maybe this had nothing to do with me ... maybe this was a punishment for Coen."

Emmy's frown deepened, her eyes sparking with warring concern and anger. If I didn't know her for the goody-sol-lover that she was, I would have thought that she was actually pissed at Coen, and the others, for bringing me into the middle of a god-battle.

"They got called up there," she said gently. Her voice almost resigned. "All five of them."

"To the god-box?"

"Yeah."

"I'm going up there," I announced, striding past her.

"And how did I know that you would say that?" She set off after me, able to keep pace with me far too easily for my fragile ego.

"Because you're secretly a rebel, and your mind works just like mine?"

She snorted, which I took for a no. "I'm glad you're okay, Will. I was terrified. I thought that Coen would kill you. I feel like your bad luck has gotten so much worse since we arrived here."

"Nah." I shook my head, peering up a few different stone staircases, trying to figure out which was the way back up. "We're friends now, even if they won't admit it. And I've only stabbed one person since we came here. *One!* I mean ... yeah ... it was a god. But still. Coen wouldn't kill me."

"I came to the closet early this morning to check up on you, but you weren't in there. I assumed you told them everything."

"I didn't have much of a choice. Five let me sleep in his room."

"Five?"

"Siret. Trickery. The one who's always kind of smirking."

"Five as in Dorm Number Five?"

I finally found the right staircase—with no help

from Emmy—and grabbed her hand to drag her after me, which was a nice reversal of sisterly roles. "You're so smart. Why can't all people be as smart as you?"

"Most people are."

"Does that make me dumb?" I asked, faking an offended tone.

"It makes you special," she teased, squeezing my hand and taking the lead, because I was definitely floundering all of a sudden. So many hallways. Barely any light. Plus, my legs were sore, so I kept trying to avoid stairs. Which was stupid, because we needed to go *up*.

Eventually, the pain in my chest began to lighten, and my body seemed to naturally turn in the direction of the Abcurses, intent on delivering me straight to them. They would have loved that. I needed to make sure they never found out. I had planned on reaching the room and planting myself outside, sticking my ear to a wall or notching the door open just enough to hear things clearly. I had hoped that both the gods *and* the Abcurses would decide to utilise their apparently private moment to spill all of their secrets, and that those secrets wouldn't be harmful to me in any way, shape, or form.

Willa Knight's involvement in all of this is just a random accident. Yeah, that's what they were going to say. Wait, no. *Who is Willa Knight?* That was better. They wouldn't even know my name. *That dweller we made you fight? You're crazy. That sign was supposed to say Willis Ninny. Silly Abcurses.*

I was so happy about what I was expecting to hear, that I barely even noticed the door in front of me opening. I stopped when I caught sight of Aros, who exited the room followed by Yael, Siret, Coen, and then Rome. They all lined up, facing me, and Rome shut the door firmly behind him, not admitting any more people into the hallway.

"Oh hey." I scuffed my shoe against the carpet. "Fancy seeing you guys here. You all done with the secret meeting?"

"We heard you," Yael announced, flicking his eyes to Emmy for a moment, before returning them to me. Oh, right. They heard my thoughts. *Oh shit. Why didn't I think of that?*

"You're still doing it," Aros added, walking over to me, grabbing me by the hips and swinging me over his shoulder. "Bye, dweller."

He strode past Emmy, and the guys started to follow. I pulled my head up, giving Emmy a hopeless look. She waved me away, obviously aware that I couldn't physically separate myself from them, even if I had wanted to, but there was still a kind of despair written all over her face as she watched me being carried away. I thought about what I would have done in her position, and cringed a little bit. I would have been kicking some sol ass. Attempting. I would have been *attempting* to kick some sol ass. Maybe she was thinking that this was out of her hands now, that *I* was out of her hands now. That she couldn't protect me anymore. Maybe in time, she would be thanking the Abcurses. Probably around the same time as the Abcurses started begging her to take me back under her wing. I was a pain-in-the-ass to look after, and Emmy had big things ahead of her. She had a glamourous dweller career, and an honourable future.

I didn't have any of that.

I had ... well ... shit. I was probably going to be a Jeffrey, but I didn't want to dwell on that. Not right now. Not when Aros's hand was splayed over the back of my thigh, because if there was anyone who had the power to distract you from unpleasant thoughts, it was the golden, seduction-gifted sol.

"I can walk," I told him, tapping on his back.

He pulled me back, but his arm tightened across my back before my feet could hit the ground. "Sure you can," he muttered, his golden eyes falling over my face. "You okay?"

"Sure I am." I grinned. "I got to fight Pain-Master-One, and I'm pretty sure I almost won. I totally almost won."

"Not even close." He laughed. "But I'd give you a participation award, minus a few points for the ball-shot. That was a little unfair, don't you think?"

"Nah." I looped my arms around Aros's neck, cuddling closer and notching my chin against his shoulder.

I really wanted to wrap my legs around him again, but I supposed I had learnt at least half of a lesson last time. I didn't think they realised how awkward it was for me to just *hang* like that, with my legs dangling. The others were still walking behind Aros, so I was able to cast my eyes over them now. None of them looked hurt. Or happy. Or angry. Or any emotion really.

"Why did they call you up to the god-box?" I finally asked, my eyes coming to a rest on Coen. I figured he owed me more than the others, on account of making me pass out and everything.

"They didn't," Coen grunted. "We called ourselves up."

"Oh. What for?"

"To find out why the hell they made me fight a dweller."

"And?"

"Do all dwellers ask this many questions?" Rome muttered.

"*And*?" I pressed.

"And it was Rau," Yael answered, sounding bored. "Trying to mess with Coen. Nothing serious. Nothing to worry about."

"Except that every sol at the academy is going to hate you now," Siret added.

"Why?" I groaned. It wasn't actually a question. More like a lament. Why did this shit have to happen to me?

"You can stop asking questions now," Rome grumbled. "My head hurts and I feel like breaking something."

"A little questioning never hurt anybody," I protested half-heartedly. I didn't actually want to fight with Rome, but there was a stubborn switch inside my mind that seemed to be stuck in the *on* position.

"Seduction," Rome snapped. "Do something about her."

"You could just ask me nicely!" I demanded, as Aros secured his arm more tightly around my back, his free hand coming to rest on my thigh again.

He manoeuvred my leg, drawing it around his waist, allowing me to wrap my legs around him properly. I was a little bit distracted. Especially when his hand gripped my ass to hold me up. *Especially* when a rush of feeling flooded through me that was far too strong to be anything but magic. I tightened my whole body around him, my head falling into his neck, my teeth sinking into his skin. I was mostly just trying not to whimper or anything pathetic or girly like that, but I suppose I also wanted a little bit of revenge. He stumbled, and then stopped walking, a light groan sounding in my ear.

"Did she just bite you?" Rome's face was suddenly right in front of mine, his fingers threading into my hair and lifting my head from Aros's neck.

"Yes," Aros gritted out.

"She's like a wild animal," Rome muttered, his

glittering eyes locked onto mine. "Every *single* time you poke her, she fights back."

"She can hear you," I said.

"Give her to me," Rome demanded. Since he was still staring at me so intensely, I actually thought that he was talking to me.

"Fuck off, Strength," Aros growled, moving forward so that Rome was forced to release me, my hair tangling in his fingers and forming a brief bridge between us, before it fell over my eyes.

I quickly pushed it off, and by then, Rome was already back in my face. He reached over Aros, hooking his hands beneath my arms and hauling me up and over Aros, who spun around, looking pissed.

"Whoa!" I tossed my arms up as my feet hit the ground, trying to separate the two of them. "I get that all the arena fighting probably has your adrenaline pumping, and you're itching to get into another fight right now, but if you—" My pitiful pacification attempts died off as the breath was literally crushed right from my chest.

Aros had advanced on Rome, and the both of them seemed to have forgotten that a dweller stood right between them. Someone grabbed my shirt, wrenching me free and ripping the material in the process. That someone had been Yael. He shook his head at me, put a finger to my lips, and started dragging me away. Siret and Coen were busy trying to wrench Aros and Rome apart.

When we were clear of the others, I expected Yael to stop walking. Maybe to give me a lecture, too. But his pace only increased.

"Where are we going?" I asked, my breath surprisingly steady as I tried to keep up. *Huh*, that was weird.

"That wasn't normal," Yael muttered thoughtfully, causing me to look up at him in surprise. "Rome and Aros," he clarified, reading the question in my eyes. "They don't normally fight like that. Or ... well, ever, really. Something is going on. That looked like *chaos* at work. Rau is still messing with you. I need to know why."

Good news, then.

He chuckled, some of the tension easing from his stunning face. "Don't worry, Willa. I won't let anything happen to you. We liked you before, because you're so abnormal it's actually somehow funny ... but now? After seeing you take on Coen like that? Well yeah, now we're keeping you. It's final."

Warmth bubbled inside my chest, happiness almost exploding out of my body, but I quickly smothered it. "I'm not a toy." I figured he needed reminding. "You can't just keep me to play with whenever you want."

"We can if you don't run away."

Why the hell would I run away?

"Exactly, Willa-toy."

"Now you're just being mean," I accused, a frown on my face.

He grinned, casting a sideways look at me. "I'd make it up to you, but I don't want to start fighting with my brothers just yet. Maybe later."

What a dick.

"Now you're just being mean." He laughed.

FOURTEEN

Yael led me back into the main part of Blesswood and up to the dining area. It was time for breakfast and I realised that I was starving. Fighting a sol and being knocked unconscious does that to a girl. As we walked the long hall toward the double doors, I turned my head to look back a few times. No other Abcurses were in sight.

"Rome and Aros ... are they okay?" I asked. "They're not going to actually beat each other up, right?"

Somehow, I thought Yael would know. I was relieved that he didn't seem to be concerned, but it was hard to read him; it always had been. He kept his emotions tightly bound, unless of course he was being competitive and losing or something.

"They'll be fine, they just needed a little distance from you."

I snorted. "Nice. That's just what every girl likes to hear."

Yael slowed his walk and faced me fully, his eyes glinting in the well-lit hall. "You're coming into a group of gifted beings, Willa, not your average friendship. One girl and five men? You're going to have to get used to that dynamic causing some problems. Especially while we're all riding the wave of whatever curse Rau hit you with."

Five! Holy crap. He was right, that was a hell of a lot of guys to have in my life, and yet, I almost couldn't imagine them not being there. Like they had always been a part of me and the sun-cycles before were nothing more than a dream.

"If my soul is split five ways, how come I only have to be with one of you and not all of you?" I had thought this earlier, but there never seemed to be enough time to voice every question that crossed my mind.

Yael's face went blank, very carefully blank. I knew then that he had an idea of why that was, but he wasn't going to tell me about it. Instead, he turned and pushed back the double doors to the dining hall. Up until now, we hadn't seen that many other Blesswood students. Most of them had long-ago left the Sacred Sand arena. Of course, they had left the arena to come to the dining hall. A hall I was now standing in the doorway of with a thousand glares shooting in my direction.

Yael strolled in like he didn't have a care in the world, heading for their usual table, which was always empty and waiting for them. "Come on, Willa-toy, it's time for us to eat. I'm starving."

I backed up and out of the room. No way in hell was I walking in there. Even though Yael was hard-core as all hell, he could not take on a thousand sols if they decided to tear me limb from limb. I liked my limbs right where they were.

The double doors closed in front of my face and the pace of my breathing began to speed up: in and out, in and out; the air shuddering past my lips. I couldn't do this. The gods were going to mess everything up and there was a high possibility that someone was going to get hurt. What if it wasn't just me? What if Emmy or one of the Abcurses were caught in the crossfire?

The ache in my chest was present again. Yael wasn't close enough to me now and my stupid broken soul was letting me know. Plus, I was still backing up. Fear had my feet moving before the reasonable side of my brain could catch up. Of course, there was one problem ... backing up meant that I wasn't looking where I was going. Thin, graceful arms wrapped around my middle and before I could call for help, a ball of material was shoved in my mouth and a heavy cloth dropped over my eyes. Darkness shrouded most of my senses as I fought against whoever held me.

They were far too strong for my struggling, and

more than one set of hands grabbed me as they moved away. I heard shouts, more than a few actually, but a stern and familiar voice shut them down quickly.

Elowin.

Holy crap. The dweller-relations committee had just kidnapped me. No need to worry about the rest of Blesswood. This was the moment I was turned into bullsen fodder.

Yael! I screamed for him through our mental link. He was the closest, with the best chance of reaching me. My concentration felt a little shaky though, probably because the pain in my chest was threatening to tear me apart. After a few more hurried steps, the fine tendrils of light which had been seeping through the woven material of the bag over my head lessened, and we were now descending. The air was cooler, the light almost non-existent.

I'd stopped struggling a little, hoping that they would ease up on their tight grip. So far, though, Elowin and her hench-dudes were staying diligent. If anything, their grips were getting tighter, which was more discomfort to add to my pain.

"Hurry," Elowin's cold voice echoed around, sounding creepy as hell. From the muted echo of their footsteps, I guessed that they were leading me down into an area of stone. "The distraction will only work for so long before they realise it isn't actually the dweller."

What distraction? I tried to scream out again, but the

gag was wedged in my mouth crazy good, and my chest was also trying to splinter into a million pieces, which made doing anything difficult. Tears ran down my cheeks, soaking into the fabric surrounding my head. I knew that I needed to stop crying before my mouth filled with liquid and I suffocated, but the pain was so intense that my tears continued to fall without any hope of stopping them.

The descent levelled out after a few more steps, and whoever held me let go, flinging me easily across the room. All of the air was knocked out of me when I hit the floor, skidding a few feet across the stones, pain now screaming up my back and sides. It fit in well with the chest pain. They were all friends coming together for a little pain-party. It had been hard enough to breathe through my gag, but the blow to my body had me gasping and wriggling around like a dying dweller. Probably something I was about to become.

Forcing myself to calm, trying my best to ignore the pain, I focused on the simple task of getting air into my lungs. Simple and easy. In and out. Except of course my attackers were still in the room, and they were so not done with me yet.

The bag was ripped off my head, and since I hadn't been expecting it, I ended up smashing my skull into the stone floor with the sudden motion. Stars danced before my eyes and I fought through whatever darkness was trying to claim me. If I blacked out, I was definitely going to end up dead.

Rome! Coen! Abcurses ... come on assholes. Hear me!

The screaming for the sols continued in my head, even though I had already resigned myself to having to get out of this mess without any help. That was the way of Willa Knight. Lone Soldier. Professional Escaper of Death. Once the ringing cleared in my head, I was able to scramble up to my feet and back away from the three sols across from me. When there was a little distance between us, I tore the material from my mouth, licking out with my tongue in an attempt to moisten my lips. They tasted salty, my tears still trailing along my cheeks.

I didn't have to wonder why Elowin was letting me back up, from what I could see, the room was small, circular, and made of thick stone. She stood with her muscle-sols in front of the only entrance: a heavy stone door with metal bars for reinforcement.

She took a minute step closer to me, her face creased in lines of dark fury. "I warned you, dweller. You have meddled in things which should never have been touched. Crossed lines which have already started a wave of trouble that will probably take us entire life-cycles to repair."

I tried to speak but my throat was so dry that nothing more than a squeak emerged. It took me two attempts but finally I managed to say, "What are you going to do with me?"

They hadn't just killed me, which meant that they either wanted something from me or else they wanted to brag *before* killing me. Neither option gave me any great hope of escaping this alive.

"As far as anyone in Blesswood is concerned, you ran away. We have witnesses. Your belongings have been packed up. No one will know the truth. You see ... if we killed you now, the gods would notice. They have an eye on you and for whatever reason have chosen to ... *indulge* this little fantasy world that you've created with the Abcurse sols. A fantasy which is causing more problems than your stupid little brain can even comprehend. The gods don't care about routine life on Minatsol. But I care. I see how important it is, and my entire life is dedicated to making sure that dwellers and sols have a distinct place in this world. Distinct, and purposeful. So you'll stay in this basement. No one knows about this wing of Blesswood, it's long forgotten. We'll feed you for a few dozen sun-cycles, until this all dies down, until the gods forget about you, and then you'll go ... back to your village."

Yeah, right. I could see in those icy eyes that I was never walking from here free. She just wanted to make sure the gods no longer cared about me before she ended my life. She was afraid of hurting her chances of going to Topia.

"Pretty sure the gods won't like you chaining me down here like an animal," I lied.

She laughed. The light and airy sound made my skin crawl. "Don't overthink your importance here, dweller. There is a slight possibility they are monitoring your energy, which would mean they'd know if you died. But they aren't going to be literally watching every move you make. They don't care about you. They care about the Abcurse brothers, which means that as soon I remove you from *them*, I remove you from the attention of the gods."

Yep, Elowin had a touch of the crazy going on. "What about the Abcurses?" There had to be something she feared enough to let me go. "They'll look for me. They're not going to be happy about what you've done."

She waved my concern away. "I'll deal with the brothers. They're in need of a little reminder that they're not yet gods ... that they're still sols and students of this academy, *subject* to the power of those employed by the academy."

I fell silent then. Arguing with crazy got you nowhere—even though she was very wrong about the Abcurse sols. They were as close to gods as one could get on Minatsol, before actual death turned them into full gods. They would destroy Elowin when they got their hands on her, and then they would come for me. I knew it. They would tear this academy to the ground, because I had accidently forced myself into their group, and they protected their own.

Hope ... it was scary to let myself have any, especially when things looked grim, but if I didn't have something to hold on to, I would lose my mind. Or ... *more.* I'd lose it even more.

Elowin, Henchman Number One, and Henchman Number Two stepped back, each of them bestowing one last look on me before the door slammed shut behind them. I ran at it, fast as I could through all the pain my body was currently in, and wrenched the handle. No movement, nothing at all to indicate that there was even a door there. It felt as solid as the stone wall surrounding it. There was no opening for me to look out of, and something told me that screaming would not help. Everything would be deadened by the acoustics of this place.

I slammed my hand against the stone and fought back another sob. "Don't leave me here alone!" My yells echoed around, just as I had predicted. Doing nothing but tormenting me with my current situation.

Turning around, I sank against the wall, my arms wrapping across my ribs as I attempted to keep it together. I was not someone who dealt well with being alone, just my own company, no distractions. I think it was half the reason I was always causing trouble in the village.

The ache in my chest intensified. The Abcurses were moving further away from me. I wondered how much distance it would take before I died, because I could feel that possibility sawing away at my insides. I was beginning to gag, and my vision was becoming blurry, my breath rasping with each dry heave. I was right now teetering on the edge of death. I hadn't told Elowin that her plan had one very real flaw: I was connected to the Abcurses, and I couldn't be separated from them, which meant that they were either going to find me soon, or I was going to die. Both of which would not be good for her.

It didn't take long for my legs to give out beneath me, and I slumped to the stone floor, my head falling into my hands.

"Come on, Soldier," I muttered to myself, the words getting stuck in my throat. "You've been in trouble before. It's no big deal. You can find a way out of this ..."

Except ... no. I really couldn't. The room was completely sealed-up. No windows. No rat-holes. There wasn't even a crack in the wall where the door frame should have been, as though it had been sealed right to the wall with magic. I screamed, slamming my fists against the door again, and then I drew away.

I had to do *something*. The Abcurses should have found me by now. There had to be a reason they were staying away. Someone had to be *keeping* them away.

What if they're in danger? Why can't they hear me?

I paced around the edges of the room, the pain tearing at me a little more with each step, my heart thudding painfully hard. It was working overtime, it seemed. Beating so fast, so heavily, that I couldn't help but feel like I was starting the dying process already. My skin was feverish and my pulse fluttered weakly. It was a familiar feeling, because I had almost died from a sickness that ate away at me from the inside when I was nine life-cycles old.

Back then, it had been caused by a cut on my leg. I'd torn my skin on a piece of metal sticking out of the metalworker's stall, and three sun-cycles later, I could no longer walk. The healer had come to our home and covered my legs and arms in leeches, giving Emmy special brews of tea to keep me sustained, since nothing else would stay in my stomach.

Now ...

Now, it seemed to be caused by another cut. More than one, even. The five slices through my soul that had separated me into pieces. They were slowly becoming infected, slowly poisoning my body, slowly trying to take me from the world of the living.

I *had* to do something.

The door handle kept catching my eye, since it was the only thing in the room that glinted silver, standing out against the bleak, stone backdrop. I moved back to it, slumping against the door, my eyes assessing every angle of it. There was a small mechanism attached to the base of the handle, almost like a tiny pin, popping out. I frowned, picking at it with my nail. It clicked out of place, and the handle moved, just a little bit. I grabbed it triumphantly, yanking it downwards, expecting the door to magically become a door again and swing open.

Instead, the handle snapped off.

"You guys are so freaking funny," I cursed, directing

my eyes heavenward, to the asshole gods who might have been watching ...

But that wasn't possible. Elowin had even admitted that the gods were keeping an eye on me, so why would she hide me within Blesswood? It must have had something to do with the stone room. It must have been under some kind of magical influence—that was already obvious, by the way the door seemed to have disappeared. It would also explain why the Abcurses couldn't find me or hear me calling out to them. This *forgotten* wing of the castle must have been drowning in dangerous enchantments.

Unfortunately for Elowin, I had life-cycles upon life-cycles of half-lectures piled up in my head, all narrated by the voice of my best friend, Emmy The Sol-Lover. They were only half-lectures because I usually worked to tune her out pretty quickly, but half-lectures were enough. They were enough for me to know that physical materials put under the strain of magic for too long were always weakened by that magic.

I looked down at the broken door handle, turning it over, and then I kneeled, taking a moment to close my eyes and concentrate through the worsening agony. After a moment, I refocused, gripping the stem in my hand and scraping the handle part against the stone. It had the effect that scraping something partly metal against rough stone would have. Both showed signs of wear. I scraped harder, wearing the handle down on both sides until it was tapered off at the end, and sharp. It didn't take as long as it normally would have, because both the handle and the stone had already been weakened by the heavy burden of magic. I moved back to the door, inserting the sharp point against the spot where the door should have met the stone, and stabbed.

A jarring *clang* reverberated right up to my shoulder, but I repositioned the handle, and slammed it down again, over and over, until a crack started to appear. When it was large enough, I wedged the battered point of the handle into it and used it as leverage to widen the crack. My hands were getting sore, blisters covering my palms, so I worked on getting the crack to spread all the way to the ground, and then I sat, wedging it in harder so that I could notch my foot against it and kick it toward the wall.

The sound of splintering wood was like music to my ears. I kicked again, my energy renewed, the adrenaline of a possible escape rushing right through me, making it so much easier to ignore the pain. Eventually, I managed to separate the door from its lock entirely, and then I was prying it open.

Take that, bitch-face, I growled internally, not even sure if I was aiming the curse at Elowin, or the door. I slipped through, turned around and flipped the room my middle finger, before sprinting off down the hallway. If anyone else had been stuck in there, I was sure that they never would have found their way out;

the hallways all looked the same, and some of the stairways led to nowhere. The wing wanted to keep people locked up. That much was clear. But the wing couldn't do shit against a soul-splintered dweller, with an in-built tracking device leading right back to her Abcurses.

I mean, not mine. The *Abcurses.*

I spilled out into a main corridor of the academy just as another girl passed by, colliding with me.

"Oh, gods, I'm so sorry—*Willa?*" Emmy screeched, before grabbing my shoulders and shaking me, far too violently for my protesting bones. "Do you have *any idea*—*ugh*, you know what. Never mind. Tell me what happened. I saw Elowin throw a bag over your head and drag you this way like three rotations ago, but then she disappeared and I couldn't follow her. Your ... sols were nowhere I could find so I've just been scouring these hallways ..."

I pushed her hands away and pulled her into a hug. "Thank you," I muttered, pressing my face into her shoulder.

It felt good to hold her. To celebrate the fact that I had battled not only a pain-gifted mega-sol, but also a magical room. A magical damn *room!* Hugging my almost-sister seemed like the best way to celebrate, and she didn't seem to mind. Until she realised that I was crying.

"What did they do to you?" She jerked back,

pressing a palm to my cheek, her murderous eyes flicking over my shoulder.

"Happy tears, that's all," I choked out, mostly lying. Her gaze narrowed, clearly disbelieving, but I started to move past her. "I need to find the Abcurses. This pain is killing me, and I don't mean that in the way I usually mean it, because I'm pretty sure it's *actually* killing me."

I let my body drag me in the right direction, and Emmy trailed behind, occasionally tossing a glare to whomever dared to get in our way.

"Are you skipping some kind of cleaning duty or something right now?" I asked her, concerned. It wasn't that I didn't think she would drop everything if she thought I was in danger, but I didn't want her to jeopardise her future just because I seemed to have a gift for trouble.

"No, I finished everything early, and then I came looking for ... *watch out!*" she suddenly exclaimed, but it was too late.

I smacked into another body and the sounds of silver serving dishes and cutlery clattering against the stone made me wince.

"Willa?" a familiar voice questioned, before hands steadied me.

"Oh, hey, Atti." I crouched down, helping him gather up his stuff ... except that I wasn't really helping, because he wasn't doing *anything*. He was staring at Emmy with the weirdest look on his face.

"Thanks for coming to get me earlier," Emmy said softly, returning his weird look with a weird look of her own.

What the hell? When did that happen?

"Did you get to the arena in time?" he asked, stepping around the fallen crap that I was still trying to gather, and looking down at her, the absolute picture of gentlemanly concern.

Maybe I should just leave all of his stuff and give them a bit of privacy, except ... well, it was kind of hard to look away. Besides, I was right there. Right in front of him. So she *obviously* got to the arena on time. Seriously.

My chest throbbed again, distracting me from Emmy's answer. I dropped the platter I had been holding, glancing at Emmy over Atti's shoulder. Emmy and Atti. *Hah*. Even their names rhymed. That was so lame. And cute. I clearly had mixed feelings about it. Emmy wasn't even looking at me. Her eyes were stuck on his, pink rising in her cheeks. I quickly turned, hurrying down the hall in the direction of the five idiots who had accidently stolen my life-force.

FIFTEEN

I stormed back through the castle like some kind of wild buckhorn, with the huge, cumbersome antlers that topped their deer-like heads. Except that my antlers were my arms, and they kept swinging out and accidentally whacking all kinds of people and things. If I didn't already know it to be impossible, I would have said that my clumsy-curse had suddenly gotten a whole lot worse, but that really was impossible, because it was already about as bad as clumsy-curses got.

After another run-in with a dweller, I found myself covered in *some* kind of sudsy water. I didn't even want to know what they were using that water to clean. I just didn't. I disentangled myself from the ground and the bucket and the girl, taking off at a run again, barely sparing her an apology. It was lucky that night seemed to have fallen, and so all the sacred little sols were tucked up in their sacred little beds.

By the time I crashed into the circular common area that headed their dorm level, my chest was heaving, and the water had evaporated a little bit, leaving my fresh—albeit already ripped from Yael's manhandling—shirt all uncomfortably squishy and soapy. The boys were all standing around the common area, the only sols still out-and-about on their floor. They didn't turn when I clamoured into the room. They were all facing inward. Facing *someone*. I frowned, creeping around to the side, shock slowly dropping through me as the female became visible.

It was me.

Except it sure as *hell* wasn't! Because I was standing right where I was standing, and not over there!

"What are you trying to say?" Rome growled, taking a threatening step toward the pretend-Willa, who was even wearing the same clothes as me, sans soap.

"I have to leave," Fake Willa replied, her voice deeper than I had expected. Almost husky. I supposed I sounded different when I wasn't hearing the words as I spoke them. "I *want* to leave," she added.

"Like hell you're leaving." Coen's scowl was dark, a shadow passing over his face.

Fake Willa swallowed, her hands trembling behind her back as she eased a few steps away from him.

Those idiots! They should have known that the girl wasn't me. When did I tremble? Okay, maybe when one of them touched me for too long, or when Rau turned up ... or those few other times that I had almost died ... but *not the point*. I rarely trembled like a scared child.

And fake Willa was looking a hell of a lot like a scared little girl, with that wild mop of curls surrounding a face that was dominated by the tawny pools of her eyes. I kind of wanted to punch her in the face.

"What the hell did you say to her?" Siret demanded, bearing down on Yael, who immediately decided to do a little bearing-down himself. Okay, now I understood why this was taking them so long to get. Men were stupid. Too much testosterone had fried their brains and they were completely useless to me.

Although, surprisingly, Yael halted the attack, managing to use his mouth instead of his fists. "I didn't say anything. She just ... decided this, all of sudden. We were having dinner, everything was fine—I mean, a few sols tried to start some shit, but I headed them off, and then I took her for a walk, because I knew you guys needed to cool off for a bit. Then she came out with this nonsense ..." he cut a glare to Fake Willa. "I brought her straight here. Straight to you guys."

This was getting weird. Too weird for me to stand back and watch. I marched up, tapping Aros's back. He turned around, his golden eyes passing right over me as though he didn't see me. His eyes narrowed, for a moment, and then he was facing Fake Willa again.

What. The. Hell.

I tried again, and this time he swung around with a scowl, his golden eyes darting all around the room as if he was trying to discern what had just happened. I jumped up and down in front of him, waving my hands. No reaction. I pulled up the hem of my clean-once-upon-a-time shirt, outright flashing him.

Nothing.

He couldn't see me.

How was this possible? What else had Elowin done? *Hold up* ... Emmy and Atti had been able to see me just fine, so had a few other dwellers I'd smashed into when I was running through the halls. *Dwellers could see me!* Maybe that was the key to this, I was only invisible to sols. There was no one else around to test my theory on, but for now it would have to suffice.

"Hey, Rome ... Siret ... Aros ... any of you!" I started shouting their names, but none of them turned to me.

You are all dumbasses! I shouted as loud, mentally, as I could, and there was an immediate reaction.

Yael growled, wrapping his right hand around the back of Fake Willa's neck. "What's with the name calling, dweller?"

Okay, mental link still in place, but it wasn't that much use to me. They just thought it was this imposter speaking. I needed to figure out why I was selectively invisible. *What had that bitch-face done to me?* I also should probably use the mental-link to let the Abcurses know that I was standing right behind them, but I kind of wanted to see what else Fake-Willa had to say for herself. Or myself.

She blinked her big, stupid eyes up at my Abcurses. "Guys, can you all just please back up? I'm feeling a little weirded out right now." She had my teeth grinding as she tried to slip out from the middle of them. Before she could escape, though, Rome let out a grumble. It shook his huge chest, and possibly even the floor that we were standing on.

His hand wrapped around her throat, the other under her arm as he lifted her into the air. The movement was considerably more violent than when Yael had reached for her. Even I was surprised. Rome had never attacked me like that before.

He growled out five low words. "Who. The. Fuck. Are. You."

His brothers started forward, as if to wrest Fake Willa from him, but he turned his head slightly, never taking his eyes from Fakey. "This is not our Willa," he snapped. "Can't you sense the difference? She reeks of Trickery's energy."

Siret laughed. It was a mean, rasping sound. "Not even close to my power, don't ever get confused about that ... but there *is* something there. Goddamn those asshole gods." He closed in on Fake Willa, who was going a bit red in the face. I had a feeling she couldn't actually breathe. "You're good," he sneered. "I'll give you that. I wasn't paying close enough attention, but now that Rome has pointed it out, I can see you didn't quite get Willa right."

Damn right she didn't. Took you idiots long enough.

Five heads spun around, and I knew that they had heard me and this time they knew it wasn't from the girl clutched in Rome's heavy grip. A girl who was now clawing at his arm and gasping for air, both actions that were being largely ignored by the Abcurses.

"Willa?" Aros frowned, his eyes flickering around the room.

Siret stepped over to stand beside the golden sol, his back to Rome and fake Willa. "Where are you, Soldier?" He held one hand out. Aros did the same. Both of them standing there with a hand toward me.

I stepped up to them and placed my hands into their outstretched ones. Siret yanked me into him, his body wrapping around me pretty well considering he couldn't see me at all. Aros made a small sound of annoyance, but didn't fight as my hand was torn from his.

As I sank into Siret, everything inside of me sighed. It was a literal sigh of relief from finally being back with the Abcurses. Closing my eyes, I let myself go limp; it had been a long sun-cycle. Very long. My body was done. Siret supported my weight with ease, and I knew he was gearing to pick me up when Coen stepped out from behind his twin and said in my direction, "What happened to you, dweller?" His flat, heavy words and the look on his face were crazy-scary. It was that death-look again, the one he'd given me in the arena. Only this one was about a million times worse.

Elowin. Kidnapped and locked me down in this magical stone room. I couldn't reach any of you mentally. Managed to break out by smashing the lock on the door. It was weakened by all the spells.

The room virtually rumbled then, and turning from Siret, I realised why. Rome had dropped fake Willa right on her fake ass before slamming his fist against a nearby pillar. The room shook, dust sprinkling down from above.

Heavy footsteps sounded and I spun my head back the other way to see Emmy and Atti sprinting into the room.

"Willa! Stop running off on me!" She was shouting as she skidded to a halt right in front of me. "Swear to the gods every time I turn my back on you, you're disappearing. I *will* chain you down."

Yael was in her face before she could say another word, and even though she didn't step back, wariness still crossed her features.

"What?" she muttered, her eyes flicking across to Atti's for half a click. She might not have even noticed that she did it, but I noticed. I had a feeling Atti didn't think she was *uptight* anymore.

Yael drew her attention with his words. "You can see Willa?"

Emmy turned her gaze back to me. "What is he talking about, Will?"

Wiggling my way free from the absolutely blissful comfort of Siret, I faced my best friend. "I'm apparently invisible to sols. They can't see or hear me. Our mental connection is okay, though, so they know that's a fake Willa there." I pointed to the ground where the imposter was still sprawled.

Granted, she was trying to crawl away, but Rome planted one foot on her back, making sure that she wasn't going to actually get anywhere.

Emmy's face went red, which was always a bad sign. If the red had just been on her cheeks, I wouldn't have worried, but it was everywhere. Her forehead, her chin, her neck, and even the backs of her hands. She was about to explode. Two steps around the Abcurses and she had kicked off Rome's foot and hauled up Fake Willa by the neck of her fake shirt.

"Who the hell are you?" she snarled. "What did they do to Willa? Why is she invisible to sols?"

Fakey started to sob. Not just normal sobbing, but huge, open-mouthed, ugly-crying sobs. *Holy father of the gods.* That was a terrible look for me. I had to remember to never cry like that.

There was even snot. Running down my ... her ... *its* face. *Wipe your damn face you stupid idiot!*

Siret's chuckles washed over me, the effect of his laugh actually calming my anger.

"We should have known straight away that this wasn't you." Aros wasn't even bothering to mask his sarcasm as his eyes travelled over Fakey, right from her snivelling face to her feet.

Yael nodded, his voice surprising me, since he had been mostly quiet since I burst into the room. "Nothing crazy happened the whole time she was with us ... that really should have been our first indication."

Emmy started shaking Fakey then, and I had to reach out and halt my friend before she rattled Fakey's brains too much to get any useful information. "Can you see me, Fake Willa?" I asked. There was no response. No recognition of the fact that I had spoken at all.

"She's a sol," I said to Emmy. "Probably one gifted in illusion, or disguise. Maybe trickery? Siret can do this sort of thing. Is it possible for her to have a gift like his?"

"Oh yeah, a definite possibility," Atti jumped in, his voice sounding from behind our little group. "Those are all pretty rare gifts, but I can still think of two or three who are in Blesswood right now with some variation of Trickery. A few more in the community. I've only heard about them, though, I don't actually know them myself."

Well, great. He'd have to make himself so much more useful if he really thought he was going to get it on with my best friend. I was standing right beside Emmy, close enough to touch fake me, and it was so weird staring into my own face from this angle. I was seeing things that I had never noticed before. A little birth mark right above my right eyebrow, and the weird silvery strands littered throughout my hair. My eyelashes were dark and stuck together from all the dampness, my nose was red from bawling like a baby, and there was colour high in my cheeks. *This is so wrong.*

I focused on the task, trying to ignore our identical faces. "Ask her what Elowin did to me." I nudged Emmy. "Why am I invisible and what the hell was she supposed to be doing? How long was she going to pretend to be me?"

Emmy jumped in immediately, shooting off those questions one after another. Fake Willa's face crumbled. For a moment, it looked like the ugly cry was about to come back, but then she let out a dramatic sigh and all tears evaporated. Actually, the entire frantic expression evaporated, leaving only boredom and impatience. *Whoa. That* was scary. It was almost like she just couldn't play the part any longer.

Her voice was even different when she spoke, more toneless. "I'm actually glad you caught me out. The thought of continuing to pretend to be that stupid dweller for one more click was actually painful."

My fist shot out and I punched her right in the nose. The crunch of cartilage and the spurt of blood was immediate and satisfying. And what did you know, my face was much more attractive when bleeding, rather than crying.

I watched her clutching at her face, trying to stem the flow of blood. I sighed, looking heavenward for a moment. I should probably apologise. It was unfair to surprise-punch people.

"Sorry I hit you. I thought you were going to keep talking, and I panicked."

Of course, she didn't reply, because she couldn't even hear me. The Abcurses, however, were losing it as though they *had* heard me. All five of them were choking on laughter. Well, except for Rome, who only cracked a smile, but that was close enough for him.

"There's our little dweller." Yael grinned, looking satisfied at the fact that I'd punched my own image in the face, which was a little bit weird, but I wasn't going to dwell on it.

Meanwhile, Fake Willa was darting her head around frantically, trying to figure out what had just hit her.

"Answer my damn questions," Emmy said again, drawing her gaze.

She sneered, droplets of red flinging from her face as she shook her head. "You're all going to pay for this. This was supposed to be an easy job! Distract the Abcurses with some simple seduction—clumsy-like, dweller-style—and then when I got the signal, I would cause an argument, act like my heart was breaking and then quietly slip away. It would have seemed as if the stupid dweller ran away."

I'm sorry ... did she just say seduce my sols? My hand moved before I could think about it, and this time, my punch landed on her right cheek, snapping her head to the side.

"Holy hell that was satisfying!" I jumped up and down a little on my feet, totally ready to have another go. I could do it. I could take her. Especially while I was invisible and she couldn't punch me back. Actually, that was probably the only time I could take her.

One of the guys reached out then and hauled me back, fitting my spine to their chest. Somehow, they all knew where I was now, like they were tuned into me. I tilted my head up, looking at them upside-down. It was Aros. Our eyes met and I froze.

You can see me?

He laughed. "Now that we know this is some sort of Trickery, we just look with more than our eyes. Our gifts are multi-functional."

Naturally. Ugh. Annoying, multi-talented sols.

"Why is Willa invisible?" Emmy started in on Fakey again, and this time the imposter didn't hesitate to answer. I think she was afraid that I'd hit her from nowhere again.

"There should be something on her," Fakey snapped, stepping back from everyone and brushing off her clothing as her mirage rippled, transforming right in front of us. "Something which is rendering her invisible to any gifted being. That was the easiest way to ensure that no one of importance saw her kidnapping."

I should have started looking for the device as soon as she mentioned it, but I was too busy staring at her. At Fakey, who had looked like me a moment ago, but now looked completely different. She was standing taller, her body thinner—almost painfully thin, though she managed to make it look graceful, somehow. Her hair was a silky black curtain around her face, her features delicate, but tight, as though she didn't smile very often.

The longer I stared at her, the more 'herself' she seemed to become, until I was taking an involuntary step away from her. Her light-blue eyes skipped right over me, the icy shade of colour making my skin crawl. I was thankful that she wasn't quite as adept as the Abcurses at seeing through my invisibility, because I really didn't want her to become the kick-ass female in the room. I wanted all of my backbone from a moment ago to come flooding back into me, but it seemed to have skipped away as soon as the sol in front of me had manifested.

She was terrifying-looking. There was no other way to describe it.

I finally shook off the weird sensation that her icy eyes had given me, pulling away from Aros and running my hands quickly over my body in an attempt to find that device. I didn't want to just stand there, cowering and invisible. I could at least fake that I was brave and kick-ass. It was better than nothing.

I searched my shirt and my shorts, before bending down to search my shoes. I could feel nothing out of the ordinary on me. Aros pulled me back again, and then his hands were skimming over my shoulders and down my sides. I shivered, trying not to focus too much on how his hands felt. With Aros, every single touch was purposeful. There was an energy behind it, begging me to lean into him, to press my body back into his fingers. Just as his hands reached the curve at the base of my spine, I was yanked away by Yael.

"Come on, Seduction," a deep voice grated, right above my head. "You know this isn't a job for you."

Aros's golden gaze went a little black around the edges as he stared his brother down, but he didn't fight back. "It's the perfect job for me, but I understand what you're saying," was all he said in response, folding his arms over his wide chest. So reasonable was that response that ... *now I was worried I had some fake Abcurse brothers to go along with the Fake Willa.*

Coen must have noticed my expression, or heard my thought. He gave me a lazy smirk. "Rau won't mess with us so easily again." Some of that smirk vanished with his next words. "Especially since we almost lost you right out from under us because we were too busy fighting. We have survived the insane politics of these worlds because we stick together. Chaos knows that. We won't let him win."

Since when did sols care about the particular politics of the gods?

I stared at their faces, waiting for a response to my thoughts. Conveniently, they pretended that they hadn't heard that one. Yael, who had been running his hands along my clothes, stood up and took the length of my hair into his hands. As his touch shifted through the strands, a very small device fell out. It was like a tiny, jewelled bug. I frowned, swooping down to pluck it from the floor. It looked so real. And then it moved.

Emmy squealed and jumped back, but I was able to pretend that I was unfazed, because Emmy's reaction had shocked me out of my own. All that really amounted to was the fact that Emmy reacted to shit quicker than me, but I grinned at her anyway. Like I was superior, because I didn't scream like a girl. As I turned my eyes back to the beetle, Rome stepped forward and swiped it off my palm.

"No!" I quickly followed his massive hand, grabbing at his fingers and prying them open again to rescue the jewel-coloured little thing. "That's mine. You can't crush it."

"It's not *yours*," he corrected, and I could tell that he was trying not to roll his eyes. "It's Elowin's. And she was using it to play with us, so I *will* crush it."

I managed to regain custody of the beetle, and Siret was at my side in an instant, holding his hand out to me. I gave him a narrow-eyed glare, but he only met my suspicion with a smirk that said *trust me.*

Technically, Siret was the least trustworthy Abcurse, but he was usually on my side if it would annoy one of his brothers, so I handed over the beetle and he slipped it into his pocket.

"Isn't it going to suffocate in there?" I asked, as Rome folded his massive arms over his chest and set himself to switching his glare between me and Siret, clearly unimpressed.

"It didn't suffocate in this mess," Siret returned, his hand winding around the wild curls that tumbled over my shoulders, tugging on the strands. It forced me to fall forward a step, and I gripped his shirt to stop myself from smacking into him.

"You guys?" Emmy spoke up, her voice dry—sarcastic almost. "She's walking away."

I turned toward Emmy, who was pointing at Fakey ... *who really was walking away*. She was heading for the door, her shoulders pinned back, her head held up high, her gait almost leisurely. She arched a dark, winged brow at Emmy as she passed, delivering her a look that was full of vile promise. Atti moved behind Emmy, and I thought that he was just trying to get out of Fakey's way, but then I saw his hand on Emmy's shoulder, his fingers clamping down possessively. Protectively.

What in the actual fu—

"Aren't any of you going to stop her?" Emmy pressed, her voice rising to a squeal, her finger pointing again. Jabbing, really.

She seemed terrified now that Fakey had revealed herself. It was the first time she had ever stood up to a sol, and the sol she had chosen was obviously a powerful one.

"We already have," Rome grunted, his eyes *still* glaring at me and Siret. He hadn't even bothered to turn around.

I blinked, having no idea what he was talking about, and watched as Fakey reached the doorway and then stopped, a frown stuck on her face. After a single click, she was on the floor, folding in on herself as though the air around her was trying to crumple her into a ball. Her head *thwacked* back, hitting the stone, and her mouth open wide on a silent scream. I started forward, toward her, but Siret grabbed me back. None of the Abcurses seemed surprised to see Fakey arching against the stone floor, apparently in so much pain that she couldn't even scream. None of them were even paying much attention to her. Except Coen, who was giving her his Glare of Death.

And then it hit me.

Holy shit. "Coen!"

His head snapped around, his eyes slamming into mine. The darkness there was so deep that even though I wasn't actually moving, I had the oddest sensation of falling forward. Fear slammed into me, but it wasn't a fear for myself. It was fear for Fakey, who I didn't even like. Coen slowly turned his eyes from me, as though he had given me that bare moment to speak out against Fakey's torture, but when I hadn't said anything to stop him, he had taken it upon himself to continue. The second time his power hit her, the scream finally escaped her body, grating up through her throat and echoing eerily around the walls. Siret released me, his gaze becoming focussed, and I figured that he was shielding the sound somehow. I had no idea if that was something he could do. When none of the dorm rooms burst open, I assumed that it was.

Come to think of it, we'd been making a hell of a scene for a while now, and not a single person had showed. Siret must have been doing something to hide us the entire time.

Fakey screamed again, drawing my eyes immediately back to her. It didn't look like anybody was going to rush to her rescue.

Which left ... Dammit. It left me.

"Coen." I called his name softly this time, walking over to him, reaching out for his arm.

"*Willa—don't!*" Yael's warning was sharp, but the words were delivered too late.

My skin was already touching Coen's, and the fire of agony flashed right through my body. An arm hooked me from behind, golden fingers wrapping around my wrist and pulling my hand away from Coen. A pathetic sound travelled out of my throat as my legs buckled, flashes of colour racing over my vision and obscuring the faces around me. The pain was burning and wild, ripping me apart with the sharp sting of fire that only seemed to worsen, instead of fading away. The voices around me swelled, the arms cradling me tighter, and then another feeling swept into me. The fire was still there, ripping through my limbs and searing my blood, but it was ... different. Almost ... I almost ... *wanted it.*

My body was confused. It hurt, but it didn't. It burned, but it only burned in all the right places. Hands spun me around, and while I suspected that I kept spinning, that was impossible, because I was anchored against a hard chest and there was a grip at the back of my head, pulling me up. The fire swelled, becoming something *more* as lips pressed against mine, hard and coaxing. I reacted on instinct, because my mind didn't seem to know what was happening. I still couldn't figure out what I was feeling. Whether I was hurting or not. Why I was arching into the hands, why my mouth was parting, my own hands grasping, almost-silent sounds sparking up from somewhere inside me.

Somehow, through the intense meld of pain and pleasure, my mind began to register details. The pain was slowly leaking away, and it was being replaced by other sensations. The burning smell of sugar-plants. The hard feel of muscle beneath my fingers. The taste of something addictive.

Aros.

A rough, rumbling sound seemed to echo from his body, passing through me.

And then he was gone.

Or ...

I was gone.

I tumbled to my knees, blinking around the sudden darkness, my hands finding the floor, words breaking up in my throat before I could get them out into the air.

"W-Willa?" The stuttered question had come from Emmy, which meant that I was still in the same room, and so was she.

"What ... what happened?" I managed to ask, my hand wrapping around my throat, my eyes still trying to adjust to the darkness.

"Nothing out of the ordinary," Siret muttered, somewhere right above me. He sounded strained. "Just an average sun-cycle in the life of a dweller who really wants to get herself killed."

"Where's Aros?" I squeaked.

No answer.

I flung out a hand, my fingers wrapping in material. I started to pull to my feet, but Siret grabbed my arms and set me before him quicker than I would have managed it myself.

"Where's Aros?" I repeated, the concern in my voice carrying.

"He stepped out for a bit." This had come from Siret again.

"Emmy?" I asked the darkness.

"Still here." Her voice was stronger this time. "Thanks for making me watch that, by the way."

"Why the hell is it pitch-black right now?" I grumbled, ignoring her sarcasm.

Just as I said it, the real world flickered back into focus. All of the other Abcurses had disappeared. Only Siret remained.

Fakey was also gone.

SIXTEEN

I was trying not to admit it to myself, but there was a pretty good chance that I'd just done something really bad, and now we were all standing in the aftermath of it. It was hard to come to terms with, though; after all, I *had* been trying to save a girl that definitely wouldn't have tried to save me in return—or to begin with. So that wasn't a 'bad' thing. Aros had used his gift on me to drown out Coen's pain, and that wasn't a 'bad' thing either.

Yet ... something 'bad' seemed to have happened. *That* much was clear. They had all disappeared, and Siret was covering for them.

"We should go," Emmy announced, staring at me, trying to convey some kind of secret message.

Unfortunately, no matter how often she tried to teach me the art of silent conversation, it wasn't something that I was ever going to master. I wasn't even good at normal conversation. I thought she was telling me that *I* should go with *her*, but she flicked her eyes to Siret and then grabbed Atti's arm, quickly striding out of the room.

"I have no idea what kind of secret message you just tried to give me!" I shouted after her, just in case she wasn't already aware.

I saw her head shake as she left, but she didn't turn around.

"Why do I feel like everyone knows something that I don't?" I spun to face Siret, planting my hands on my hips.

"Because that's usually the case?" He arched a brow, not even a little bit intimidated by me.

"Where are the others?"

"Strength went after Karyn, Persuasion saved Seduction from ruining you, and Pain is standing right there." He jerked his chin forward, indicating a spot behind me.

I turned, jumping a little bit when I noticed Coen standing in the corner, half obscured by shadows.

"Who the hell is Karyn? And what do you mean by *ruining* me?" I asked Siret, though I was still looking at Coen. We seemed to be locked into some kind of staring battle.

He had this scarily blank expression on his face, and his eyes were still too dark, too full of pain. Also, he was standing in a shadowy corner and that was suspicious and weird enough in itself.

"The girl who was pretending to be you," Coen answered, probably thinking that I had been asking him the question. "And the level of power we have ... you should know, Willa, it isn't normal. It isn't safe for you. For a dweller. If Seduction had taken complete control of you, it would have destroyed you." His voice was too deep, too low. Like he was hurting in some way.

I walked over to him, almost surprised that Siret didn't hold me back ... but then I stopped. Surely ... surely it didn't have anything to do with the kiss.

Coen didn't *like* me, did he?

Almost as soon as the thought flitted into my brain, I brushed it aside, a derisive laugh fighting to escape through my lips. Yeah right, the super-sol totally had a crush on me. Probably had ever since he almost shot me nonchalantly with a crossbow. *Gods*, I was such an idiot. I was an idiot to even *think* that one of them could have feelings for me that went beyond the obvious enjoyment they got out of watching me do something life-threatening every sun-cycle. They seemed to have accepted me into their group—they even seemed to *want* me in their group, and they definitely seemed to think that they had ownership of me in some way. Like I was *their* dweller-slave to look after. I supposed I kind of was, even without the stupid rules that governed Blesswood and our society as a whole. Even if dwellers and sols had been given even-footing in this world, I still would have belonged to them, because I literally couldn't walk away from them. They were technically keeping me alive.

I moved the rest of the way to Coen, laying my hand on his arm again. I didn't even flinch. It didn't even occur to me that I might get hurt again. He seemed surprised that I hadn't hesitated. He was looking down at me with a furrowed brow, his arm tensing beneath my fingers. Without a word, he swept down, hooked an arm around my legs, and tossed me over his shoulder.

"Oh," I huffed, as the breath got knocked out of me for a moment. "We're back to this, are we, One?"

Siret shook his head, the look on his face bemused, as though he had expected something completely different to happen. He followed behind as Coen strode down the hall, passing by the doors of all the people who had no idea what had just transpired so many feet from where they were sleeping. They stopped at Dorm Number Three. Aros's room.

I couldn't see much from my position as we stepped inside, the door closing behind us. But I could hear Aros and Yael murmuring to each other very quietly. Everything came back into sight as I was dropped to my feet. Coen moved away from me quickly, as if *I* was the one who could cause debilitating pain with nothing more than a graze of skin. I wanted to follow him, with my eyes mostly, because his behaviour was confusing.

Aros springing to his feet distracted me and I lost

sight of Coen as he disappeared somewhere. The seductive sol closed the distance between us and then he was all I could see, and smell, and feel. Why the hell did he smell so sweet? It muddled my mind and made me think crazy stuff. Like the fact that I wanted to feel his lips on mine again. I had to forcibly grip the side of my shirt to stop myself from reaching out for him.

His face was gentler than I'd seen it before, and yet also strained. "Are you okay, Willa?" He wasn't using his gift on me, I knew that—but his words still wrapped around my body, sinking into me. Aros didn't need to actively use his seduction—it was infused into everything he did and said. And now that I had tasted it, it was so much harder to resist.

"Yes, I'm fine. I feel ... fine." It wasn't even a lie. My head was a little fuzzy, my body felt a bit disconnected —which was odd—but otherwise, I felt the same. Like me. A really tired version of me.

My yawn must have taken up half of my face, or more. I couldn't even bring myself to care that my mouth was wide open for everyone to see.

Siret, still standing close by, shook his head. "Half the time you act like we aren't even in the room. What are you, dweller? How do you exist with us so easily?"

What kind of a question was that? I opened my mouth to say something else, but another yawn took over before I could speak. Aros's hand draped across my lower back as he guided me toward his bed. A monstrous, four-posted, silk-draped thing, which took me forever to change the sheets on. Speaking of ...

"Who's been cleaning your room?" Because I sure as heck hadn't been.

Aros's golden head swung around as if he hadn't even noticed. "No idea, just another dweller, I'm sure."

For some reason, that bothered me. *I* was their dweller, and while cleaning was never going to be my thing—and frankly I had zero trust for anyone who thought that cleaning was their thing—except maybe Emmy, she was my exception—but it was still someone stepping on my turf. I made a mental note to find out who had been in the Abcurses rooms. Atti or Emmy would know. Those two super-dwellers knew everything.

I managed to haul myself up into the huge bed, and Aros's hand remained on my back as he gave me a semi-boost. "Get some sleep, Willa. We'll wake you when we find Elowin and those who helped her. She'll never touch you again. You can rest easily, knowing that." He draped a warm, woollen throw over me, and then turned back to his brothers.

I almost asked him to stay, because his words had triggered all the memories of the past sun-cycle. Somehow, until this moment, I had completely forgotten about being kidnapped and impersonated. That was what the Abcurses did to me. They wiped everything else from my mind and made the whole world revolve around them. Although ... now that Aros had brought it back up, I couldn't get the memories out again. The feel of the gag. The suffocation of a bag tied over my head.

I felt a sick sense of satisfaction that the boys were going to deal with her. They could do things which were far beyond me and I knew that if she wasn't stopped, Elowin wouldn't rest until I was wiped from this world.

Good luck to her.

The gods had been trying to wipe me out for eighteen life-cycles and I was still there. I would not be brought down by someone like her.

My mind was crazy with worries, and despite the fatigue plaguing me, I just couldn't shut down long enough to sleep. I was about to give up on the whole sleep thing when a warm body slid into the bed beside me, pressing heavily along my side. Small prickles of pain-energy caressed me.

Coen.

Opening my eyes, I found him on his back, staring up into the ceiling above us.

"Go to sleep, dweller-baby. I'll kill Elowin as soon as we find her." He didn't sound like he was kidding. Each word was low and laced with truth.

"Next time, just say like ... *sleep well*, or something normal," I said. "Not *go to sleep, I'll be murdering someone in no time.* It doesn't sound as comforting as you think it does."

He chuckled, a small spark zapping up my spine in

retribution. It felt nice. *How did he do that?* Pain was supposed to feel bad.

I wanted to keep my eyes open, to stare at him for a bit longer, but the broken part of me relaxed immediately with the contact of an Abcurse, and the slight prick of his energy was almost hypnotising me as it continued to whisper along my body.

Before I knew it, the darkness spread and I lost the last threads of my consciousness. I had no idea how long I slept for, but it was one of those sleeps where you don't move from the same position for many rotations and nothing registers in your subconscious at all. The moment the darkness eased—the moment I would usually have been pulled to wake up—I found myself in the head of an Abcurse. And judging by the view of the other four, it was Siret.

"We have no idea what Willa has become, but there is no doubt ... she's affected by our power."

Aros groaned, his golden head hanging low. "It was instinct; I just reacted. Her pain called to me ... Pain and I have shared our women for so long, I just ... I needed to counter his energy with mine. It's the way we keep the sols alive when we need something to fuc—"

Yael surged out of his chair, a snarl rising to his lips. He looked almost animalistic, but Rome only planted a hand on his shoulder and shoved him back down again. Typically, he didn't stay there. He was back up again in a flash, shoving Rome out of the way and advancing on Aros again. Rome grabbed him just before he got there, and Aros jumped up to face him, holding up his hands, the palms facing outward.

"I wasn't going to ..." he shook his head, grimacing. "I'm trying to explain this, Persuasion!"

Rome shoved Yael back again, biting out a curse, his thick arms folding. "Ever since *she* came, it's been chaos between us." He jabbed his finger, and my—Siret's—head swung toward the bed.

Once again, I found myself staring at my own image. This time it was even more eerie, because the face set against the pillows on Aros's bed was sleeping soundly, almost peacefully. For a moment, they all fell silent, watching me sleep, and then Siret was turning back, his voice low when he spoke again.

"Let him explain, Persuasion."

Yael gave a single, sharp nod, and Rome stepped back, giving him space.

"You all know that we share," Aros muttered, glancing at Coen quickly, who didn't seem to be likely to offer him any kind of assistance. "And you know *why*. Our power isn't like yours. Our power is directly physical. If Pain loses control, the girl dies. If I lose control, she becomes obsessed, and usually ends up killing herself—so in either scenario, she dies. I just *reacted* to Pain's power trying to destroy her, and I used mine to counter it. And then ... she ..." He trailed off, and I could see that Coen's face was darker than ever.

He looked like he wanted to rip something apart, but he still wasn't saying anything.

Siret made a grunting sound that was part-acknowledgement, and part-annoyance. "We know why you and Pain do that shit together, and it's the very reason it can't happen with *her*. She's not even a sol. You both need to balance out your powers with each other for a *sol* to get close ... so how the hell do you think a *dweller* is going to live through it? It's not possible. We're lucky she's alive."

"She touched me," Coen finally snarled. "Seduction didn't *start* it, and I didn't start it either. And I've known you idiots for an eternity; you would have reacted the same way if she'd kissed you like that—"

"No more fucking kissing!" Rome roared, shocking Siret's eyes over to him.

Rome blinked, as though surprised by his own outburst, and the others hissed at him to be quiet. Coen walked over to the bed, checking that I was still asleep, and then they all seemed to settle a little bit, sitting back in their chairs and taking a moment to think.

Eventually, Siret let out a sigh, picking up the conversation again. "So to save future problems, and probably Willa's life, we need to make a binding pact. The deal was only for one life-cycle. One life-cycle at Blesswood and then we would be able to go home. There's no reason why we can't keep her with us, but it can't go any further. I never thought I'd be fighting with my brothers over a dweller ... but there it is. We can't leave her—we're going to have to figure out a way to take her with us when we go home, but the only way she can stay with us is if she isn't tempting us to tear each other apart to get to her. We share her equally. As friends." He broke off, laughing. "Our friend, the dweller."

"If I have to be her friend to keep her around, I'll be her friend," Rome grunted.

Nobody looked surprised, but I was a little bit shocked. I had been under the impression that Rome had started resenting me for the fact that my soul was trespassing on his soul's territory.

"I'm already her friend." Aros rolled his eyes, his expression caught between resignation and annoyance.

"As am I," Coen added.

"I want to keep her around," Yael murmured, glancing toward the bed. "She makes me laugh. I can't tell if she's stupid or brave. I want to figure it out."

"We're in agreement, then." Siret stood, and so did the others, all taking a step toward each other.

"No kissing," Rome declared.

"No sex," Coen corrected, shaking his head.

"No corrupting the little dweller in any way," Aros countered, his brows inching up in challenge.

"All of the above," Yael stated. "No kissing, no sex, and no corruption. Nothing that goes past friendship.

From now on, we treat her like one of us. A sixth brother. A sixth girl-brother—"

"A *sister*?" Coen interrupted, his face creasing up in disgust.

"No." Yael shook his head. "*Fuck* no. A girl-brother."

"That sounds like a sister—"

"*A girl-brother and that's final!*" Yael snapped.

The others looked at him, some of them in frustration, some in amusement. I noted that none of them seemed shocked. Maybe Yael had a habit of demanding that people believe in contradictory things —*what was I saying?* He was *Persuasion*! Of course that was a habit of his.

"Are we in agreement?" Siret wanted to know.

Although more than one expression crossed their faces, not one of them disagreed. In fact, all of them slammed their hands out into the centre of their circle and did some sort of shake. It was fast, I couldn't quite see what was happening, but it was clear that they had all agreed.

Sweet Topian gods, were they for real?

Those five assholes were standing around making *pacts* about not kissing me? About treating me like a ... like a *girl-brother*? It was ... *what the actual freak*?

I would never admit it to them, or myself really, but deep down a part of me was hurt. Okay, so yeah, I *had* just admitted that to myself. I knew I was just a dweller; that fact had been slammed into my head more times than was really necessary. So I knew my place in this world, but the Abcurses didn't generally treat me according to my place in the world. Not really. Now it seemed they were making this decision without even consulting me. Sure, they had apparently done it to save my life, but it was *my* life.

Rome spoke, distracting me momentarily. Although 'spoke' was a bit of an understatement. His words slammed out into the room like stones smashing into a brick wall. "Elowin needs to be destroyed. As soon as the dweller finds us our information, we can take care of her. It has to be fast, our powers are starting to strain. We're going to have to cross over again soon, and this time we know that someone will be waiting for us."

I had no idea what he was talking about with his powers, so I decided to focus on the one thing that I *did* understand. Their pact: it was pissing me off in a way I hadn't expected. I fought against being in Siret's mind. I didn't want to see anymore; I was too mad. I wanted to wake up and kick all of their asses. I was distracted from my struggle, however, when the door slammed open and a small figure burst into the room.

It was Emmy. Coen was at her side in an instant, and even her unflappable confidence faded under his glare. "Did you figure out where she is?" he asked, his voice a rumble of menace.

She nodded quickly. "Yes, Atti gained entrance to her office. He found her address in Soldel. She apparently put in for some time off and is no longer in Blesswood."

Coen turned his back on her, dismissing her in one motion. "We need to find her now, and her companions."

Sounded like Fake Willa was still on the run too. All of them skipped out of Blesswood; they already had this little escape planned. I was afraid they were going to bail then, leaving me behind, but thankfully they hadn't forgotten about our connection. I was sucked from Siret's mind the moment Aros put his hands on me.

I shot up in the bed, my heart pounding as I tried to bring my mind back to itself. It was so disorienting being in someone else's mind, even just for a little while.

"You're fine, Willa ..." The seductive sol started to say, but before he could finish, I had already lunged from the bed, prepared to storm out of the room.

A plan which went badly astray as my legs tangled in the bed sheets and I took a head-first dive into the floor. Or I would have, at least, if Yael hadn't been there to scoop me up. I wiggled against him, wanting to stay mad, but as always ... I just couldn't. My stupid, co-dependant soul just wanted me to like them. That was my story and I was not budging from it.

"You okay, Willa-toy?" Yael's moss-green eyes missed nothing as he let me stand on my own feet. "You're looking flustered, even for you."

Breathing in and out, wanting to scream and yell, I decided there was no point. They had made their choices, and to some degree, I understood them. I didn't like that they had decided without me, but I understood that it wasn't exactly a conversation that we all needed to have together. And the conversation itself made sense, even it if *was* hurtful. We couldn't actually get involved romantically. It was impossible because there wasn't a single one of them that I preferred over the others, which would mean that ... well, it would mean that I would be getting involved with *all* of them. It was taboo enough for a dweller to get involved with a sol in Minatsol in the first place, let alone *five* of them.

So instead, I just pointed to the front door. "Need to use the bathroom."

It was the only thing I could think of to get a moment awake to deal with what had happened. In Siret's head, I had been mainly angry, but now that I'd had a moment to think things through a little more calmly, I found that I was a mix of emotions. None of which I wanted the Abcurses to know about. Thank the gods Emmy was still in the room. She stood near the door and when I got close, she linked her arm through mine.

"She'll be fine with me," she declared over her shoulder to the five sols, all of whom were closing in on us. She looked a little bit confused.

Coen shook his head just once, and I knew that there was going to be a fight.

"We can protect her, dweller." He had that look again. The murder one. "She needs us."

I was one click away from rushing outside and slamming the door in their faces, but even though he'd declared it in that way, he was still right. I couldn't separate myself from them.

"I can pee alone, guys. You can wait right outside."

Coen kicked the door open and stepped out. "Come on," he said bluntly, striding down the hall in the direction of the bathing chamber.

Emmy and I hurried after him, my best friend whispering to me as we went. "We aren't allowed to use their bathing chambers, Willa. We'll get in trouble; they'll send us back to our village."

I snorted, and she shook her head, realising what she'd been saying. "Right, no one is taking you from the Abcurses." Her voice got even lower. "They're a little scary, Will. Are you sure—"

Her words were cut off by Coen swinging to the right and opening the door to the bathing chamber. He disappeared inside and by the time we reached the entrance, he was striding back out. "All clear. I'll be right here." He glanced down at me, a frown on his face. "Shout out if you need help. Don't be a hero, dweller-baby."

I narrowed my eyes until they were surely no more

than slits and tried my best to mentally shout every ounce of my annoyance at him. He shocked the hell out of me by slightly tipping his head back and laughing: a deep rocking laughter that sent shock waves of a strong emotion through me. He was beautiful. Perfect. Just like his brothers. And they didn't want me. A lot of my anger fled then, because I was used to accepting this sort of disappointment. It wasn't their fault; they had done far more for me than anyone else ever had. I should have known and I should have seen it coming. I needed to be okay with it. I *was* okay with it.

I forced a smile across my face. It was almost a real one. "I'll be right out, One, you don't have to worry about me."

There was not a trace of laughter on his face when he said in a low voice, "If only it were that simple." He straightened to his full height of 'giant' and gestured to the time-piece around his neck. "You have three clicks before I come in there after you."

"I might be peeing," I said in pretend-horror.

Coen nudged me into the room. "I'll take my chances. Three clicks."

I knew he wouldn't let us keep the door closed, but luckily there was a second door past the sinks which meant that I wasn't actually being watched in the bathroom. Emmy went into the stall next to mine, and both of us had a whispered conversation while we peed.

"Tell me everything that happened while I slept," I said quickly. "The boys got you to spy for them?"

Her reply came back without hesitation. "How did you ... never mind. Yeah, they weren't really taking no for an answer and they seemed to be dealing with something else. It was pretty easy for Atti to get access to her room. He cleans for the dweller-committee."

She paused for a brief moment, and I could sense her building up to asking me something big. Finally, she whispered, her voice really muffled on the other side of the wall. "You're going to leave Blesswood again. Will you come back again this time?"

My heart ached a little at the sadness seeping from her. Our lives were being wrenched apart and there was nothing much that could be done to change that. "I'll always come back for you, Emmy. You're my sister."

Normally this would be the point where we hugged, but being separated by a wall, we just finished up our business before busting out of the stalls. Emmy's eyes were slightly red-rimmed and misty, but she cleared her throat and changed the subject as we washed our hands. "So, do you like Aros? I mean ... you *did* kiss him. I don't think the others are going to let you choose, though. They seem to like the dynamic they have going on, and sols aren't allowed to get involved with dwellers, so an illegal lover would really mess up that dynamic."

I flinched, the memory of their little pact coming

back to me as pain once again slammed into my chest. It felt a little like when our mental link was stretched too thin and my heart was shredding through my ribs.

"Will ..." Emmy knew me too well; she could read the sadness. "What happened? What did they do to you?"

I had to tell someone, so I spared a quick glance toward the door. I hadn't even realised that Coen had closed it until then. I leaned in close and whispered, "They made a pact. A pact to not ... want me."

They didn't want me.

In hurried words, I told her everything I'd heard during my time in Siret's head. My best friend listened closely, one hip notched against the sink, her expression remaining calm. I knew our time before someone barged in on us was running out, so I did my best to stay on point.

When I finished up, her calm expression had morphed into something else. It was a look Emmy wore a lot: one I had seen a million times growing up. The one which said she knew something that everyone else didn't. Since Emmy was a genius, it had happened far too often over the past dozen life-cycles.

When she didn't speak, I growled at her. "What? Just tell me!"

She straightened, taking both of my hands into hers. "Will, you have this terrible habit of thinking and expecting the worst from everyone. Like you push them away before they can do it to you. I mean ... how many friends have you had over the last eighteen life-cycles? Besides me. And I think the only reason you never kicked me out of your life was that I literally had nowhere else to go and you eventually had to get used to me."

"That's not true," I burst out. "I love you."

Emmy chuckled. "You love me now, but don't you remember when my mum first died and I moved in with you? You shoved rocks under my side of the bed on the floor for weeks. Not to mention that sleeper incident."

She was still smiling and I couldn't help but return it. "Yeah, okay, I was pretty sure that the moment you moved in my mum was going to realise what a terrible, clumsy child I was and that it would be much nicer just to have you as a daughter."

Emmy surprised me by pulling me into a hard hug. "I knew, and I understood. I was determined to break through that wall you kept around yourself, and it took me forever, but once I did." Her eyes were definitely misty now. "When you let me in, Willa ... it was beautiful. You're the best friend I could ever imagine having and my life is so much richer with you in it. Before you, there was no laughter in my life. There was no *goodness*."

Now I was the one with a thick throat and misty eyes. I swallowed a few times before I managed to speak. "You were ... I thought you were going to steal my family from me. But instead you became the only true family I've ever had. And as much as I've enjoyed our heartfelt moment, I would be a liar if I said I understood what the point of this last conversation has been."

She threw back her head and laughed, the tinkling sound filling the bathroom. "Will, please ... Never change."

Yeah, that was never going to happen. I had tried. Most of my teachers had tried. It was impossible. I was stuck with my personality, with every negative thing the gods had cursed me with, and none of it was going anywhere. I was going to have to be *me* for the rest of my life.

"And my point was," Emmy interrupted my mostly-useless train-of-thought. "You act like the Abcurses are so far above you. That you could offer them nothing and therefore you're not surprised that they don't want you. Any one of them would be lucky to be with someone like you, Will, and whatever pact they made, I don't think it was about you not being good enough. There's something bigger going on here, something about them we don't know."

Before I could push her further or ask about this mystery she thought the Abcurses were hiding, a banging on the outside door had us both jumping.

"Come on, dweller!" Coen shouted. "It's time to go."

Emmy stopped me before I could leave, whispering in my ear. "They don't look at you like you're nothing. They're going out now to take on

Elowin because she hurt you. They care ... maybe try to let them in."

I closed my eyes briefly, fighting down the emotions, before I opened them again and smiled sadly. "The problem is, I already have let them in."

They were more *in* than anyone else had ever been. Even Emmy. They all literally held a piece of my soul in their hands, and it scared me on a primal level that I had never experienced before.

SEVENTEEN

Apparently, we hadn't moved from the bathroom fast enough because the door slammed opened and Coen was suddenly filling the space. His eyes were extra bright as they bore into me, before his gaze dropped slowly to run over me.

"Are you okay, dweller-baby?"

Those low, gravelly words grazed across my skin, igniting it as though my whole body was straining in anticipation of the pleasure-pain that his touch could bring. Emmy nudged me in the back, and when I glimpsed her from my peripherals, she was grinning like a crazy person. I turned to glare at her more fully and she mouthed *told you* before turning to make her way from the room.

Coen moved aside to let her free, and then there was more than just his giant form filling the area. Siret,

Yael, Rome, and Aros pushed inside, each of them taking a moment to inspect me for injury.

I decided right then to not worry so much about their pact. For now, this worked for us, whatever this was, and I wasn't going to ruin it by thinking too hard about it. They were my kindred souls. The rebels. The rule-breakers. The guys who gave the middle finger to the gods, the same way I had, my whole life. They were the friends I had been born to find, and I wasn't going to let my annoying feelings push them away.

"So," I said, smiling at the Abcurses.

Eyes narrowed, brows furrowed, and suspicion crept into their features.

I let out a huff. "What? It's not like I never smile. I was hoping one of you could fill me in on the plan."

Yael shook his head, before reaching forward and dropping a stack of clothes at my feet. "We'll explain on the way. Put some proper clothes on. This isn't the time for your usual penchant for nudity and those clothes look off, like you tried to mop the floor in them."

That would have been the bucket of dirty soap water that had been poured all over me—*wait, say what now?*

I so did not have a penchant for nudity.

It just happened to me. The rest of the asshole-brothers were grinning at Yael. *She so does have a penchant for nudity*, the looks seemed to say.

How dare they unwittingly counter my thoughts!

I was so riled, I whipped my shirt up over my head and tossed it across the room without any hesitation whatsoever. My bra was next as I flicked it free, shorts and underwear following soon after. Well, kind of. I got them to my ankles and then as I tried to kick them free, I tripped over backwards, clipping the edge of one of the sinks and landing flat on my face. My shriek would have been loud and piercing, if it hadn't been muffled by the shirt I'd landed on. The one I'd just flung off my body. Like a stubborn idiot with a penchant for nudity.

I really need to think things through more often.

There was a beat of dead silence, before one of them groaned. Aros's words were far less smooth than usual. "I'm out, guys."

The sound of steps and then a door shutting followed. I knew I should roll over and get back to my feet, but now that I'd managed to make a fool of myself for the hundredth time in front of them, I really didn't want to move. My ass was showing, but nothing else. Which seemed like something I could deal with.

Something warm draped over my body, and I lifted my head to find Siret crouched right beside me. "I thank the gods every single sun-cycle that you tripped into our lives, Soldier." His smile was so bright, like he was on the verge of laughing. "But you really need to get dressed now, otherwise Chaos might get his wish." He stood and was almost out of the room when he turned back and said, "Move that perfect ass. You have one click or I'll be back to dress you myself."

He was gone then, and the room felt so empty without them in it. I pulled myself up from the bathroom floor, praying to the gods—except Rau, that asshole was getting no prayer from me—that the floor in there was cleaned by a super-dweller like Emmy or Atti, and not a lazy, face-planting dweller like me.

Stumbling across to the pile of clothing left by the Abcurses, I found clean sets of everything I usually wore. Underwear, dark fitted pants, and a simple black shirt. My boots were sitting a little further away; I pulled them on when I was dressed.

I pushed the door open to find the Abcurses lined up and ready to get out of there. I caught Coen's eye, since he was standing closer than the others. His gaze dropped from my face for a moment, settling on my chest and then flicking lower, before he quickly pulled his head up and stormed off down the hall. He really needed to stop looking at me like that. I was kind of regretting the nudity now, because my legs were a little too weak. It wasn't good to have weak legs right before a kick-ass mission. Not that I had any experience with kick-ass missions. But ... I assumed.

"Let's do this," I announced, filled-to-the-brim with a confidence that didn't really make sense, since I had no idea what we were actually *doing*.

I knew that we were going to hunt down Elowin, and that she was going to wish she'd never messed with me on account of the five badass sols apparently hell-bent on defending any threat to their pack—a pack that I was now a part of. But that was where my knowledge reached a bit of a hurdle, because I didn't know how we were going to get our revenge, and I didn't even know if it would be possible. The boys weren't normal, but they weren't *gods*, and Elowin was older than them. Older—with more experience, and enough of a brain to get herself out of Blesswood. Just in case.

Maybe she was trying to draw them out. Maybe they also presented a threat to her *natural order* of things. Maybe she was pissed at them for dragging me out of my place and standing me above the dwellers; for excusing me from the duties that she had given me, and refusing to accept the repercussions of their actions.

Maybe ... *shit, maybe this was* her *revenge-plan.*

"Her who?" Yael asked, as the others spun around and strode off. He must have been assigned Willa-duty.

"Elowin," I said, hurrying to catch up with the others. "What if this was her plan all along? To draw you guys out of Blesswood—to get revenge on you for upsetting the hierarchy here at the academy?"

"What, and ambush us with a couple of sols?" Rome shot over his shoulder, flashing me a rare grin. He clearly found the concept amusing, so I shut up about it.

"Could you guys maybe stop hearing my thoughts?" I asked, only just realising that Yael had questioned something that I'd said to myself. "It's bad enough that you've all seen me naked, and that you're keeping the poor pieces of my soul prisoner—do you really need to butt into my private conversations too?"

"Firstly, it's your own fault for talking to yourself so much," Siret countered as we hurried through the abandoned hallways. "Normal people aren't constantly speaking to themselves like they're actually expecting an answer. Not that you should change it. It's damn entertaining."

I scoffed, choosing to ignore him. The anxiety was beginning to claw into me as the streaks of dawn sunlight began to flicker through the windows. I had felt some safety in the darkness, but now I was afraid that the world was waking up. Or, more specifically, that the *gods* were waking up.

"And secondly," Aros added, glancing over his shoulder at me before following Rome up the staircase ahead, jumping four steps at a time without even a puff in his breath, "we aren't keeping your poor soul prisoner. It's keeping *us* prisoner."

Yael fit his hands around my waist, pulling me off my feet as he jumped up the stairs after Aros, setting me down again at the top. Coen and Rome were pulling ahead again, since I was holding the other three up, but they paused at the archway leading outside, waiting for us to catch up to them.

"And thirdly," Yael pushed low on my spine, encouraging me to move faster, "it's not like we tied you down and ripped all your clothes off. You chose to be naked. It's your thing. You have something against clothes."

"I do not!" I countered, falling to a stop and holding up my hand to catch onto Coen's shirt so that he wouldn't immediately go bounding off again like the most annoyingly agile giant in all of Minatsol. "And you might as *well* have tied me down and ripped my clothes off! You should have stopped me. I'm not the responsible, intelligent super-sol around here. I make bad decisions. I'm a dweller. We have flawed minds like that."

"What the hell are you four talking about?" Coen groused, gripping my wrist and untangling his shirt from my fingers.

"Can't remember," Siret said, completely deadpan. "My mind is stuck on that last visual."

"Pact," Rome grunted, flinging out an arm and punching Siret right in the stomach.

Pact, I thought derisively. Now I was angry again, because they'd reminded me of the stupid thing, and because they were talking about it right in front of me, even though I wasn't supposed to know a thing about it. It made me wonder how many other things they spoke about right in front of me, assuming that I was too dumb to understand. Which ... actually would have been pretty accurate, because I hadn't picked up on any other hidden meanings yet. I realised that they were all staring at me, then, and I squared my shoulders, yanking my wrist out of Coen's grasp and striding right past him. He grabbed the back of my shirt as I swung my leg out, ready to take another defiant step, and I glanced down ... at the staircase. A staircase I definitely would have tripped down, because I hadn't noticed that there was yet *another* one right there in front of me.

"Why the hell is there a staircase going down?" I muttered, like it was the staircase's fault that I'd almost fallen down it. "We just climbed *up*, and now, immediately, we're going down again? This academy makes no sense. This is a stupid academy. You'd think with how blessed it is and how all the best and most sacred sols come here, and what with the gods visiting and everything—"

"Can I kiss her just to shut her up?" Rome grumbled, brushing past me.

Nobody answered him, which was good, because I would have been forced to punch them in the face to defend my honour—if honour was a thing that I had. I would have punched Rome for saying it in the first place, but I didn't want a broken hand. It was bad luck to break your hand before a kick-ass mission. See? I was learning so much already.

"Come on, Rocks," Yael re-captured the wrist that I had freed from Coen, his tone sombre, as though he had taken Rome's question as a threat of some kind.

Evidently still on Willa-duty, Yael pulled me down the stairs and we were running again—except faster, this time. Rome led us to a small, cobbled pathway which wound a crooked path along the side of the academy, eventually leading us to the very front. To the courtyard where I had first encountered Coen and Siret. The memory seemed ... odd. I couldn't quite piece together the version of me who had dropped to the ground a mere click before a bolt would have pierced her chest with the version of me that was now running alongside the five arrogant sols who had become, somehow, the most important people in the world to me.

Not that Emmy wasn't important. Emmy was *family*. But those Abcurses? They were ... they were the missing piece. It was like coming home. I wouldn't call them family, the way Emmy was family, but I belonged with them, and they belonged with me. It was that simple. We were six shades of weird, all stitched into the same cloth, and without even one of us, the whole thing would unravel.

But ... I still had to file away a reminder in the back of my mind that it ended there, as per *their* preference. We weren't ever going to be anything more. Not that it would even be possible. Not with one of me and five of them. And I was thinking about this again ... *why*?

We passed through the courtyard and started down the long line of steps that led back down to the water. I almost expected the giant, floating platform to come and take us away, but instead, Coen turned off to the side, following a wooden boardwalk that edged the water.

"We're not taking the platform?" I called out.

Siret, a few steps in front of me, snorted. "The barge? No. They save that for dwellers and bullsen."

Wow. Ouch.

"Wait, how are we getting across the water, then?"

"Train," Aros answered, pointing in front of us, his arm raised almost to the line of the horizon.

I glanced up, taking in the tall, thin bridge that stepped all the way over the water, and then seemed to go on and on ... even over the land. I had no idea what a train was, but if *that* was a train, then I would have actually preferred the bullsen barge. I could see gaps in the steel, like it had no proper space to walk across the bridge, only steel rods and steel bars and steel bolts. The gaps were massive, almost too big to jump over. I had always thought the sols were a little too obsessed with showing off their bravery for the gods, but this was something else entirely.

"That can't be safe," I muttered, just loud enough that the Abcurses *might* hear me. I didn't want to be the wimpy one of the group, but I felt it needed to be said.

"Just you wait," Aros promised, his lips curling into a smile that immediately sent my mind spinning.

He's talking about the train, I had to remind myself.

His golden eyes momentarily darkened, since he had clearly heard that last thought, and I coloured, quickly turning my head away and pretending the moment never happened. The others didn't react, so it was relatively easy. As we walked along the boardwalk,

I worked on trying to muffle my inner dialogue. It had proven impossible to stop the thoughts before they formed, so I needed a new technique.

Five, four, three, two, one. I visualised the numbers, counting them out over and over again. It was something that Emmy used to make me do when I woke up from a nightmare. She'd say, 'Count backwards from five, Will, and take a deep breath with each number. By the time you get to one, everything will be okay.'

Five, four, three, two, one.

Five, four, three, two, one.

Five, four, three, two—

The sol in front of me had stopped walking, and I smacked into him, bouncing backwards. I didn't go far, though, because Yael had been walking right behind me. I blinked my eyes up, rubbing my face. Rome turned around, staring down at me. The others had stopped, and were similarly staring.

"What?" I demanded, looking back down at myself. I was still clothed.

"You were calling out to us," Aros supplied.

I waved a hand in the air. "Just counting. Proceed."

They didn't proceed. Probably because I was ordering them to and they'd never taken orders from a dweller before. *Whatever.* I started walking on my own, heading toward the big, steel train. Someone fell into step beside me. I didn't glance over, but then the back of my shirt pulled tight across my chest, and my forward motion halted. Four of the Abcurses passed me, which left one behind me, holding me back.

"Five," I grumbled.

Siret chuckled, releasing my shirt, and we started walking again—this time at the back of the group. "It's not that we don't like watching you walk in front of us, Soldier—especially now that we can visualise you without clothing ... but you have no idea where you're going."

I was about to open my mouth and declare that there was only one possible direction to walk in, when Coen suddenly changed direction, splitting from the main boardwalk and beginning to climb a steep set of stairs that seemed to lead to the steel train. I shut my mouth, then, and followed. Halfway up, I started panting, which was actually pretty surprising since I'd tackled almost five flights of the rickety wooden stairs that stepped up the side of the mountain.

The higher we climbed, the faster I fatigued. "Is the air harder to breathe up here?" I huffed out, not caring who answered.

"Yes," was the reply shot back from what sounded like all five of them.

Well, okay then.

Finally, I could see the end of the staircase approaching; I dragged myself up the last few steps on hands and knees, collapsing onto the platform. My face felt hot and flushed, my breathing was ragged, and my hair was falling in messy curls around my bent head. This was it: the place where I finally met my end. Luckily, I seemed to have a penchant for nudity, because I was about to become a Jeffrey.

Heavy black boots stepped into my line-of-sight and I was picked up and placed on my feet by Rome. "You're not going to die; just give your body a few clicks to adjust to the altitude."

My wheezing did seem to be improving slightly, the stabbing pains in my lungs abating. "Why did they ... build this damn thing ... so freaking high, if the air is so bad up here?"

Rome nudged me forward, pushing me toward his brothers who were nearby, standing on some wooden planks beside a huge metal beast. *Holy god monsters.* What the hell was it? Was this the train? Because it looked like a metal monster and I was pretty certain that it was staring at me. I was pretty certain that it wanted to eat me. I was pretty certain—once *again*—that I was about to die.

Rome shocked some of the fear out of me when he answered my previous question. "They built the train platform closer to the gods, Willa. Everyone wants to be closer to the gods."

I still wouldn't take my eyes from the train-monster, but I did manage to murmur back, "Someone should tell those idiots the gods live at the end of a dingy cave."

Siret, who was close enough to hear that, laughed. "That was just the dingy back entrance, the other one is much nicer. Of course, very few will ever get to see that."

I definitely wouldn't, that was for sure. Unless of course they rolled out the welcome wagon for the Jeffreys, lured them in with a false sense of shiny awesomeness, and then once they got them inside it was all about the mind-washing, shaved heads, and degrading, ugly skin-clothes.

"You know they aren't all called Jeffrey, right?" Yael had apparently picked up on pieces of my inner chatter, and was once again amusing himself with what he had heard. "Last time we were there, there was definitely a Bob and a Linda helping out."

"Sandy and Mitchy, too, if I remember correctly," Aros added.

Seriously ... Now this was something that was going to steal my full attention. "How is it that you five know so much about Topia? Like you even know the names of the servers?"

They had far too much knowledge for a bunch of rebels who occasionally broke through the dingy back entrance into Topia.

Yael just shook his head at me, that damn amused smile still on his lips. "We have friends in Topia. We know how to cultivate relationships. All of which will help to keep you safe, Willa-toy."

Blah, blah ... sounded like a whole lot of deflection, which was something that worked very well on me. Deflection and distraction. Which happened then as the train-monster let out a loud whooshing sound, and steam suddenly filled the air above us. And I was back to staring at the beast. It looked like a massive, metal furline—one of those fuzzy, cylindrical-shaped bugs, with way too many creepy little legs. The train-monster had way too many legs too, but they were more like hollow metal wheels, hooking over the metal tracks that ran along the base of the bridge. Its body was hairless, too, the shape long and bulbous, with carts scattered back along the path which led out over the water and into the distance.

"Come on, Soldier." Siret placed his hand on the small of my back, pushing me toward the door which was now open on the second carriage. "Time for a little trip into Soldel."

My breath caught in my throat and I wondered if the air had gotten even thinner all of a sudden. There were three small steps leading up to the door, and I couldn't stop thinking about what I was going to find inside.

"This is not natural." I tried to backtrack, but Siret wouldn't let me move an inch. "Like how does it move? Why is no one driving it like the carts? Why are no bullsen pulling it like the carts? Can't we just take the damn carts?"

Arms wrapped around me and before I got a single answer to my very important questions, I was hauled up and into the dark interior. My shriek was stuck in my throat, but that didn't stop my panicked hands from clawing at whichever sol held me.

"Pain will get you nowhere with me, dweller."

Coen's low, growly voice was enough to have my hands calming. My body calmed too. In fact ... I felt downright calm as he strode with me down the cart, dropping me into one of the chairs which spanned along each side of the carriage. Yael smirked at me as I sat down, indicating that my sudden calmness had much more to do with his sneaky Persuasion than my own adaptability. A huge window stretched along the wall beside me, and I was gifted an absolutely jaw-dropping view of the valley below. And ... *wow*, Blesswood was huge. Despite having been there for a few dozen sun-cycles now, I'd had no idea that it was that size. I certainly had not explored even a small percentage of it. But I had been to Topia, so I was officially the most well-travelled dweller in the world. Unless you counted the Jeffreys.

Warmth settled into the seat beside me, and I turned to find Rome. His huge body was blocking out the sight of his brothers, but somehow I knew they were sitting in the seats in front and behind me. *Thanks, soul stealers.*

I turned back to the view, pressing my hands to the glass. "Is this what the gods see every sun-cycle?" My words were low, husky. For a click, I let myself bathe in the beauty which was right before me.

Rome leaned in closer, his head resting close to

mine as he followed my line of sight. "The gods rarely look beyond their own noses. Sols are the same, always striving to become gods. That's all either of them see. It's always the dwellers who stop and appreciate the beauty. The gifts. Why do you think that is?"

I swivelled in my chair so that I could see him better. Rome pulled back a little, the intensity of his eyes dazzling. "What are you dweller? What makes you see the world the way you do?'

I found myself shaking my head, blinking a few times. "I ... I don't know. I guess when this is the best you can hope for, you appreciate it. Gods have Topia. Sols have the hope of Topia and dwellers ... we just have Minatsol. This is the best for us."

That was such an Emmy answer. She would totally be so proud of me right now. Rome didn't say anything more, but I could tell my words had struck something within him. He seemed thoughtful, his brows furrowed and his eyes searching mine. I jumped as the train let out another loud whooshing noise, and with a jolt we started to move. I settled back into my seat, Rome did the same, and we both kept our heads turned toward the view. The valleys gave way to massive expanses of water, the same water we had crossed in the barges, but this time I got to really see the vastness. It formed a huge circle around Blesswood, the early morning rays of sun highlighted colours across the surface, shifting from the deepest cobalt blue, to the lightest of turquoises.

"I want to learn how to swim." The demand burst out of me before I could think about it.

Yael's head appeared above the seat in front of me. "Is this another excuse for you to take your clothes off?"

I glared, narrowing my eyes as far as I could whilst still being able to see him. "*No!* I will be learning to swim fully clothed. I love clothes. I'm never taking my clothes off again."

Siret's mutters drifted up then; he must have been sitting beside Yael. "That's really disappointing, Soldier."

Crossing my arms, I dismissed them all, and focused on my water. Unlike the Abcurses, I was going to claim that beauty. It was worth claiming.

EIGHTEEN

The train ride was close to the most awesome thing that I had ever done in my life. Sitting just behind my first view of Topia. Topia was more beautiful, but it also had asshole gods and Jeffreys. Neither of which were comfortable to be around. On the train, it was just me and the Abcurses, and a view which drifted from one beauty to the next. The metal beast climbed up the cliff with the multitude of waterfalls, across the plains of Blesswood's territory, and then into the rolling hills of Soldel.

A crowd of sols and dwellers were on the platform when we emerged. Siret, Yael, and Coen went out first, and I was next, followed by Rome and Aros. The sols appeared to be waiting for the train. I supposed that it would continue on to Dvadel and Tridel, after leaving Soldel. The dwellers were there to load bags and to clean the station. I knew this because that's exactly what the few dwellers present were doing.

Of course, there was no time to stop and chat—we had ass-kicking to do and sols to get revenge on. The usual for a sun-cycle with the Abcurses. They moved as a single unit of zero-fucks-given through the crowd. They didn't get out of the way for anyone ... actually they didn't even have to attempt to avoid anyone, since sols and dwellers alike moved for them. They were striding quickly and with purpose—two things that would have tripped me up, if it hadn't been for the fact that I was wedged right in the centre between Aros and Yael, both of whom had a hand on me, half carrying me.

We moved off the train platform, which I now noticed was located right on the side of the Minateurs' training facility: the shiny, extra-perfect building I remembered from my journey with Emmy. We didn't go inside, but passed the wide-open double-doors, and I could see enough to know it's interior was not quite as fancy as some of Blesswood's academy buildings, though it came close. Definitely designed by the same sols. No time to think about that though, we were out in the streets now, walking the same path I had driven in the bullsen cart with Jerath. I hadn't seen that dweller-on-a-power-trip for a while. I wondered where he'd gotten to.

Rome and Siret had taken point now—I knew that

because they told me, and since I had no idea what 'point' was, I just nodded and smiled. *Seriously, was there a damn name for everything people did*? Anyway, apparently 'point people' went in the lead and ran the risk of being taken out by angry Elowins. The Points veered off the path, and we all followed a few steps later. We now walked between small hut-style homes, and interspersed were some of those larger houses with the gates and fences. I still had no idea what they were trying to keep in ... or out. Either way, this was a fancy part of town, even in the already-fancy Soldel.

Siret held up a hand and everyone knew that signal. Everyone except me, that was. When Point People hold up a hand, you stop. I, on the other hand, did *not* stop and ended up crashing right into a pole. *Where the hell did that come from?*

As I rubbed my face, Aros lifted me up and into his arms. "Quiet," he murmured into my ear, before he moved with his brothers backwards, right into the shadow of a huge house. "Minateurs on patrol." The seduction-gifted sol added, before wrapping a hand around my mouth.

Come on, I wasn't going to talk. Probably not anyways.

His chest moved in a silent laugh, his arm wrapping around me a little tighter. I rested against him, allowing the calming nature of his closeness to soothe my rough edges. I seemed to be more rough than smooth right now, and any comfort was good.

I finally picked up the sound of the patrol, a good five clicks after the Abcurses. I was totally built for this world of stealth. I was a little surprised that they were hiding, though. That didn't seem like their style.

Coen answered that question once the five guards were past, and we were moving again. "We don't want Elowin to be warned of our approach," he said, his voice brittle. "She'll run again and I'm not in the mood to track her down."

Yeah, me either. No mood for that.

Siret was back in his position of Point, and from there he cut a straight path to the entrance of a skyreacher.

Holy crap! Emmy was going to lose her mind when she heard about this.

"Don't let it collapse on me," I pleaded, my voice a little high as we walked through the door. Or stalked, more accurately. We were all badass again, stalking and shit. Elowin was going down. I would be the sixth in line to take a shot at her ... no need to go first, Point had already been claimed. We approached a large, polished cage, and I found myself distracted by the dweller who was standing beside it, his hand resting on a huge, wooden pulley. I was staring at him because he was by far the biggest dweller that I had ever seen. He had muscles upon muscles, and height to go with it. I might have even mistaken him for a sol, except that other than his size, he was typically plain-looking. His clothes were dull and modest—and he was staring back at me, I realised.

I glanced down at myself, at the clothes that were far too fancy for a dweller, even though they were simple and dark-toned. The material was still sol-quality, meaning that the boys had robbed some poor girl who was around my height and stature, or else the clothes were another manifestation of Trickery's magic. Which was actually a little weird ... because that meant that he had designed my underwear. Actually, it was weird in either scenario, because the alternative was that I was wearing some other girl's underwear.

Muscle Dweller was still staring at me, his mouth popped open a little bit. It must have been obvious that I was a dweller. It was probably the wild curls that hadn't been brushed in a few sun-cycles, and the way I barely even topped the triplets' shoulders, even though they were shorter than the twins.

"Eyes on the wheel, dweller," Coen snapped to Muscle Dweller, herding us into the cage.

"And eyes on us, Willa," Siret added. He sounded serious, which was a new tone for him.

I gave him a surprised look, but he only met my eye stubbornly. Challenging me to argue with him. Well ... I wasn't going to argue with him before, but he *challenged* me, dammit. I opened my mouth, ready to shoot off some retort, but the cage chose that moment to lurch, and I tumbled sideways into Rome. He looked down at me, planting a hand on my shoulder to keep me steady as the cage began to rise. I tried not to squeal, but some kind of a sound must have escaped me, because one of the crazy sols stuffed into the cage with me laughed.

"She's never been in a cage before," Yael noted, sounding amused.

"I've been in plenty of cages," I returned, huddling into Rome so that I didn't accidentally fall out of the cage—even though I probably wouldn't fit through the bars. "I got stuffed into a cage by my mother that time a visitor came over to *talk* to her in private, and Teacher Fern used to lock me in a cage every time we had physical fitness classes. She wasn't allowed to actually ban me from the class, since attendance was mandatory ... so she just put me in a cage in the middle of the back field, and all the other kids ran laps around me—"

"You're getting off-track again, Rocks," Coen interrupted.

"Right." I shook my head. "Point is, I've just never been in a moving cage, because cages aren't *supposed* to move!"

"It's how you get to the higher rooms." Rome's voice rumbled through his chest, vibrating against my cheek, and I turned my face up a little to look at him.

His hand slipped from my shoulder to the middle

of my back, pressing me closer for a moment, before his gem-like eyes flicked away.

"So what's the plan?" I asked. "Are we going to wait outside her home for her to leave and then ... what?"

"We don't wait. We break in, and then we kill her," Coen informed me stoically.

"What?" I managed, choking over the word. "I thought you were just saying that. Like being dramatic and stuff."

Coen spun as the cage groaned to a stop, his intense eyes glittering down at me. "I'm never *dramatic and stuff*," he said, grabbing the front of my shirt and hauling me out of the cage.

We ended up in a hallway, with several, numbered doors spaced out right to the end. They were like the dorm rooms back at the academy. Coen took the lead, dropping my shirt to grab my hand instead, and we stopped in front of Number 113. He dropped my hand, and I knew that he was moments away from kicking the door down like a crazy, deranged sol, so I quickly raised my fist and knocked. They all turned to stare at me, looking like I'd just stolen their favourite toy and ripped its head off.

"What?" I asked defensively. "Just trying to be polite."

"We're here to kill her," Siret reminded me, his voice a frustrated groan.

"Don't see why we can't kill her politely," I

muttered back. "And ... I mean ... don't really see why we have to kill her at all."

The door swung open then, and Elowin's shocked eyes took us in for a moment, before she tried to slam the door back in our faces. Coen pounced forward, knocking the door fully open and, as a result, knocking Elowin to the ground as well. I hurried in after Coen, the others at my back. I wasn't so excited about the kick-ass mission anymore. I didn't really want to murder anybody, even if they *had* locked me in a magical dungeon with the intention of eventually getting rid of me.

"Guys—" I started, a little hesitantly, scrambling to Elowin's side and trying to help her up.

I never got to finish my request, however, because Elowin seized me, dragging me upright as she stood, and a flash of silver was the only warning I got before there was a dagger at my throat. The five Abcurses froze, staring at the knife. I could have sworn that they even stopped breathing.

Elowin laughed. "That's right. Good boys. You don't want me to kill your little toy now, do you?"

Yael started forward immediately. I guessed it was only okay when he called me a toy, and not anyone else. I tried to suck in as little air as possible, not wanting to push my throat out against the blade, but it didn't seem to be working. Either that, or Elowin was beginning to apply pressure. I winced, feeling the break in my skin, and Yael paused, his chest heaving with the heavy motion of his breathing.

"Nobody fucking move," Aros instructed quietly, as if even the sudden sound of his voice would convince Elowin to cut me deeper.

"Yes, nobody move," Elowin parroted, skipping over the swear word like a complete, knife-wielding snob.

I could feel the dribble of blood that was creeping down my neck, catching on the material of my shirt. Yet another shirt ruined, not that it was important right now. I wondered if Elowin would actually kill me. It didn't seem likely, but the tighter she pressed the knife to my skin, the more the likeliness grew, and the higher the panic clawed up through me.

Until Yael spoke.

"Elowin." It was just the one word, delivered so precisely, so calmly, but it dropped right over my head and knocked me out a little bit.

Suddenly, everything was okay. The panic evaporated, the world slowed down around me, and the pain of the blade against my neck eased.

"Release the dweller," Yael suggested, his tone almost conversational.

I blinked, trying to figure out why the pleasant suggestion sounded *off*. I was suddenly sure that Yael and Elowin were close friends, and that we had all come over for a friendly visit. The insistent thought was pushing into my mind, warring with the fact that she was holding a knife to my throat. That didn't seem like a thing you did on casual visits with your friends. Elowin seemed to come to the same conclusion, because the knife drew further away.

"I'm ... I'm so sorry," she muttered, releasing me.

I stumbled forward a step, and all hell broke loose. Rome grabbed me, lifting me into the air and tossing me to the side. I yelped, sure that I was about to land flat on my face, but hands plucked me from the air easily, catching me against a hard chest. I looked up at Aros, completely disoriented, because it seemed that we were suddenly on the other side of the room, and I couldn't figure out how we had gotten there so quickly. I wiggled and twisted, trying to see the others, and Aros set me on my feet again, though his hands came down on my shoulders, anchoring me back against him so that I couldn't actually go anywhere. I fought off the lingering dizziness in my brain, focusing on the other four Abcurses as they surrounded Elowin in an angry circle.

"Good girl," Yael cooed in approval, even though Elowin had to be about twice his age and the look on his face was more 'I want to crush you into pieces' than 'I approve of your actions'. *Still*, he said it so persuasively, it was difficult to resolve his expression with the words that came out of his mouth. He reached down, taking the knife out of her hand. "Now why don't you tell us why you took our dweller, and tried to mess with us, hmm?"

"She doesn't belong here!" Elowin was back to panicking, even though she hadn't tried to keep her knife. She actually wasn't moving at all, her arms were hanging limply by her sides and she was staring up at Yael with a pleading expression, trying to appeal to him as though he would understand her. "She's just a dweller! You can't change all the rules for her and expect everyone to be fine with it. The rules are there for a reason!"

Yael exchanged a look with the others, and Siret grinned, taking a small step toward Elowin, so that her attention flicked directly to him.

"What's the reason?" he asked, conversationally.

"It is how the gods wish it," she spat back, regaining some of her fire, now that her eyes weren't locked on Yael. "You'll all be punished for going against them."

"It's true," Coen agreed, grabbing Elowin by the shoulders and spinning her around to face him, "the gods *do* like their punishments."

I knew that he was about to kill her. I could see it in his eyes. He had death-eyes again. I really needed to learn to step back and stop defending people who only wanted to hurt me, but I couldn't seem to help myself. I shouted Coen's name in my head, and his attention wavered, his eyes seeking me out in the corner of the room. As soon as he was distracted, Elowin screamed something that sounded like a cry for help, before erupting into flames.

"*Holy crap!*" I screamed unnecessarily, pointing right at her. "*The lady is on fire!*"

The other Abcurses took a step back, but it definitely wasn't a big enough step to avoid getting killed if Elowin decided to give one of them a hug.

"That's her gift, I guess." Aros's hands tightened on my shoulders. "And stop distracting them, you'll end up getting someone hurt."

Elowin lunged for the knife in Yael's hand, but he pulled it out of the way, side-stepping her. There was a laugh in his eyes. Actually, they *all* looked amused.

Seriously?

Did nothing ever frighten them?

The door burst open before Elowin could lunge again, and a group of people spilled inside, along with a billowing rush of red smoke. For some reason, it reminded me of Rau—of the scarlet-red cloak that he had worn on both occasions that he had appeared before me. Aros shoved me behind his back, basically squashing me between him and the wall, and I saw boots move in front of us, turning to face the rest of the room. I couldn't see much else, because of the smoke, but I recognised Rome's massive feet.

Someone screamed—a woman. It didn't exactly sound like Elowin, but it was hard to tell. Things started crashing around, and I could see that Elowin's fire was starting to catch onto things. The flames were licking up the fabric that covered her windows, adding to the smoke that already choked the room.

"I need to get Willa out of here," Aros muttered, as one of the guys grunted, and a body flew into the wall right beside us, collapsing the plaster.

"Rau is blocking the exit," Rome spat back. "Turns out Elowin wasn't smart enough to come up with this plan all on her own."

Rau! AGAIN?

"So we'll knock him the fuck out of the way," Aros countered, grabbing my arm and dragging me across the room.

I tripped over a lank leg—which had been dangling half across the floor, courtesy of the body sticking out of the wall—but Rome caught my other arm, and they carried me between them the rest of the way to the door. I caught sight of the dark-haired sol who had impersonated me back at the academy. She and three other sols were fighting against Coen, who seemed to be playing with them more than actually fighting them. But Fakey was holding a candlestick and it looked like she might actually manage to hit him, so I untangled myself from Aros and Rome, running over to her and yanking the thing out of her hand before she could use it.

She spun, her eyes narrowing, and I knew that she was about to get her revenge for all the times I had punched her. Or ... she would have, if Rome hadn't grabbed me again, dragging me back to the front door. He pushed me through in front of him, and Aros kept an arm outstretched in front of me, like I might attempt to run off and attack Rau all on my own.

Which actually wasn't a bad idea. I mean ... I had a candlestick, and Fakey made it look super easy to use as a weapon. I could totally take Point on this. And, let's not forget that I had stabbed a god before. That practically made me an expert in god-fighting.

Rau manifested before us, standing against the opposite hallway, his oily black hair stuck to his square-shaped skull, his muddy, red-brown eyes trained on me. He looked happy to see me. He even released that horrible, high-pitched laugh that I was starting to think was *actually* the worst sound in the world. It was more like a giggle. The giggle of a maniac.

I dropped the candlestick. I was so retired from god-fighting.

"Hello again, dweller." He pushed back his scarlet cloak, revealing the red robe beneath. He was probably even wearing red underwear. Not that I really needed to picture his underwear.

"What? You're ignoring us now?" Aros drawled, managing to sound offended, even though I knew he wasn't.

Rome slammed the door behind him, closing out the smoke and the fire and the battle within. It made me nervous, because I was almost certain that the boys weren't fireproof. I mean, they were gifted, but they weren't invincible.

TRICKERY

"Your father forbade me from speaking to you," Rau replied, his eyes still focussed on me. "*This* little girl, however. Nobody gives a shit about you, do they? It's beautiful, really. It wasn't what I had planned. I left as soon as the curse hit you, so I didn't realise that you had lived through it. I'm so sorry, little dweller. If I had known that you would survive it, I would have stayed."

"Say what now?" I stuttered, as the door burst open behind us.

Coen and Yael stood there, covered in soot and blood, chests heaving.

"We've got a situation," Coen announced, completely ignoring Rau.

Or ... not completely ignoring Rau, because Rau wasn't standing there anymore. He had disappeared, and the red smoke had disappeared with him. Elowin's home was now utterly silent. Rau had taken away the chaos with him.

"What is it?" Rome asked, looking over Coen's shoulder.

I actually had the better vantage point, because I could peer through the small gap between Coen's and Yael's torsos. It was a gap just barely big enough for me to glimpse Siret, crumpled up on the ground.

"Five!" I pushed Coen out of the way, stumbling back into the room.

The floor was blackened and grimy, and there were bodies strewn everywhere. I only made it a few steps before my feet were flying out from under me, but this time, I was flying forward and none of the guys could catch me in time, so I landed on my face. I crawled the rest of the way to Siret, reaching him by the time the others had already surrounded him.

There were tears streaming down my face, and I didn't even know what was wrong yet. I pushed between two of the big legs standing around Siret, until I was crouched over him.

There was a knife sticking out of his chest, right on the left side.

Some mothereffing effer stabbed him in the heart.

I was caught between an intense wave of fury, and an equally intense pull of terror. Would he survive this? He was a sol! He had to survive this!

"Five?" I grabbed his face, trying to get him to open his eyes. His skin was still warm, but there was so much blood. I could feel it now, warm against my knees, soaking up into my pants. "Please ... please open your eyes ..."

He grimaced, his eyelids flickering, and his hand rose, catching mine. "Calm down, Soldier, I'm going to be fine." He choked as he spoke, and a spot of blood landed right on the side of his mouth.

The terror fighting my rage won, and I started shuddering, my bones veritably knocking together with the thought that I could lose him.

"There's a knife in your chest, you idiot!" I realised that screaming at him probably wasn't going to help the situation, but I couldn't seem to control myself.

He laughed—he actually *laughed*—and someone grabbed me off the floor, raising me up. I fought against them, but Yael stepped in front of me, his hands cupping my face.

"Calm," he muttered, his moss green eyes flinching, as though he didn't like using his power on me.

It swept through me with the force of a gentle breeze, wiping out my emotion and leaving me hollow. The sol holding me—Aros—bundled me tighter into his arms, and I only watched as Coen bent over Siret, blocking his chest from view. Siret groaned in pain, and a moment later, Coen flicked the blood-covered knife aside.

"We need to get him back to Topia," Coen declared, hooking his hand beneath Siret's arms, while Rome picked up his legs.

"You need to get him to a healer," I countered calmly.

It felt strange, seeing this sol bleeding and limp in his brothers' arms. As though I should have been doing something about it. As though it should have been tearing me up inside, or driving me halfway to insane with fear. I could feel the *pings* of emotion, barely sparking up inside me before hitting a barrier and fizzling into nothing.

"He's going to be fine, Willa." Aros spoke while carrying me out of the room, away from the mess that we'd all left inside.

I caught a glimpse of Elowin's face before we made

it clear of the doorway. Her head was bent at an awkward angle, her legs twisted beneath her. It looked almost accidental, as though she had tripped while falling backwards, and hit her head on something.

But maybe I was just fooling myself.

Maybe I was trying to convince myself that all of this had been an accident. Another product of my clumsy curse.

NINETEEN

The trip back to the train was a dizzy dream. My emotions were still frozen, courtesy of Yael. He had to top up the Persuasion every so often, because occasionally the panic would burst through and I would start bawling like a baby. Something which seemed to cause a lot of brow-creasing in the Abcurse brothers.

The train was apparently the quickest way back. We had piled into the empty carriage—there was no one on it, courtesy of Rome, who tossed them out without an ounce of remorse. As it started to move, I remained glued to Siret's side; I might have been numb, but my brain still knew it was bad. Really bad. He was no longer conscious, despite my constant yelling at him to wake up. There wasn't even a flutter of his eyelashes. No glimpse of beautiful, mischievous eyes.

The tears just wouldn't stop flowing. I had been batting them away, but that got tiring so I just let them fall, soaking his already blood-soaked clothing.

"I can't take this any longer." Coen's mutters had my head lifting up from Siret's chest.

The massive sol was up front, where he had been standing guard. He strode down the aisle and with hands far more gentle than I was used to from him, lifted me from his brother and hugged his big body right around me.

"It's going to be okay, dweller-baby. Siret is tougher than you think, and this isn't his first knife in the chest." I pulled myself as hard as I could into him, burying my head into his warmth. His words got a little strangled then. "Please, for the love of my sanity, and the safety of this train's walls, stop crying."

"Stop getting stabbed," I shot back, a flicker of emotion surging through me again.

Coen held me like that for the rest of the journey. I only lifted my head to check on Siret, but otherwise I remained in his comforting embrace.

Finally, the train crossed the water and pulled into the station atop the massive mountain.

Rome carried Siret, moving with ease, and I was set on my feet to walk between Coen and Aros. The golden sol brushed his hands across my face, and as he pulled them away, I realised that not only were my cheeks covered in tears, but they were also streaked with Siret's blood.

There was no time for me to fall apart again, though. It was just a little blood. Or a lot of blood, which was leaking out of one my Abcurses.

They were so mine.

No point in denying it any longer.

I was thankful that Aros kept a tight hand on my shirt, because his grip stopped me from plummeting down at least eight times. Once we hit flat ground, Rome took off at a run, and that was when Yael's persuasion wore off completely. Those assholes! How dare they mute my fear and pain! How dare they lessen my worry about Siret! It was serious ... it had to be. Rome would never run like that unless it was serious.

I took off then too, as fast as my clumsy legs could move. Running was not my thing, I'd said that more than once, but right then I was a freaking athlete. Ignoring the burn, I was actually keeping pace with the brothers. Probably they were keeping pace with me, but it was much better for my sanity to think the pace was theirs.

We circled around the outer areas of Blesswood; it was later in the sun-cycle now, the sun was lowering itself to make way for night. When we reached the dingy back entrance to Topia, Aros reached out and threaded our fingers together. I glanced down, my eyes widening slightly.

He caught my look. "You have to touch one of us, remember?"

Oh, right. Of course, this was nothing more than

necessity. They had a pact, I couldn't forget that. A pact to keep our pack together.

We crossed over with ease and then we were back in the land of pretty and weird. Rome, who had gone through first, was waiting for us. Siret was still in his arms, and I rushed across so that I could make sure that he was still alive. I placed my fingers on his face, sliding them along his cheeks and down to his throat to feel for a pulse.

His skin was hot, almost burning, but there was a steady beat in his throat.

"He's feverish," I said, lifting my head to the others. "Why did you bring him here? Who will help him in Topia? We should have gone to Blesswood healers."

Rome shifted his brother higher in his arms, before shaking his head. "Trickery is going to need a little more help than a sol healer." Then he tilted his head back and roared into the sky above. *"Abil!"*

I didn't understand ... what was more than a sol healer and who the hell was Abil? The name sounded familiar. *Wait* ... wasn't Abil the god I had *stolen* from? Just as I thought it, purple robes burst into view as a god stepped out of thin air. Nifty trick that one. I ducked my head down and tried not to stare at him.

"Uh, Rome," I whispered. "That's the god I stole the cup from. Is it a good idea to call him down here?"

His mouth twiched, before he strode around and walked straight up to the massive god. Abil—or *D.O.D.*

—had a face like beauty and perfection smashed together, and then some shiny sprinkled on top of it. I hadn't paid much attention last time, all I had seen was purple robes and the cup, but now I could see him so clearly.

His hair was fiery red, but with a darkness to it, almost like a ruby had been spun out and made into hair. His eyes were green, though it wasn't the usual green; his were whatever colour green would have been if it had been touched by magic. His skin was bronze, dark enough to be thought of as copper in the right lights.

I was distracted from my god-gawking by Rome's words. "Hit by a blade forged in Crowe's workshop."

Abil's beautiful face darkened then, and actual clouds washed across the previously perfectly-clear sky. "How is a blade from Death on Minatsol?"

"Rau and his dammed chaos." Those words came from Siret, and my heart leapt for joy as I dashed closer.

He was awake!

I had forgotten that a scary-ass god was standing there, and I pretty much barrelled him over trying to get to Siret. Before Abil could react though, Coen and Yael were stepping in front of me.

I pushed at their backs. "Let me through, I need to see him."

Abil's low, eerily powerful voice washed through

me. "Yes, let her through. I am very curious to meet the dweller my sons guard so diligently."

The world around me went a little pear shaped, and it took my brain a few moments to register what he had just said.

Sons.

Had I misheard him? How could the Abcurses be his sons? The gods have no children, the Originals were created by the Staviti guy, and then the others were born of sols with enough power to be accepted in Topia. Right?

Right?

Where the hell was Emmy when I needed a history lesson?

"Ignore Willa. She isn't your concern." Rome's voice was bite of command; I'd never heard him so angry before. I heard a thump then, and I tried to wedge my head through a small gap to see what was going on.

The thump had been Siret. He was back on his feet, although he looked very pale as he fought to remain upright.

Abil forgot about me then, reaching out and placing a hand on Siret's chest. At first I thought he was just touching him, but then I realised there was something in his hand. A jar, or a small glass object. It shattered as it came into contact with Siret, and something misty emerged. The huge gash, which was still visible across Siret's chest, slowly closed, and my knees almost buckled when he let out a relieved sigh.

"I'm going to kill Rau," he said to Abil as he straightened. Finally looking like the sol—uh godspawn, or whatever he actually was—that he usually did. "You let him know that if he tries to send his chaos down again, we *will* end him. If he messes with our dweller again, I will make sure his ending is long and drawn out."

Abil's expression grew even more serious. He looked between the five of them. "I will deliver the message, but you five need to get out of Topia. You know the rules; your punishment is for one life-cycle, no less. I will forgive this infraction, and not extend your time."

His eyes flicked across to me then, where I was still wedged between two of his sons. "I have a feeling I'll be seeing you soon, dweller." His promise rang across the land, and then he was gone.

I couldn't even bring myself to care right then—I was more interested in getting to Siret so that I could double-check he was okay. No one stopped me as I flung myself at the Abcurse, who now looked like he was in perfect health. He lifted me up and against his body, holding me tightly.

"You didn't need to worry, Rocks. It takes more than a blade to bring me down."

I pulled back, my eyes narrowing on him. "Apparently." My angry eyes flicked between the other four as well. "I think you *sols* have a little explaining to do."

The explaining didn't happen until we left Topia—which was much faster and easier through the dingy entrance than the banishment cave—and were back in Siret's room at Blesswood. Before anyone could change out of their bloody clothes, or even sit down, I had my hands on my hips as I stood at the centre of them all.

"Start talking." My voice was a snap of command.

I actually didn't expect them to say anything, since they never obeyed any of my other commands, but surprisingly enough, Siret spoke.

"What Abil said is true. He is our father and Adeline is our mother. Both gods of Topia."

"So ... you're actually gods. Like real gods. A hundred percent, special cupcake, *god*-gods."

Aros snorted. "Yes."

"What the hell are you doing on Minatsol then?" None of this made sense. My head was spinning as I tried to wrap my tiny mind around the fact that my soul was merged with the souls of five gods. "You guys have seen my ass!"

This was bad. So, so, *so* freaking bad.

Siret smirked. "Your ass has almost been the best part of this entire series of events."

"Pact," Rome grunted, nudging Siret's shoulder. The gesture was almost gentle. I guess he felt bad about Siret getting stabbed.

Fatigue from the fight and stress washed over me

and I basically collapsed onto the floor. I needed to sit. "I still don't understand," I said. "Explain everything to me."

"There's only so much we can tell you without you becoming an even larger target for the Original Gods," Coen said. "You've already made yourself known to Rau and Abil. That's bad enough."

I was about to start losing it, Willa style, when Aros at least gave me a little more information.

"All you need to know for now is that we are gods, that we are stuck on Minatsol for the rest of this life-cycle, and that Minatsol weakens us—which was why we had to get Siret to Topia."

Somehow, I was on my feet; and then somehow, I was out the front door. I couldn't even remember moving, but running was happening and then the chest-shredding was happening and I found myself collapsing near the supply closet that had once been my temporary sanctuary.

Crawling inside, I curled up in a ball and tried to assess everything I now knew. The Abcurses were gods ... their parents were Abil and Adeline. Abil was scary beautiful and scary deadly—and I was pretty sure that Emmy had called him a god of Trickery. Rau had hit me with some sort of curse and he was creepily acting as though I was special, somehow, because I survived it. It was almost as though he had a particular kind of interest in me now ... almost as though he saw me as *useful*.

A heavy thud against the door made me jump. "Get out here, Soldier." Siret commanded. "Don't make me crawl into a supply cupboard; that shit is for dwellers."

"I *am* a dweller," I yelled back. "I don't belong out there with you guys!"

The door slammed open and a long arm reached in and hauled me out. I found myself being held up off the floor, evil green cat-like eyes boring into me. "You've never been a dweller, Willa. And if you couldn't play with the gods, Rau's curse would have killed you."

Oh for fuc—

"Do you assholes have to be right all the time? And stop listening to my thoughts!"

The other four were down the hall a little, waiting for me to get my shit together. Siret set me back on my feet, and I held both hands up in front of me. "Sorry about that, minor panic attack—I'm okay now."

And funnily enough, the moment I said it, I knew it was true. I was okay. I was more than okay, actually. I must have been having some kind of a delayed reaction to everything that had happened. Maybe it was Yael's fault, for repressing my emotions. Either way, the freak-out seemed to be over, and I could feel a calm beginning to settle into my bones. Elowin was dead, Rau had fled, and Siret was alive. In the greater scheme of things, everything really *was* okay.

"So what's the plan?" I asked, looking between the perfect, arrogant faces of the five males who had rapidly become the centre of my world.

Siret tucked me in under his massive arm, and we walked toward his brothers. "Classes tomorrow. Hope you're prepared, because you're going to learn everything the sols get to learn."

I groaned. *Learning* ... that was the worst plan ever.

Rome laughed. "We'll keep you safe, Willa. Even if Rau comes for you again, he won't get through us."

And what about when they leave? When their exile has ended?

"You'll be coming with us," Siret whispered, close to my temple.

"Why are you guys being punished anyway?" I asked, thinking about all the things they could have done wrong to make the gods angry enough to banish them from Topia.

"Trickery thought it would be a good idea to—" Yael started, but Siret cut him off.

"We don't need to talk about it right now."

I nudged Siret's side, the motion gentle because I didn't know if there were any lingering effects of his injury still bothering him or not. "What'd you do?"

Siret sighed, his arm falling from my shoulders, and he muttered something incoherent.

Rome laughed. "We can't hear you, Trickery."

"I tricked Staviti into trying to mate with one of Bestiary's creations, okay!"

I stopped walking, my mouth falling open, my words tumbling out on a squeal. "You *what?*"

Siret tossed his hands up in the air. "You wouldn't

understand! It's a running joke, between the gods. Staviti has been in love with Pica—the goddess of Love—since the beginning of time; she was the first companion that he created. But she didn't love him. She eventually fell in love with Rau, and so Staviti banned all of the gods from pairing up, or having children together. He thought that it would be better for *nobody* to have a partner than for Pica and Rau to be together. Anyway, so to get around his rules, D.O.D.—our *dear old dad*—used his magic to disguise our mother as Pica. She ran to Staviti and asked him to gift her with children. It's the only way to have children, in Topia, since Staviti controls everything. So she told him that she would finally love him, if he allowed her children. He agreed, and gifted her two pregnancies, on the condition that she not seek out Rau to be the father of her children. He obviously thought that if he took Rau off the table, she would turn to him instead."

"Uh ..." my brain seemed to be short-circuiting. That was all a little hard to swallow. "So he thought Adeline was Pica, and he *allowed* her two pregnancies?"

"That's right." Yael was the one who answered, this time. There was a wry smile twisting his lips. "By the time he found out that he had been tricked, it was too late. And being the asshole our father is, he manipulated the magic to get as many sons out of those two pregnancies as possible."

"That's ..." *Really messed up.* "Impressive?"

Siret snorted. "Over the life-cycles, you'd be surprised by how many times Staviti has fallen for the *Pica Illusion*. It's like he's deluded, and every time it happens, he convinces himself that it really is her. That's how desperately he loves her."

"So you ... disguised a beast of some kind as Pica," I surmised, trying to keep my tone bland.

He grunted, and I took that as an affirmative. The other boys were smirking. They clearly still found it amusing.

"But wait ..." I frowned, looking from one of them to the other. "If Siret is the one being punished, then why are you *all* down here?"

We had herded back into Siret's room, since it was the closest, and Coen grabbed me by the shoulders, spinning me around.

"We stick together," he said firmly. It was almost a warning, or an ultimatum.

The others were staring at me, but trying to be covert about it, like they were waiting to hear my response, or to see my reaction. A tiny smile hooked the side of my mouth, and I bit down into my lip, trying to curb it.

"Okay," I said casually. "We stick together, then."

Coen smiled—a real smile, wide and beautiful and completely disarming, almost knocking me off my feet as an answering happiness welled inside me, filling me to bursting with emotion.

For the first time in my life, as I stood surrounded

by the Abcurses, I wasn't worried about what the next sun-cycle would bring. Whatever the world of the gods threw at us, we would face it together.

And nothing would defeat us.

To be continued ...

ALSO BY JANE WASHINGTON

Standalone Books

I Am Grey

The Bastan Hollow Saga

Book One: Charming (Dec, 2018)

Book Two: Disobedience (Jan, 2019)

Book Three: Fairest (Feb, 2019)

Book Four: Prick (Mar, 2019)

Book Five: Animal (Apr, 2019)

Curse of the Gods Series

Book One: Trickery

Book Two: Persuasion

Book Three: Seduction

Book Four: Strength

Book Five: Pain (Oct, 2018)

Seraph Black Series

Book One: Charcoal Tears

Book Two: Watercolour Smile

Book Three: Lead Heart

Book Four: A Portrait of Pain

Beatrice Harrow Series

Book One: Hereditary

Book Two: The Soulstoy Inheritance

ALSO BY JAYMIN EVE

Secret Keepers Series

Book One: House of Darken

Book Two: House of Imperial

Book Three: House of Leights

Book Four: House of Royale (September 15th 2018)

Storm Princess Series

Book One: The Princess Must Die (September 1st 2018)

Book Two: The Princess Must Strike (October 1st)

Book Three: The Princess Must Reign (November 1st)

Curse of the Gods Series

Book One: Trickery

Book Two: Persuasion

Book Three: Seduction

Book Four: Strength

Book Five: Pain (October 2018)

NYC Mecca Series

Book One: Queen Heir

Book Two: Queen Alpha
Book Three: Queen Fae
Book Four: Queen Mecca (2017)

A Walker Saga

Book One: First World
Book Two: Spurn
Book Three: Crais
Book Four: Regali
Book Five: Nephilius
Book Six: Dronish
Book Seven: Earth

Supernatural Prison Trilogy

Book One: Dragon Marked
Book Two: Dragon Mystics
Book Three: Dragon Mated

Supernatural Prison Stories

Broken Compass
Magical Compass
Louis (December 2018)

Hive Trilogy

Book One: Ash

Book Two: Anarchy

Book Three: Annihilate

Sinclair Stories

Songbird

CONNECT WITH JANE WASHINGTON

Website:
www.janewashington.com
Email:
inquiries@janewashington.com
Facebook:
@janewashingtonbooks
Instagram:
@janewashingtonbooks
Twitter:
@TheAuthorPerson

CONNECT WITH JAYMIN EVE

Website:
www.jaymineve.com
Email:
jaymineve@gmail.com
Facebook:
@JayminEve.Author
Instagram:
@jaymineve
Twitter:
@jaymineve1

Printed in Great Britain
by Amazon